CAST OF CHARACTERS

Five extraordinary siblings. One dangerous past. Unlimited potential.

Maxwell Strong—Keeping his identity hidden from the world is his number one priority, until a beautiful stranger with dangerous secrets sweeps onto his shore.

Honey Evans—Her parents control her life, so what better way to get back at them than to fall in love with a penniless drifter...?

Jake Ingram—On the remote island of Brunhia, he's gathered the siblings he's found, but will this long-awaited family reunion end in disaster?

Samuel Hatch—The retired CIA agent holds the key to unlocking the mysteries of the Extraordinary Five, yet can he be trusted?

About the Author

BEVERLY BIRD

loves quirky, slightly outrageous heroines and was thrilled by the chance to write the story of Honey Evans, Extraordinary Five Marcus Evans's often-in-trouble younger sister with a vulnerable heart.

"The other authors were great to work with," she says, "always willing to accommodate my zany Honey-isms in their own books. I also enjoyed breaking Maxwell out of his millionaire shell. I like love stories where the characters are opposites in fundamental ways so their love tends to take them by surprise."

Beverly lives on the New Jersey coast and admits to being computer addicted. You can write to her at BvrlyeB@aol.com.

THE BILLIONAIRE DRIFTER

BEVERLY BIRD

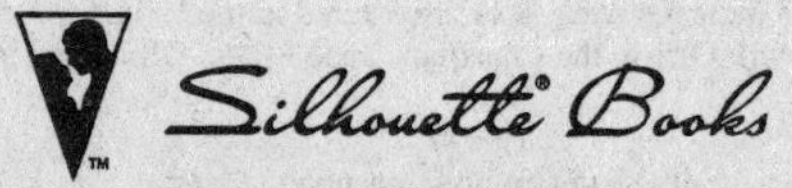

Published by Silhouette Books
America's Publisher of Contemporary Romance

Special thanks and acknowledgment are given to Beverly Bird for her contribution to the FAMILY SECRETS series.

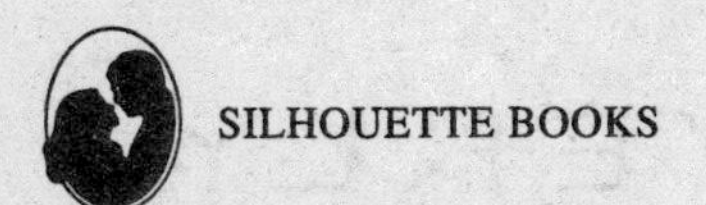

ISBN 0-373-61374-1

THE BILLIONAIRE DRIFTER

This edition published by arrangement with Harlequin Books S.A.

Visit us at www.silhouettefamilysecrets.com

Printed in U.S.A.

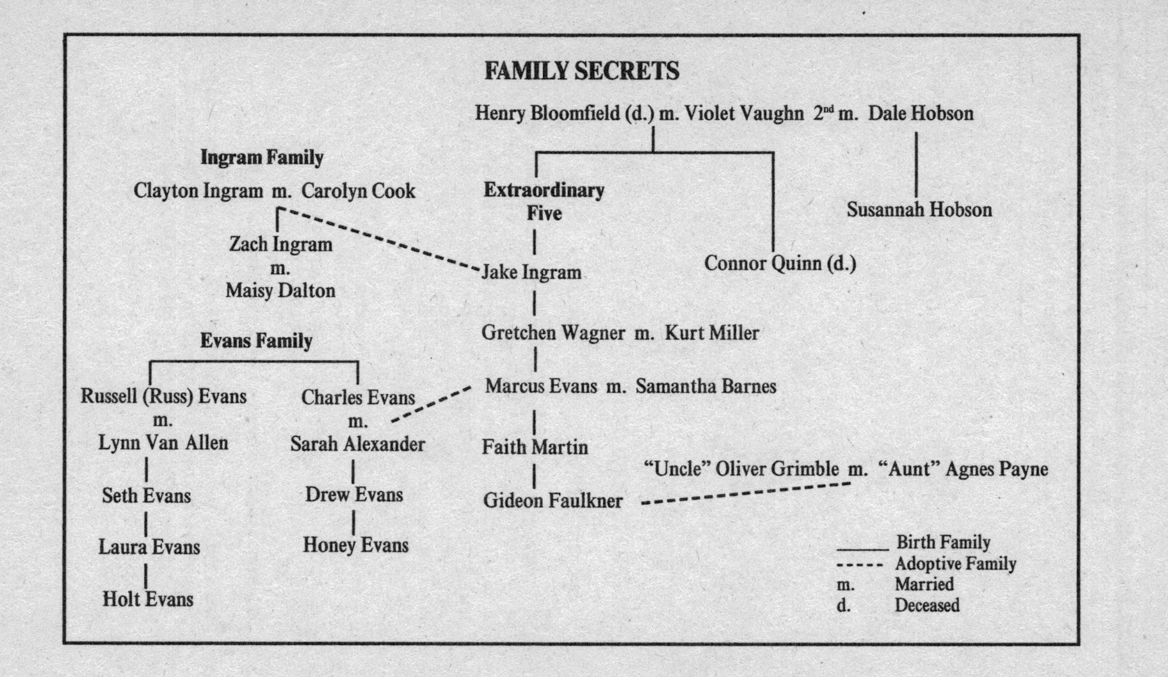
FAMILY SECRETS
Henry Bloomfield (d.) m. Violet Vaughn 2nd m. Dale Hobson
Ingram Family
Clayton Ingram m. Carolyn Cook
Extraordinary Five
Susannah Hobson
Zach Ingram
m.
Maisy Dalton
Jake Ingram
Connor Quinn (d.)
Gretchen Wagner m. Kurt Miller
Evans Family
Russell (Russ) Evans
m.
Lynn Van Allen
Charles Evans
m.
Sarah Alexander
Marcus Evans m. Samantha Barnes
Faith Martin
"Uncle" Oliver Grimble m. "Aunt" Agnes Payne
Seth Evans
Drew Evans
Gideon Faulkner
Laura Evans
Honey Evans
Holt Evans
Birth Family
Adoptive Family
m. Married
d. Deceased

One

Honor Elise Evans was on a tear, and she rather liked it.

The beat of the music in the Woodley Park nightclub throbbed as deep as her bones as she grinned at the man standing next to her. When the tempo of the music changed, turning sinuous, she decided to dance. She snaked her arms over her head and brought them down again to slick her palms over her ribs. When she reached her hips, she took handfuls of her tiny Caribbean-blue dress. The guy caught her at the waist and pulled her close.

His mouth found the soft spot beneath her left ear. Something like a shiver tickled in the pit of her stomach. Shivers were good, she thought. Then his mouth slid to her ear.

"I want you!"

Preferably those words would have been whispered, she thought, but he had to shout to be heard over the music. Her shivery feeling started to vaporize. She had to get him out of here. Then things could progress as planned.

She backed off, easing away from him, and crooked her finger at him until he began to follow her to the door of the club. He caught her there and dragged her close again, grinding himself against her. Out of patience now, she grabbed him by the neck of his T-shirt and hauled him toward the door.

It was September in Washington, D.C., and the heat was liquid. Summer hadn't yet given up its ghost. The humidity reached out for them as soon as they left the air-conditioning. She could feel her curls zinging even tighter. No matter. They'd be a mess anyway when she was done with this guy.

"What do I call you, baby? What's your name?" he asked, rooting for her mouth again as they stood on the sidewalk.

"Do you want me, or do you want to talk?" She pressed herself against him and hooked one foot around his calf to slide it up and down. So far, so good.

"I get your point. Just don't blame me if I call you Linda in the heat of the moment."

She felt the quick little bam-bam of that nasty fist in her chest. She did *not* want him murmuring words of passion to Linda. "Call me Honey. It's what those who know me best don't call me."

She pulled away from him and did a quick pirouette on the pavement, enough to have her very scant hem doing one of those Marilyn Monroe things and billowing up a little. Honey loved old movies. On rare occasions she actually stayed in at night, nuked herself a bowl of popcorn and watched them on the digital wonder her parents called cable.

Her parents weren't in Georgetown tonight—they rarely were—and she had the townhouse to herself. She planned to share it.

She turned away to her car, a candy-apple-red Mercedes SL500 parked at the curb. She went to the driver's side and turned around to slide her bottom onto the door edge. She'd left the convertible top down with just this moment in mind. She swiveled nicely, bringing her legs inside the car. He was ogling her now. "Well? Are you coming, or aren't you?"

"Jeez. That's yours? You're rich."

"Got a problem with that?"

"Uh...no."

"Good. Then let's blow this pop stand."

"Let's what?"

Damn it. "Never mind. Just a line I picked up from an old movie." *Rebel Without a Cause,* she thought. Or maybe *American Graffiti.* Honey couldn't remember exactly which at the moment. She slithered and dropped behind the wheel. The keys were in the car. The valet came running. She slid a hand under her skirt to the top of her thigh-highs and extricated a roll of cash. She peeled off a twenty and gave it to the guy.

"See you soon, Honey," the valet said.

"Count on it." When she looked over at the passenger seat, her catch was there. She peeled away from the curb.

"Where are you taking me?" he asked.

"Heaven." Please, please, please, she thought, let it be heaven this time.

Conversation was kept to a minimum because of the backlash of air that batted at them with the top down. On one hand, that was too bad, Honey thought. She would have liked a few sweet nothings exchanged between them. On the other hand, maybe it was good. His conversational abilities seemed somewhat limited.

Honey screeched to a halt in the driveway of her townhouse and levered herself out of the little car in pretty much the same fashion that she'd entered it. Using doors was pedestrian. She had a very big stake in being anything but.

He was slower getting out. He looked a little dazed.

"You drive like a..." He trailed off. Probably searching for a word over four letters, she thought.

Don't start that, damn it!

Honey headed up the walkway. She heard him behind her. She unlocked the front door, stepped inside and trotted her fingers over the alarm keypad to turn it off. When she turned to face him again, she hooked a finger in his collar and drew him closer.

"Now, where were we?" she asked.

He opened his mouth to answer and Honey swallowed his words. She did a little hop into his arms, wrapped her legs around his waist and plastered her mouth to his.

All systems go, she thought. And then it happened. Again.

At first it was just the bam-bam-bam of that fist in her chest. She ignored it, so it hammered harder. She made a snarling sound of protest in her throat, warning it off. That seemed to turn the guy on. He cupped her bottom, holding her to him, and that was when she stopped being able to breathe.

No, no, no!

He was sucking the air right out of her lungs, she thought. She tried turning her face to the side, letting him feast on her neck.

Maybe it was his aftershave. She tilted her head back, letting his mouth roam her skin, trying to pull in air that wasn't contaminated with whatever it was that he was wearing.

And then it got worse. This time, it got worse. This wasn't just a fist in her chest. It turned into a jackhammer and it was pointed with something sharp. *Rat-tat-tat-tat-tat.* Pain actually splintered through her lungs with every breath she tried to draw in.

And oh, dear God, she was sweating. How mortifying.

She jumped down, letting him go, backing off. "Wait, wait."

"You got me too hot."

"You've—" She gasped. "*You've* got me too hot."

"You, too? Good."

"No, I meant..." What the hell was she doing? Correcting his grammar?

Honey needed to breathe. If she didn't breathe, she was going to...

She was going to pass out.

The foyer started spinning around her, her mother's collection of Hoger and de Hooch artwork on the walls, and over there the picture of Marcus all dolled up in his military garb. Two frames down from that there was Drew...then her parents...and, lest she miss it, the President of the United States shaking her Uncle Russ's hand.

The edges of her vision started going to shades of pearly white and gray.

"Wait," she croaked again. She kept a hand planted on his chest to keep him at a safe distance. "I need to...go...to go outside."

Honey fled. She reached the gardens in the backyard and leaned against the sundial there, its stone damp with the night. She breathed. In, out. In, out. Okay, she thought, I'm fine now. Then she felt his hands sneak up on her from behind, wrapping around her waist to pull her back against him again.

And her heart started pounding harder, and perspiration gathered in every pore she had ever been born with. The gray at the edges of her vision went positively black.

"I'm really sorry about this," Honey murmured. Then she felt her knees fold.

"Obviously, you find the sexual process to be abhorrent in some fashion."

The shrink's words hit Honey like a cattle prod in the backside. She pushed away from the wall where she had been leaning and looking out his office window. "That's what I get for three hundred bucks an hour? That I don't like sex?"

"It triggers a phobia within you. What you're experiencing are panic attacks."

"No offense, Sherlock, but I figured that much out on my own."

She was so agitated she started pacing the office and very nearly snatched her sunglasses off her face. She already had her fingers wrapped around them before she remembered herself.

Her wild blond curls were smashed down beneath a baseball cap that kept wanting to fall off because it had never been designed to corral eighteen inches of hair. She'd swiped a pair of her mother's finest linen trousers out of her closet—no little blue dresses today. She'd given the shrink a phony name and she was forking over good money out of her own pocket for this visit rather than submit it to her insurance company. If anyone caught wind of the fact that Honey Evans had gone down in her garden last night like she'd been shot from a cannon—and all because a man had touched her—she'd… Well, dying on the spot didn't seem to be an overly dramatic way of putting it.

"You're a virgin," Dr. Henkeldorf said.

Honey stopped in mid-stride and spun to face him, baring her teeth. "I am not."

"Then what happens on those occasions when you *do* manage the act of intimacy?"

"Who's talking intimacy? I just want to get laid!" Then the air went out of her as though he had siphoned it from her lungs. She dropped into the chair in front of his desk, her linen-clad legs sprawled in front of her. "Okay, okay, I'm a virgin." Then she jackknifed to sit up straight again. "If you ever breathe a word of that—"

"Whom would I tell, Ms. Benton?"

Honey winced. Her brain had gone inert when she'd called to make this appointment and the receptionist had asked for her name. Her pal Carey's name just happened to be what spilled off her tongue at the time. Carey, however, was no longer a virgin.

"Just tell me how to fix this," she said to the doctor.

"We'll schedule another appointment—"

Honey shot to her feet again. "Are you out of your mind? I have a date tonight!"

"You thought I could fix this in fifty minutes?"

"At three hundred bucks an hour? Yes!"

"This breathing problem—"

Honey shook her head to interrupt him and had to clap a hand to the cap to keep it in place. "No, no. You weren't listening. The fist comes first."

"The fist." He looked down at his notes.

She moved her hand to thump it hard against her breastbone. "Bam-bam-bam. Then rat-tat-tat."

"I'm not sure I discern the difference."

"Bam-bam-bam is hard and slow. Rat-tat-tat is sharp and fast."

"It's your heart."

"Of course, it's my heart! It doesn't want me to have sex!"

"Ah," he said, putting his pen down to steeple his fingers. "Now we're getting somewhere. Unfortunately, your time is nearly up. I suggest that you cancel your date tonight and make an appointment next week."

She was so agitated she went back to his desk and planted

her palms on the wood to lean toward him. "That is not a viable option. This is getting worse. Last night was the first time I passed out! One minute it was just bam-bam-bam-rat-tat-tat and I couldn't breathe, and the next thing I knew I was in the rose bushes! I need to fix this right away!"

"Where did your young man go? I assume he was with you at the time?"

"Yeah." One thing was for sure, Honey thought wildly. She could never go back to Murphy's now. Being a tease and backing off when the bam-bam-bam-rat-tat-tat started was one thing. She could live with that rep, could spin it to her advantage. Doing a nosedive into the roses was a little harder to work with.

"Isn't there a drug for this or something?" she pleaded.

"I would have no way of knowing that without understanding the root of your problem, which I cannot possibly do in one visit," Dr. Henkeldorf said.

Honey pushed off his desk. He had a real racket going on here, she thought. "So I come back and we talk about my childhood?"

"That would be helpful."

"And in the meantime, I remain celibate?"

"I might interject here that that is not a fate worse than death."

"Speak for yourself."

"You find it intolerable?"

"Would I be here if I didn't? I have a reputation to maintain! If this gets out, I'm ruined!"

"A reputation with whom?"

Honey slashed a hand through the air. "My friends. My family. My—" Then she broke off and stared at him. "My *family!*"

"What about them?"

She smacked the heel of her hand against her forehead, banging the bill of the cap in the process. She slammed both hands down on top of her head to hold it in place and spun for the door. "Thanks. You've been a huge help. If you ever want some kind of testimonial or something about how that three hundred an hour is worth it, feel free to give me a call."

"Ms. Benton."

Honey grabbed the door handle and looked back. "Right. That's me."

"I really think you need to make another appointment."

"No, really. I'm fine now. I just figured it out."

He watched her unblinkingly. She felt compelled to explain.

"Every single time this happens, I take my catch back to the townhouse," she said.

"Your catch," he repeated.

"You know, my hottie-for-the-night." She started to rake her fingers through her hair, remembered the cap and dropped her hand to her side again. "Here's the thing," she confided. "When I take them back to the townhouse..." She lowered her voice to a whisper. *"...they watch me."*

"Who?"

"Mom. Dad. Drew and Marcus. They're my brothers."

"You're attempting to have sex while your family watches?"

She stared at him, appalled. "Of course not. I meant that figuratively. It's the townhouse. We've got one in Georgetown, though my parents live most the year at Conover Pointe, so they never use it. And my brothers have lives of their own. I mostly live there alone. Still, I'm thinking a change of scenery here, you know?"

"Ms. Benton, the problem is inside you, not with your environment."

She narrowed her eyes at him. "Meaning?"

"Since I doubt very seriously if I can convince you to come back for subsequent visits, I'll go out on a bit of a limb here. You're suffering panic attacks when you try to engage in the sex act because you are doing so with strangers."

Honey stiffened. "I didn't say they were strangers. Did I say that?"

"I believe your exact phrase was *hottie-for-the-night.*

You're unable to engage in intimacy in order to maintain your…ah, reputation…without invading the core of yourself."

"I *want* my core invaded."

"No, actually, you don't."

"It's the townhouse! Last night when all the swirling started, I was thinking about all the pictures of my family on the walls!"

"Swirling?"

She lifted a finger and rotated it in quick little circles. "Bam-bam-bam. Rat-tat-tat. No air. A few spinning de Hooches. Then splat. Like I said, I just need a change of scenery."

"I daresay you'll reach the same conclusion no matter where you take your…hottie. If your psyche could honestly tolerate casual sex, you would not still be a virgin."

Honey opened the door. "We'll see."

She left the office and walked to her Mercedes parked three blocks away. She hadn't wanted anyone she knew tagging her spiffy little car in front of a sex shrink's office. She used the door this time and slid behind the wheel to gust out a deep breath. Then she noticed the parking ticket stuck under her wiper blade.

She still had the car's top down and she levered herself up to reach over the windshield and snag it. "Seventy-six bucks?" she shrieked. "Because I ran out of quarters?" She opened the glove box to shove the ticket inside.

The action dislodged a partially opened box of condoms and several spilled out onto the floor of her car. "If wishes were horses," she muttered. She gathered them in a fist and tossed them over the door onto the sidewalk. The homeless would be protected tonight, and she probably wouldn't need them. Honey twisted the key in the ignition, stomped her foot on the accelerator and took off.

Maybe she should meander on down to Conover Pointe this weekend until word of what she had done last night died down. She could dig out the old jodhpurs and offer to exercise some of Daddy's thoroughbreds. If she could get the head groom to turn over the reins to Heartache, *that* would sure as hell work some of this frustration out of her blood. The horse had won the Belmont by six lengths some years back, upsetting the Triple Crown favorite du jour. That was what she needed, Honey thought. Just Another Heartache. And maybe one of the lean, trim and hot Latin grooms her father employed to see after his babies before and after they were shipped off to the top trainers in the country.

Then again, if her father found out what she was up to, she'd probably get the poor guy fired.

Okay, one of the cute little preppies she'd grown up with then, Honey thought. Kyle Kilmartin, maybe, or Geoffrey Paige. "Oh, sweet heaven, what am I *thinking?*" If Drew or Marcus or Dad caught wind of *that,* no one would get fired but she'd find herself all dolled up in white lace and standing in front of an altar before she could blink. And the only thing worse than being a virgin was being her mother.

It didn't matter anyway. Her parents would be in residence at Conover Pointe, so the place would have the same effect on her as the townhouse. She needed a change of scenery, she thought again, if she was going to fix this mess.

And then it hit her. Marcus's wedding.

Honey whooped aloud and punched a fist in the air. Her brother was getting hitched next week on some island off the coast of a European country. She couldn't remember which one at the moment, but it was a safe bet that the place would be crawling with continental types. A guy like that could get her right over the hump, she decided.

She ran the SL500 into the townhouse driveway and hit the front door like a filly breaking through the starting gate. She threw her sunglasses on the tiny good-for-nothing cherrywood table her mother kept in the foyer and galloped up the stairs to her bedroom. Where had she put Marcus's letter? Her room was a disaster. She'd gotten a wild hair a few weeks ago and had banished the live-in maid to days only and had asked the woman to leave her bedroom alone. It was probably for the best, Honey realized, the resulting mess aside. If Naeve had been here last night, she might have found her in the rose garden in the wee hours of the morning and how the hell would she have explained *that* to the help?

Somewhere beneath last night's shocking-blue dress, her computer equipment, the VCR, DVD player, stereo, an entire wall of books spilling from shelves and her library of old movies, the unmade bed and twenty-six teddy bears collected from various parts of the world was the letter she'd received from her brother a few weeks ago. Honey went to the nightstand and yanked it open. She pawed through show-ticket stubs, two unfinished diaries and a sweet little clay figure one of the kids at St. Christopher's Orphanage had made for her when she'd borrowed twenty-three pups from the pound and took them to visit a bunch of kids who might never know the joy of a canine kiss otherwise. The nuns were probably still cursing her name but the kids had loved it.

There was no letter from her brother in there.

Honey dropped to her knees to peer under the bed. Dust bunnies but no correspondence. She really had to rethink the whole business of banishing Naeve and her vacuum cleaner from her bedroom.

She went to her desk as a last resort—that was where *most* people would keep letters from their family. She found it tucked under the computer keyboard. Honey finally whipped the baseball cap off her head and tossed it onto the bed. Her blond curls spilled. She stepped out of the perfectly creased linen trousers she'd swiped from her mother's closet and trotted downstairs again in her white T-shirt and her underwear.

In the kitchen, she snagged a can of orange soda from the fridge. She swigged while reading the letter again. Then she choked.

How had she missed the whole beginning of Marcus's letter the first time she'd scanned this? Her only explanation for missing something so...well, *staggering,* was that she must have been in the throes of virgin-angst at the time.

"Miss Evans?"

Honey looked up at the sound of the maid's voice. ''Hey there, Naeve.''

''You're in your underwear.''

Honey looked down at herself. ''I don't care if you don't.''

Naeve almost grinned but in the end she only shook her head. Honey started out of the kitchen, still staring at the letter.

''Are you all right, Ms. Evans? You look pale.''

Honey glanced back at her. ''Marcus is superhuman.'' The help—at least those who had been with the Evans clan for any length of time—knew that Marcus was adopted. After her parents had had Drew, things had stalled. They'd adopted Marcus and then—voila!—Honey had made her appearance.

''Superhuman,'' Naeve repeated.

''He says he's sort of found his natural family. And his parents were like...test tubes or something.''

The maid started looking around the kitchen as though seeking something to defend herself with. Honey shoved the letter at her. ''Here, read it yourself. I'm going to pack and fly to a place called Brunhia.''

Two

Maxwell Strong woke to the throaty cluck of a rooster.

He rolled his legs over the side of the fore-cabin berth of his Dufour 3800 and remembered to lean forward before standing so he didn't whack his head against the teak molding of the low-slung ceiling. He was getting the hang of onboard living. It had only taken him the better part of six months.

He could have purchased something newer and much larger, but that would have negated his entire purpose. Max Strong would not be expected to travel about the world in a twenty-year-old thirty-eight-foot sailboat. The *Sea Change* kept him anonymous.

Max ducked through the doorway into the salon and moved past the navigation table and two more single berths to starboard. The galley was portside. He rooted through a cupboard there for the tin of coffee. Amazing what they thought of these days, he reflected as he plucked out a dose already enclosed in its own little filter. He would never have known about this trifling convenience had he not left Pittsburgh. And New York. And Paris. And Cairo. But there you have it, he thought, dropping the filter into the coffee maker. He'd gone wandering—some said off his rocker—and he'd discovered that the world had come a very long way from his mother's kitchen.

He poured water into the machine, smacked the button to turn it on and went topside to deal with the rooster. The bird was pacing the sailboat's deck, his head thrusting arrogantly with each step as though he was proclaiming his turf. Max got the plastic container of chicken feed he kept in the transom seat, lifting a blue leather cushion to dig it out. The rooster stopped moving to stare at him with small black eyes. Max sprinkled the feed over the deck in the hope that it might shut the thing up long enough for him to enjoy his coffee.

He went below again and poured himself a mug, standing against the thin counter in the galley to savor the first sip. No espresso in Milan had ever tasted better, though he might have enjoyed a newspaper to go along with it. But what for? He already knew what would be in it—the international economic fallout of the World Bank Heist, some speculation about a U.S. governmental genetics experiment gone awry and the bizarre disappearance of one renowned and filthy-rich real-estate developer named Maxwell Strong. The society pages would probably carry a blurb about who his ex-wife was currently screwing, but at least Camille was no longer doing it on his money.

He didn't need a newspaper, Max decided. He had his boat, the rooster to deal with and hands that were nicely callused again for the first time in ten years. He had—

—coffee all the hell over the place because a wave had hit him portside.

The sailboat rolled a little with the slap of the wake and jolted Max against the sink. Bay water sprayed against the windows on the left side of the cabin. The coffee sloshed in his hand, spilling over the rim of the mug, scalding him. He swore, swore again and finally dropped the mug into the sink where the ceramic broke into pieces.

What the hell? He'd been anchored in the Gulf of Cadiz since June, give or take a few excursions to Portimao on the mainland. In all that time he'd never encountered a wave larger than what might result in a swimming pool after a 350-pound man did a belly flop.

Max hightailed it topside again. His heel hit some chicken feed and he went skidding. The rooster, alarmed, tried to peck at his bare toes. He yelled and grabbed the main mast to catch his slide. When his legs were steady again, he looked for the source of the ruckus.

It was the outboard skiff that carried people back and forth between Brunhia and Portimao. It was at full throttle and a crazy woman was at the helm.

Max stared, wondering what the hell had gotten into Amando to turn the wheel over to a woman who piloted as if she was out for the joyride of her life. The wizened little Portuguese stood beside her, clapping ecstatically. No one knew the sandbars and shoals and boulder-strewn shallows around the island except the local fishermen—and Max himself because he'd had the good sense to learn after Amando had brought his *Sea Change* in here the first time. Max knew Amando, and to his knowledge Amando did not ever clap.

As Max watched, the skiff came catastrophically close to a sandbar at full tilt. Amando stopped celebrating long enough to reach and cut the throttle. The boat stalled. The woman hugged him. Amando allowed it. Max stared.

He couldn't see much of her—they were at a distance now—but he did note that she had a pretty fantastic body and a great deal of hair. To the best of his calculations, this made the third new arrival on Brunhia this week. None of the visitors seemed to be Portuguese. This woman's copious curls were as blond and bright as the sun.

Something was going on up at the big house. Max didn't like the feel of it. His isolated, nobody-knows-about-it Utopia was being invaded.

The thought depressed the hell out of him. Max went below for another cup of coffee before dealing with the rooster.

When the boat stopped rocking enough that she no longer needed to grip the rim of the dashboard in white-knuckled hands, Honey planted those hands on her hips and let her gaze roll over the coastline. Brunhia was not even remotely what she had expected. She did not spy anything resembling a hot European lover moving along the rugged beach.

What had gotten into Marcus anyway? Why in the world would he choose to get married *here?* Maybe it had something to do with the new voodoo-gened siblings he'd found.

Getting here had been an exercise in the damned-near-impossible, she thought. She'd flown into Lisbon last night and had caught a shuttle flight into Portimao. From there everything had gone to hell in a...well, a sea skiff. This little guy, Amando, had come to the hotel looking for her at six-thirty this morning. An hour later—an hour that she'd had to beg for—he'd tossed her luggage into his boat to bring her to Marcus's hideaway.

The ride had turned out to be a kick though. Halfway into the three-mile span of gulf that separated Brunhia from the mainland, she'd convinced Amando to let her take the wheel. He'd kept his hands on it along with hers, of course, especially as they'd gotten closer to the island. "Rocha! Rocha!" he'd yelled. Rock! Rock! She'd managed to miss them and a few sandbars and shoals as well. When they'd gotten clear of the worst of it, he'd let go of the wheel to cheer.

The boat finally bobbed to something close to a standstill in the current and Honey turned on one hip to grin at Amando. "Thanks. That was a great time."

"You are very *bonito*. How I say no?"

His English was choppy but she caught his meaning. Beautiful? Her nose was a tad too long and she'd spent twenty-three years aching for straight hair, but she'd take the compliment. "Thanks."

"No one ever my boat ride say great!"

"No one likes your boat ride? Then they need to lighten up. Which brings to mind a question."

"Voce esta pensando de umo pergunta?"

"Whoa. Hold the thought, amigo." She dug her English-Portuguese dictionary out of the back pocket of her favorite vermilion shorts. For the first time in her life, she blessed the Spanish classes she was forced to take in high school. Though Portuguese was a bit different, it was essentially close. "Say again?"

Amando repeated himself and she flipped pages.

"Ah, gotcha. Yes, I am thinking of a question." She flipped more pages until she thought she had the translation straight to get her point across. With any luck, she wasn't asking for cheese on the moon. *"O que esta la fazer ao vedor para o divertimento aqui?* What is there to do for fun around here?"

"The *senhora* would like fun?"

"Fun! Yes! Fun!"

He began laughing so hard it was entirely possible he might wet his pants. The concept of fun on Brunhia was apparently hysterical. This, Honey thought, was not a good sign. "I changed my mind. I want to go home."

And then, for reasons beyond her, she felt compelled to look over her shoulder. It was a substantial, physical pull, like warm fingers gripping the back of her neck. When she did, she saw him. Her Portuguese lover. Made to order.

He was standing on the deck of the boat she'd noticed coming in, the *Sea Change.* She was too far away to see his face, but his black hair gleamed in the sun and he had what looked to be very decent pecs. There were a few other nice parts and pieces of him, too. She could tell because he appeared to be wearing blue-and-red plaid boxer shorts.

Amando stopped laughing long enough to get a pole from the bottom of the craft. He stuck it overboard, using it to pull them closer to the shore. Honey felt the little bump that told her they were beached.

"You can jump, *senhora,* no? *Salto?*" Amando pantomimed his intent.

"You betcha." Honey climbed up onto the bow, gathered herself and leaped. She cleared the shore line with inches to spare, then she planted her hands on her hips again and looked around.

There was a rutted dirt road straight ahead, trees crowding it tightly as though to protect it from trespassers. To her left, about an eighth of a mile down the beach, were several cabins of aged wood. They hugged the tree line and, though the day was warm, one of the chimneys belched smoke that smelled of fish, though not unpleasantly. Bayberry bushes crowded the fronts and sides of many of the dwellings.

Down the other way, five or six kids splashed naked in the surf. A woman with long inky hair sat on the sand, her knees drawn up, her dark skirt pooled around her thighs. Every once in a while she shielded her eyes to count heads. The sun was turning the water to a million shifting, glaring diamonds.

Honey was inclined to admit that it was beautiful. Primitive, but beautiful. Then she heard a creaking sound coming from the direction of the road and her gaze snapped that way.

Marcus!

Honey hooted and ran for him. He sat on the plank seat of a mule-drawn wagon and as she approached, one of the mules flattened his ears. Marcus cautiously reined the team in and jumped down. "Honey, for God's sake, I've got no idea how these beasts react to—"

It was all he got out before she leaped at him. He braced himself and wrapped his arms around her and Honey peppered his face with kisses.

"Well," he said, setting her down. "Hello to you, too."

"It's been forever! Tell me *everything.*"

"I already did. In my letter."

Honey looped her arm through his and led him back toward the cart. "That wasn't everything. That was 'my real parents were part of a government experiment and I have at least one other sister.' By the way, I'm not entirely sure how I feel about that."

"Trust me, Honey. No one can top you." He lifted her into the wagon. "You'll like Gretchen. She's here. Her husband owns part of the island."

Honey shifted her weight a little to make sure she wasn't going to get any splinters in her backside. *That* would put a damper on what she was starting to consider as her Portuguese Plan. She glanced back at the sailboat anchored offshore, but the man had gone below deck now. "Well," she said, looking around at the wagon, "her hubby must be loaded. We're really traveling in style here."

"Your sarcasm hasn't waned with the months." Marcus went down to the beach for the luggage, which Amando had deposited on the sand, then he returned to the wagon and took up the reins again. They started moving with a little jolt.

"No way to get cars over here," he explained. "A ship large enough to carry one can't get close enough to shore because of all the shoals out there."

She didn't particularly care. She wanted to talk about what really interested her. "So was this Gretchen hatched in a test tube, too?"

"You didn't read my letter."

"Sure I did. I'm here, aren't I?"

"You skimmed it on your way to do something designed to turn Mom's hair grayer."

"Only the first time. The second time I *read* it."

"If you had, you'd know that my real parents were as human as you and me."

Honey glanced sideways at him. "No offense, bro, but the jury's still out on you. You said they tinkered a bit with your genes."

"They did."

"Okay, I'll bite. Go ahead and change shape or something."

"If you insist." He stopped the wagon and left it again.

Honey watched him walk off the road. There was a good-sized boulder over there, tucked into the trees. As she watched, he squatted, braced himself...and lifted it.

"Whoa," she whispered. This was weird.

Marcus came back to the wagon.

"Have you always been able to do that?"

"More or less."

"Why didn't I know about it before this?"

"I just felt more comfortable keeping it to myself."

"So what does it mean to me?" Honey demanded.

He tucked his chin and looked down his nose at her—which was difficult to do, she thought, given that she was perched high in the wagon. "Honey, not everything in this world revolves around you. Stay out of it."

"If you wanted me to stay out of it, then you shouldn't have told me."

"I had an obligation to tell you. Several people connected to all this are going to be on the island this week. I decided the best way to handle that was to tell you the truth and advise you in the strongest possible terms to keep your nose to yourself."

Honey frowned. "Do Mom and Dad know? What about Drew?"

"I told Mom and Dad. I asked them to pass it on to Drew."

So, Honey thought, things remained a little tense there between her brothers. "Is he coming to the wedding?"

"Sam sent him an invitation." He picked up the reins and they started up the road.

Honey sighed and crossed her arms over her breasts. "I want to know more about your voodoo genes."

"No."

"That's cruel. What you did with that rock was just a...a tease." Then she thought, More of the same. "God forbid anyone in this family should ever trust me to have a reasonably working brain cell in my head."

He shot her his eyebrows-in-the-clouds look. "Something bothering you?"

"No."

Marcus heaved a sigh. "Honey, if you want to be taken seriously, then maybe stop getting arrested."

Her spine shot straight. "I was arrested *once.* And it was for a good cause."

"Twice. You got snagged drinking in that bar in Miami when you were only seventeen. And if the good cause you're referring to is the circus-animal fiasco, I doubt the beasts had any idea that you were rushing to their defense."

"Those PETA people are idiots. *They* were my cause. I was trying to prove a point."

"By riding a horse through their picket lines?" Marcus laughed.

"I got their attention."

"It landed your tush in jail."

"Only for a few hours. And it was worth it. Just because an animal is kept in a stall or a cage doesn't mean he's being mistreated. Hey, if horses had any brains they'd be lining up for the opportunity to live at Conover Pointe in Dad's barn."

"True. I'm just saying..."

Suddenly, she forgot about PETA. She sat forward to look around him to the view on the other side of the wagon. "What's that?" She pointed.

Marcus glanced over his left shoulder. "The marble quarry."

"Oh, of course. How silly of me not to have recognized that."

He gave the grin that she'd watched bring women to their knees time and again over the years. "Kurt's uncle bought this land for its marble," he said. "He pretty much mined it out, then he died and left the whole kit and caboodle to Kurt."

"And Kurt would be..."

"Gretchen's husband."

"My sister competition."

He grinned a little wider. "Trust me, you don't want to get into any competitions with her. At least nothing that involves hieroglyphics, signs or symbols."

"Are you doing it again? Knocking my smarts?"

"Jeez, Honey! I'm just *saying!* I was coded to do things like lifting that rock back there. Gretchen was engineered to be brilliant with encryptions."

Honey got a queasy feeling in her stomach again. When she'd first read the letter, it had all sounded rather cool. But, she thought again, this was really pretty off the wall. "Let me get this straight. Our government created you guys with special...powers."

He hesitated, then apparently decided he could tell her that much. "More or less."

"Are you human?"

Marcus grunted. "Of course I'm human!"

"Who were your parents exactly?"

"Violet— Oh, no you don't."

Honey lifted her brows innocently. "I don't what?"

"You're trying to snoop more information out of me."

Busted. "I never snoop. I'm very direct."

He guided the mules around a bend in the road. "Honey, trouble follows you like a retriever's tail, wagging all over the place and knocking into everything it gets close to. I'll be damned if I'm going to let you anywhere *near* this situation. Besides, you talk too much."

"I do not."

"How many people have you told about my letter?"

"None." Okay, one, she thought. She'd let Naeve read it, but that wasn't actually the same as *telling* her.

Honey took a different approach. "Guess this has Mom and Dad pretty whacked." Her father was military-rigid. Her mother was…well, exactly what the family had spent twenty-three years trying to mold Honey into—a woman who sat still, looked beautiful, knew her place and was content to be doted on. Sarah Evans did not do well with the unusual and the unorthodox.

They came within view of the house. The old marble maven had had a wee bit of taste, Honey thought, their classy chassis notwithstanding. The place was magnificently huge, of weathered wood with six chimneys jutting from the roof. There was nothing so grand as a pillared entry, but there were six sets of windows to either side of the front door, at least on the second floor. They were somewhat more spare downstairs. There was a widow's walk at the top with a small, dome-like area tucked inside it. There were windows on that as well.

"My, my," she said.

"By tomorrow night, it will be jam-packed," Marcus warned. "There are six bedrooms but we've allotted all of them, what with people coming in for the wedding."

"I'll make it easy on you and take that little room up top there."

"The bell room? What would you want with that?"

A bell, she thought, intrigued. "What did the old guy need a bell for?"

"I'm not sure. Maybe to call his people in from the quarries." Marcus guided the wagon around the house.

There were several outbuildings behind it, including a long garage-like thing with four bay doors that she already knew didn't contain anything with four tires and a steering wheel. There were also a small, windowless hut and two neat cabins. Marcus reined the mules in near the garage. He got out and hefted her luggage from the back of the wagon.

"Come on. I want to get you settled so you can meet Sam."

A smarmy feeling hit her gut as Honey hopped off the wagon, all swimming and sweet. Marcus with a wife, she thought. Who would have believed it? He'd always been so driven—though in some measure, she knew that it had been his way of trying to outshine Drew. All the same, it hadn't left him a lot of time for romance.

She definitely wanted to meet this Samantha, Honey thought. She followed him up a cobbled brick walkway, back toward the front of the house. "How did you find her?"

"Doesn't matter."

Doesn't matter? It had something to do with his super genes then, she decided. That was a little too vague for a man who was about to be married.

They went in through wide, double oaken doors and into an immense hallway that ran the length of the house. Not the *depth* of the house, she thought, but the length. Side-to-side. Different, she thought. Very quirky. She liked it and let out a quick peal of laughter.

"Yeah," Marcus agreed, following her gaze. "Come on, I'll show you your room."

There was no central staircase. What the house did have were corner stairs, tucked into the east and west ends of the front of the house—winding, circular things that delighted her. They went up and entered a corridor on the second floor much like the one on the first. It ran side-to-side, but up here, at least, there was a bisecting corridor.

Marcus led her to a door and Honey balked. "No, I meant it. I want that bell room." She had every intention of seducing that Portuguese Lothario out on the boat. She needed to keep herself as separate from her family as possible. "I like my solitude."

Marcus stared at her. "Since when?"

Honey shrugged and started up the hall to look for a way up to the bell room. "I cut Naeve down to days only. I'm even thinking about getting my own place."

She heard Marcus snort behind her. "That would necessitate remembering to pay your mortgage on time each month."

"Not if I just dig the money out of my trust fund and pay for it up front," she shot back, then she found the stairs she wanted at the middle of the hall.

The opposite side of the corridor was pretty nifty as well. On that side there was a banister, and she leaned against it. "Whoa." She looked down at a straight drop into one of the largest rooms she'd ever seen, and Honey had been in her share of big homes over the years. It took up the entire depth of the house. You could spit a whole buffalo in that fireplace, she thought. One end of the room was given over to a sitting area with four sofas and corresponding, bracketing chairs and a bar. The other end of the room sported a pool table and a small dance floor. Dead ahead of Honey's nose, dangling over all of it, was an awesome brass chandelier with a million tiny gold-tinted bulbs.

Marcus joined her at the railing. "That's where we'll have the wedding."

"The marble dude did pretty good for himself." There were plenty of specimens from his quarry in evidence, too, from the floor to the fireplace mantel.

Honey turned to the door on the opposite side of the hall. Just beyond the threshold, steps curled upward. "This is it?"

"You're seriously going to make me carry these suitcases up one more level?"

"If you wanted to pout about it, then you shouldn't have lifted that rock." Honey started up. She encountered a decent share of cobwebs on the way and batted them aside. She heard Marcus muttering behind her.

"I don't think Gretchen got this room ready for guests."

"I don't care," Honey tossed back.

"You don't—" He broke off, dumbfounded. "What are you up to, Honey?"

She'd reached the top and didn't answer. She gave a little squeal instead.

It was exactly that—a bell room, a space through which to reach the heavy velvet rope that hung down from the center ceiling. She stopped there and looked up at the bell, big and bronze. She reached for the rope.

"Don't you dare," Marcus said quickly, dropping her bags hard to grab her hand away.

"Spoilsport." But she left the rope and went to tour the windows.

They were spaced every two feet or so all the way around, offering a panoramic view of the island. Even without the hunk on the sailboat, Honey thought, she would have loved this. As it was, she could see his boat perfectly from here.

The island was long and skinny and the house seemed to be at its northernmost tip. Eviscerated earth gleamed white in the sun off to her right—the quarries. To her left was a stretch of rugged beach. The rest of the island was hidden from view by forest cover so thick it looked as though the trees were holding each other in strangling, dying embraces. But she noticed two distinct breaks in the tree cover, one on either side of the dirt road she and Marcus had traveled, close to the southern shore of the cove.

"If you're really going to do this, I'll have Rafaela bring up a cot and some linens," Marcus said. He came closer to peer deeply into her eyes. "Who are you and what have you done with my five-star-hotel sister?"

Honey laughed. "I have my reasons."

"That's what scares me."

"I'll fill you in on them later." And she decided that she would, too. Her Portuguese Plan would get a nice rise out of everyone. "I'm starved. The last thing I had to eat was some peanuts on the flight down from Lisbon last night."

"We'll be having brunch in about fifteen minutes." Marcus looked at his watch. "Downstairs in the big room."

He left her and Honey went to the windows to look out again, then she turned away to wash up. She wondered if any of those rooms downstairs had their own bathrooms, because there seemed to be a real shortage of plumbing up here. No matter. Sharing one of the bathrooms downstairs was a small price to pay for not having to bunk down next to the rest of her family. Honey trotted downstairs again and this time she kept going past the second floor. She'd already noticed that this lonely little winding staircase went down as well as up.

She landed in a kitchen. The door she stepped through was tucked between two cooktops on one side and an oven and refrigerator on the other. Right beside it was another door that led directly outside. Perfect for midnight escapes, she thought, grinning.

A woman was busy at the stove. Her black braid was heavily threaded with gray. She wore the same sort of long, dark skirt as the younger woman on the beach.

"Hi," Honey said.

The woman gasped and spun around. "You scare the devil into hiding!"

Amen, Honey thought. She spoke English. Sort of. "Sorry. I'm Honey. Marcus's sister. The *first* one."

"You be the crazy one in that bell room?"

"That would be me."

To her surprise, the woman grinned widely and came from the stove to clasp both her hands. "*Bonito* room, no?"

"Yes, the view is spectacular."

"My Ricardo and me—I am Rafaela—we honeymoon there. We marry when we work for the *senhor.* We had no *dinheiro* to go to Portimao so the *senhor* say come to big house to get away from our families." She winked slyly.

"That's the marble guy? How nice of him." Honey stood on tiptoe to look over her shoulder at the stove. "So where's the chow? *Alimento?*"

"That way." Rafaela pointed.

There was another doorway at the other end of the room, this one of the swinging variety. Honey tucked through it and stepped into the big room. It seemed even larger when you were actually in it, she realized. The four people she found there might have been grains of sand on a beach. They were all gathered at the sofa-and-bar end.

Honey headed that way. Safe guess that the almost-redhead standing next to her brother was his wife-to-be, she thought. The only other woman there was seated on a sofa beside a man whose hand she appeared to be holding, and the man wasn't Marcus. *That* wouldn't be a real auspicious matrimonial start, she thought.

Then her gaze jogged back to Samantha Barnes. And her second thought was, well, if I had boobs like that, maybe I wouldn't have a virginity problem. Maybe no guy would stop when I passed out in the thorns.

The woman seemed to inhale through her nose and her smile beamed. The smile was genuine, Honey decided, though maybe a little practiced. Marcus had said that she was the U.S. Ambassador to Delmonico, so she had to be good at smooth. But edging beyond that was an I-really-do-want-to-meet-you curl to her mouth.

Marcus, she thought, was behaving like a man who was either about to get shot or crowned king. He was jittery. He came toward her and grabbed her elbow to drag her toward his fiancée. "Honey, this is Samantha. Sam, Honey."

Samantha took her hand. "It's nice to finally meet you. I've heard a lot about you."

"I'd be disappointed if you hadn't." Honey grinned.

"This is Gretchen," Marcus said, turning her the other way, "and her husband, Kurt. Kurt was kind enough to offer us the island safe from harm for the wedding."

"What kind of harm?" Honey asked, turning away from Samantha to size up the couple on the sofa.

"Never mind," four voices said in unison.

Well, she'd deal with that later, Honey decided. She took stock of the other couple. Something thunked in her chest when she realized that there was a vague physical resemblance between Marcus and his new sister. They had the same dark hair, the same blue eyes. Maybe Marcus's hair inched a little closer to black, but still, it was there.

The woman came off the sofa and embraced her. That was when Honey realized she was pregnant.

"Hi," Honey said. "He was mine first."

"I know that. But...I'd hoped we could share."

"Give me all the dirt on this voodoo gene business, then I'll decide."

"No!" four voices said in unison.

Honey stepped back and looked around at all of them. "This is getting old. What's going on, anyway? Does this involve state secrets or something?"

No one answered her.

"Hey, I've got White House security clearance."

"You answer the phones there," Marcus said dryly.

It stung. Damn it, it actually stung. Why was she only lately so sensitive to her family's dismissal of her? They'd been doing it to her all her life—which was why she went so deliberately out of her way to underachieve. She'd been offered an internship at the White House. Since she'd never been sure if it had been on her own merit or if her father or uncle had pulled strings, she'd turned it down to be included on the phone staff instead.

Gretchen's husband stood from the sofa to join them, jolting her back to the moment. He was handsome in a rugged sort of way, Honey thought.

"You reputation precedes you," he said.

"Reputations are frisky little things," she agreed.

He threw back his head and laughed. She really liked his laugh.

"Have you eaten?" Gretchen asked.

"No, and I could tackle a steer."

"Would ham and eggs suffice? Rafaela is doing very well at learning to cook American food. We also have some fruit and oysters, muffins, toast."

"I'd commit murder for ham and eggs," Honey said wholeheartedly. "And oysters."

The woman smiled. Honey had never seen a face that was both so inherently canny and kind at the same time. All in all, she could enjoy this bunch, she decided.

They went to the buffet and Honey dug in. She eschewed a little table in one corner to sit on the sofa and balance her plate on her knees. When in Rome, she thought, do exactly the opposite of what the Romans do. Everyone else except Kurt went to the table.

"Marcus says you want to stay in the bell room?" he asked.

Honey chewed, swallowed. "It suits me to a T."

"Rafaela should have a bed made up for you there by the time we're done here."

"But as for facilities..." Gretchen said from the table.

"Yeah, I noticed there were a few missing." Honey grinned.

"I suppose the one closest would be ours, Kurt's and mine. When you come down from the bell room, it's the first door to your left. We don't mind sharing."

"Unless you're a slob," Kurt put in.

"No, I'm—"

"She's a disaster," Marcus interrupted.

It made her stomach hurt. Honey got up to put her half-eaten plate back on the buffet. She realized she wasn't all that hungry after all.

"I'm afraid there's not much to see or do on the island," Gretchen continued.

That depends on what you want to do, Honey thought. "Oh, I'll keep busy."

"If you'd like to explore, there are several motor scooters in the barn."

"There are four or five mules out there, Honey," Marcus said. "If you want to wander, stick with them."

He wanted her to ride a *mule* after their parents' thoroughbred racehorses? "I can handle a scooter."

"Please don't ruin my wedding," he said with utter seriousness.

Honey glanced at Samantha. She seemed to be enjoying the conversation. She didn't appear to be even remotely worried about her wedding. "Calm down. I have plans for this week, none of which involve disrupting your nuptials."

"Share with us," Gretchen urged.

"No, wait. You don't want to her to—" Marcus began, but Honey interrupted him. This would serve him right for the crack about her being a disaster, she thought.

"My Portuguese Plan is to snare a man," she told everyone. "Temporarily, of course, just for the duration of my little gig here on Brunhia." She grinned around at all of them. "I'm going to take myself one kick-ass, smooth-as-blues Portuguese lover."

Three

It took Max twenty minutes to catch the rooster but that was largely because the bird had been on board three times before and he was getting wise to Max's methods. He circled him with the fishing net and the bird started doing that thing with his neck again as though to lay claim to top-dog masculinity on this vessel. Max floated the net out twice and missed the little bastard. He should just eat him, he thought, but that would involve catching him, too. So he looked over both shoulders and when he was sure that no one was nearby enough to catch the spectacle, he started clucking right back at the feathered demon in what he hoped was a threatening poultry tone.

Then he thought of the blonde.

He wasn't worried about islanders catching him communing with a chicken, he realized. They already thought he was a little bit loco. Which left the crazy woman with the reams of sunlight curls, the one who had damned near beached Amando's boat into splinters and had made the wizened old guy *clap*. Truth be told, Max thought, he'd been considering her all morning. Good-looking women were a dime a dozen. But a *clappable* woman? Yeah, that got his attention.

The bird did something with its wings and came a foot off the bottom of the boat. Max pushed the blonde from his mind and lunged. This time he was successful and it was every bit as bad as the other times he'd been forced to nail the arrogant, needle-beaked, winged beast. The rooster went crazy, squawking and squirming and pecking as Max wrapped his arms around him now that he was safely in the net. Feathers floated everywhere. Max wrapped a quick knot in the net and dropped the bird into the little dinghy he kept tied to the starboard side of the *Sea Change.*

"Stew pot, buddy. This time I'm not going to plead your case." But they both knew he would.

He hopped down into the dinghy, taking care to step around the writhing, rolling net. He threw off the line, pulled the ripcord on the outboard motor and headed to shore a lot more neatly than Amando had this morning, but then again, he wasn't distracted by reams of blond hair and little—okay, very little—red shorts.

Max collected the rooster again and started off down the beach toward the tiny village of Deus Fornece—a total of twelve cabins, maybe eighty-five people whose yearly earnings equaled a miniscule fraction of what Max earned in an hour whether he was hiding or at the helm of his financial empire. He was happier among them than he had ever been with heads of state and they needed this bird a lot more than he did.

Lourdes saw him coming. She was working on the beach, scaling the portion of the night's catch that her family would keep. A small pile of glistening sea bream lay on a rock by her side. Tulio, her husband, would already be headed for Portimao to sell the rest of the haul. He'd be back by noon and sleep until sundown, then he'd head out to sea to start the whole routine all over again.

"Bird on board again," Max said, stopping beside the woman. "I'll just drop him back in the pen."

"You do that, I be very unhappy."

The people of Deus Fornece—and of Paz, the other little village on the other end of the island—did their best with English. And he did his best with Portuguese. All in all, they got by.

"Man gets paid for what he does," she insisted.

"Not this man." Max was frustrated. He had been through this so many times before. If it wasn't roosters or hens on board, then it was pigs tethered to the beach. Or a couple of sea bream or cuttlefish tied to his bowsprit. But it was always something. Three or four times a week, it was something.

The calluses on his hands—the ones he'd earned back by sheer stubbornness, lunacy and dint of will—came from mending these peoples' nets, filleting their fish, repairing a boat or two. Max knew carpentry. A long time ago, in another life, he'd staked his future on it. He helped these people because he enjoyed it, and because he had nothing better to do with his time. He helped them because they needed every hand to chip in. And they insisted upon paying him—*him,* worth billions.

The rooster in the net was getting decidedly fractious. Max carried him behind the cabins to the chicken pen. He dropped the bird inside, leaning over the fence to untie the net. The bird strutted off without a backward glance.

Max walked around to the far side of the chicken pen and ducked under a lean-to. The villagers let him keep his motor scooter there. He slung a leg over the bike and gave it some throttle. If he thought to scare the rooster when he zoomed out and past the pen again, he was disappointed.

He headed up the road toward the big house and with every kilometer his gut tightened more. Part of that was the fact that he'd spoken to no one but the villagers for months now; he'd been making it a point to lie low and keep to himself. He had no fear that his social graces had gone rusty but he resented being flushed out of isolation. The other part of it was that he dreaded how Kurt would answer his questions. How many more people would be coming to the island, people who might recognize him? How long would they be staying?

Max did not want to leave Brunhia. Kurt had told him about the place when they'd run into each other in a little bar in Cairo in May and the man had dubbed it just the ticket if Max really wanted to drop out. No phones, no televisions, no newspapers. No one in the villages—in Paz or Deus Fornece—were likely to know his name or recognize his face.

But if Amando kept bringing in outsiders, Max thought, then that was going to change. When Kurt had mentioned coming here, he'd said nothing about bringing half the continent and America with him.

Max did not want to move on yet. He wasn't ready to go back to the real world. It would start all over again—women breaking all the rules of decent behavior to become the next Mrs. Strong, paparazzi angling for that one shot, that one photo, that would mark them as The Guy Who Found Max, and his business associates descending on him, both those in his employ and those who wanted to buy from him or sell. His family would catch wind of his whereabouts and they'd start plucking at his nerves again in well-intentioned worry.

His jaw hurt from clenching it. Max forced himself to relax, and then it happened.

The scooter was more difficult to maneuver than the average bicycle, Honey admitted, but she could damned well do this. The trick was in remembering that the steering was a little more exaggerated. She figured that had to do with the fact that the scooter was going a good bit faster than she'd ever learned to pedal. Velocity equaled less reaction time so a slight easing on the handlebars more or less put the frustrating little thing into a virtual U-turn.

Honey revved up the throttle a little and grinned as the backlash of wind whipped at her hair. She was just approaching the bend in the road before it straightened out and dove straight for the beach when he was suddenly there, her Portuguese hottie.

They both shouted in the same instant. Honey twisted the handlebars. She forgot that she didn't have to go hard left to avoid him. She forgot that a gentle drift in that direction would have done the trick. When she tore her surprised gaze from his face—and man, what a face!—Honey found herself flying headlong at a pile of white rocks.

The front tire of the scooter struck them and she figured she was going to take one hell of a spill. But she was going too fast for the scooter to simply stop with the impact. It went airborne, and she went with it.

* * *

Max heard the delicate putter of her smaller bike before he saw her, but even that didn't give him enough time to react. He came around the curve and there she was, headed dead at him. He had no choice but to spill, and to spill fast.

Max leaned his weight hard right. Then the crazy blonde veered to her left and they were still on a collision course. Except she kept going, kept turning. *What the hell?*

He had an impression of the most incredibly wild hair and a face captivated with so much real and emphatic emotion that for some reason it made him ache inside. Then he was down and the gravel was shearing the skin off his arm and his thigh. His bike zoomed onward on its side, chewing up dirt and sending dust pluming. And the blonde went right over the side of the road. On the bike.

Max had explored the island enough to know that there was a ten-foot drop to the beach on that side. And the beach was as nasty as any he had ever seen in his world travels. It was craggy and rough and wild. Trees grew aslant from between boulders on the way down, angling for life-giving sun.

She was going to get herself killed.

Max forgot all about the fact that he didn't want to be recognized. He forgot that he resented the hell out of all these people landing on what he'd come to think of as his island. He launched his bleeding body up from the road and ran after her.

Just as he reached the top of the jumble of rocks on the roadside, he heard her laughter. *Laughter?* It was a sound like silver bells tinkling, light and airy and genuine, and it froze him just as he was about to leap and no doubt hurt himself even worse.

"What the hell are you doing down there?" he shouted. He realized that anger was making his voice vibrate.

"Hello?" she called back.

Max got a grip. "Are you hurt?"

"Hold on!"

"Hold on for *what?*"

"I'm checking to see if everything still works." That

laughter came again. "I'm all right but the scooter has seen better days."

Not only did he have a bunch of people descending on the island but at least one of them was certifiable, Max decided.

He began making his way down the cliff with much more decorum than he had originally intended. He no longer felt particularly inclined to play superhero.

"That stands to reason," he called down to her. "Hold on, I'm on my way."

"There's no need—" she began, then she broke off. "On second thought, ouch."

"Ouch?" She was hurt, he thought. He moved faster. Then he reached the beach.

She was sitting on a boulder, grinning at him. Max felt something deep inside himself start to shake. He told himself it was the aftermath of adrenaline. Throw in a good dose of anger for good measure. That explained it.

But he was arrested by her face.

It hit him again, as it had when she'd gone airborne, that he'd never seen such real and unrepentant emotion in anyone's expression. As though anything life could dish out, including spills over cliffs, was just one more grand adventure for her to savor, experience and chalk up on one side of the line or the other, as a lesson or a hoot. This, Max realized, this whole disaster, seemed to be falling on the side of hoot.

She scraped her hair away from her face. She did have a nasty abrasion on her cheek, he realized. She'd be beautiful without it. Maybe that was why he sat down in the sand in front of her. Beauty should have had him hightailing it back up the cliff as soon as he knew she was basically okay. But abraded beauty didn't quite stir the same panic in him.

He'd have to think about that later. He told himself he just wanted to make sure she was all right.

"Someone ought to lock you up in a padded cell." His voice came out in a growl.

"They've tried. I keep slipping them."

Max's frown hurt his forehead. "A little contrition might be in order here."

"What for?"

"For trying to kill me."

"I wasn't trying. It just happened."

"Well, luckily we both lived." It struck him that he sounded utterly rigid and pompous, and what was that about? Then he realized that things were still shaking inside him.

He wasn't European, Honey realized. The European part was important—as far removed from her own life as she could get. She had the strong sense that she needed to change *everything* if she was going to get laid this time. She had to wipe away her constants, her identity, the brackets of her real life. But, by the same token, he made her mouth water. Honey watched him watching her and felt a series of tiny little jitters dance through her blood. No bam-bam-bams. No rat-tat-tats. Just...jitters.

His body was as nice as it had looked earlier from a distance, though he had pulled on a pair of cutoffs over the boxer shorts and he wore a blue mesh tank top now that obscured that delicious chest. His black hair was wind-ruffled, wild, too long. He needed a shave in the worst way, but that just made the jitters pick up speed. His eyes were the color of her father's favorite whiskey—and they got darker as she watched.

Well, Honey thought, he was building up a good case of temper. "Oh, chill out," she told him. "No harm done."

Those beautiful eyes of his bugged a little. "No harm? You've ruined that thing beyond repair!" He waved a hand at her motor scooter. "And look at me! Look at *me!*"

"Oh, I was."

To her utter surprise, that tantalizing remark got no reaction from him at all. He was on a roll. "I left half my skin up there on the road!"

"You know, it takes two to tango."

"Two to—" He broke off and started to sputter again. Cute, she thought.

"I wasn't the only scooter on that road," she reminded him. "You came at me like a bat out of hell."

"You were in the middle of the road!"

"Who was I going to hit? A seagull?"

"Me!"

"I traveled that road earlier and there wasn't another living soul on it."

"So that means all good sense and traffic regulations go right out the window? Lady, you're a danger to yourself and to mankind."

My, he was angry, Honey thought. He stood abruptly. He was *leaving* her? He was just going to walk away from her? Men never walked away from her. She fainted or shooed them off, but they didn't walk away.

Honey's jitters took on a whole new rhythm. Slower, unsure, then speeding up again. He has no idea who I am, she realized. He doesn't know I'm an Evans and he doesn't know I'm rich. He doesn't know I work at the White House or that I drive a Mercedes. He doesn't think I'm a tease, a flirt, wild and outrageous, an accident waiting to happen. He just thinks I give validation to all those dumb blonde jokes.

She had to have him.

Not just because of her Portuguese Plan. Because it was too rich, too special, too utterly, incredibly de-pressurized. He had no preconceived notions about Honey, and he had no clue Honor even existed. He was perfect. The air that hit her lungs then was the purest she could ever remember breathing.

"I can fix that for you, you know," she said, eyeing his scraped thigh and arm.

"Don't you come near me."

"I took a first-aid course once."

"In the Girl Scouts?" he demanded.

"Then, too, but I gave up the whole debacle of scouting after the cookie incident."

"You never sold Girl Scout cookies." His voice was like a whip now, she thought. "They don't let lunatics sell Girl Scout cookies."

"Well, yes and no." Honey pushed to her feet. Was he actually inching backward on that rock, trying to keep distance between them? It flabbergasted her, but she recovered nicely. "I did sell cookies before they kicked me out."

"Ha!" he barked. He didn't want to hear the explanation, Max thought. He did *not* want to know why something as All-American as the scouting organization—who took *everyone*—might be inclined to decide they didn't want her. "What did you do?" he heard himself ask anyway.

"It wasn't my fault," she murmured, reaching for his arm.

"That's what they all say." Max reared back a little out of reach.

He watched her cross her arms over very nice breasts. Small, but begging for attention. What the hell was he thinking? He didn't want breasts. He was enjoying his celibacy. He was taking a break from the silken talons of women who looked at him and saw dollar signs.

Then it dawned on him that he was having an entire conversation with an American for the first time in months and she hadn't recognized him yet, had no idea who he was. That startled him so much that he actually let her take his arm.

Her touch was a butterfly kiss. There, but not. Gentle, but fleeting. The shaking in his gut that he'd finally clamped down on started up again. And that kept his voice rough. "What the hell do you think you're doing?"

In response, she dropped his arm and headed across the sand toward the sea. As he watched, she whipped her top over her head.

She had a bra on. Something pale yellow. His heart stopped anyway. She was insane. She bent to swish the little white French-cut T-shirt in the surf, then she straightened and turned back to him. Oh, yeah, nice breasts, he thought. Except he wasn't thinking about breasts these days. Max dragged his eyes away from the view. Maybe she did know who he was, he realized. Maybe this was all just some sort of convoluted come-on.

"It won't work," he snapped when she came back to him.

She looked startled. "Of course, it will. Salt water is amazing. It will keep any infection at bay until you get back to that boat of yours to slop antiseptic all over this mess. You have a first-aid kit on board, right?"

She was talking about first-aid kits? In her underwear? "I meant the half-naked part."

She looked down at herself. "I'm not half-naked. I have a swimsuit that puts this to shame. Of course, if I was going to wade in and go swimming, yeah, then I suppose I would be half-naked."

"What's the connection?" Max asked before he could remind himself that he didn't want to know. But God, her mind took more loops and turns than a roller coaster. He realized that he'd never found out why they'd kicked her out of the Girl Scouts, either.

"It's lace." She snapped a bra strap. "If it got wet, then I guess, sure, that would be as good as naked."

He was not going to think about this. "Normal women don't discuss this sort of thing with strangers."

"We almost got killed together. We're not strangers."

"I don't know your name," he heard himself say.

She seemed to hesitate. "Elise."

"Pretty."

"Thank you."

"Almost as nice as that bra."

"Thank you again. Now can I have your arm, or would you rather contract gangrene before you get back to your boat?"

"How do you know I live on a boat?"

"I noticed you when Amando and I came in this morning."

Well, Max thought, that makes two of us. He let her take his arm.

"I guess if I took my shorts off, too, to deal with that mess on your leg, you'd really have a heart attack."

His heart was definitely reacting to such a prospect. "Stay dressed."

"It's a little late for that."

"I'm not looking."

"Sure you are. You looked three times before I stopped counting. But I don't mind."

He stared deliberately into eyes the color of the sea in the southwest islands to avoid doing it again. "Who the hell are you?"

"I told you. Elise. But you didn't tell me your name."

Max opened his mouth and clamped it shut again. Change the subject, he thought. But she would just dog the subject if she really wanted to know the answer. Better to lie, he decided. "Joe," he said, using his brother's name.

"Pleased to meet you, Joe."

"Don't be offended if I don't return the sentiment."

"Ah, come on. I'm the best thing that's happened to you all day." She wrapped her sopping shirt around his bicep.

What really ticked Max off was that she was right. "I might have twelve Vegas dancers waiting for me in my fore cabin."

"If you did, you probably wouldn't have been riding along that dirt road on your scooter all alone," she countered. "And you wouldn't be so obsessed with one little yellow bra, either."

He almost grinned before he caught himself. "You can knock that off now." He motioned at her shirt with his free hand. "I think I'm de-germed."

She pulled it away from his arm and plastered it against his thigh.

"Ouch!"

"Be brave," she said, holding it against what was left of his skin.

It stung like hell, worse than his arm, but he sucked it up for a moment. Then he pushed off the rock and stood. "I can take care of it from here. Get dressed."

She pulled the top over her head. Wet as it was, it didn't make a damned bit of difference. "Happy now?"

"No. Yes." He stalked off toward the rocks again, then common sense filtered back into his brain along with some of the manners his mother had drummed into him. He looked back at her. "Do you need a ride to the house? That scooter of yours isn't going anywhere."

Honey thought about it. On one hand, it was a good excuse to prolong their acquaintance. On the other, she didn't want him anywhere near her home base where Honey and Honor would intrude. He was *hers*.

"You were headed there when we almost hit each other, weren't you?" she realized.

"When *you* almost hit *me*."

Honey waved a hand. "Semantics."

"And I wasn't headed to the big house."

"Then where were you going?"

"I was just out and about." His eyes shifted.

He was lying. Why? It only intrigued her. "The house is the only thing up this way. Do you know Kurt and Gretchen?"

"Who?"

"Never mind." She started toward the road. "I can walk back. It's not far."

She'd almost reached him before Max realized that the information he'd needed from Kurt, the whole reason he'd been heading for the big house in the first place, was as close as his fingertips. And getting closer. Clad in a sheer, wet top with tempting yellow-lace swells. He dragged his eyes away from her breasts again. "Ah, you're staying up there, right? Nobody's come here in months. Now all of a sudden there's a steady stream of people going there."

"Well, my brother's getting—" She broke off.

"Your brother is what?"

"My brother's getting tamed."

"That's not what you were going to say."

She blinked innocent azure eyes at him. If she told him about the wedding and he actually did know Kurt, he might put two and two together and identify her. It wasn't worth the chance.

"Is something going on up there this week besides this

taming business?" he asked. "Will everyone clear out again soon?"

Honey shrugged. "I imagine so. They won't tell me anything. But why in the world would they stay after the... taming?"

Now what did *that* mean? he wondered. It didn't matter. She'd as good as told him that he only had to lay low for a while, that all these intrusive people weren't long-term. He turned away again and began climbing up the rocks. She trailed behind him.

She gave him a little wave—not as jaunty as Honey would have done, nor as polite as what would be expected from Honor—as he righted his bike again. She turned toward the house. She'd taken four steps before his voice stopped her.

"So why *did* you get kicked out of the Girl Scouts?"

Honey turned around to walk backward. "My brother bought up all my cookies and I won the Disney World prize. They said it was fixed."

"Was it?"

"Nah, that's just the way Drew—" She caught herself. "Drexel. The way Drexel is."

"Drexel."

"My brother."

"The tame one?"

"No. The other."

He gunned the throttle. He was going to leave, Honey thought. Suddenly, she had an almost overwhelming need to keep him. As long as he was here, as long as they were trapped here in time, she was just herself and even her Portuguese Plan didn't seem to matter too much.

"I also put a snake in Marilena Morgan's sleeping bag at camp!" she called as he drove back toward the beach.

She wasn't sure if he heard her or not.

Four

In her own defense, Honey thought, she'd *tried* to get back to her bell room without being spotted.

She slipped into the kitchen with the intention of using the back stairs. Rafaela was beating the tar out of something in a large metal bowl with her back toward her. Honey sidestepped for the stairs door, then a floorboard creaked beneath her and Rafaela glanced over her shoulder. They stared at each other for a moment then the woman shouted.

"O deus bless o, aqueles motocicleta matará alguém!"

Even without her dictionary—Honey had it in her back pocket because she really had anticipated that Joe was Portuguese—she'd picked up a few key words of that. *God. Motorcycle. Kill.* "I'm fine. No problemo here." Caught dead to rights, she marched more normally through the door to the stairs.

She was on the first tread when the woman's shriek brought Gretchen, who had apparently been lingering in the big room. "Oh, Lord!" she cried when Honey turned around and she saw her face.

"It's nothing. Really. My bones are all still in one piece."

Gretchen rushed at her anyway. She pulled her back into the kitchen, took her chin and turned her face into the sun that streamed through one of the back windows.

"Well, if I didn't hurt before," Honey muttered, "I do now."

Gretchen dropped her hand fast. "Oh! I'm so sorry!"

Honey was instantly contrite. "I was just jiving you. Please, don't ever take me seriously. No one else does."

The door to the big room swung open again and Kurt came in. "Wow," he said, "you're going to have a shiner. How'd you get wet?"

"I went over the cliff on the scooter. The seawater is just left over from a little first-aid effort."

Rafaela called on God and cursed scooters again in Portuguese. She zeroed in on Honey with a towel and looked for all the world as if she was going to start dabbing it at her cheek. Honey backpedaled fast. "The body replenishes skin cells every twenty-four hours. This is really no big deal."

"But the pretty face be mess for the wedding." Rafaela clucked.

"The pretty face never goes to weddings without makeup," Honey assured her.

"How's the bike?" Kurt asked.

She thought about lying, then gave it up. "Maybe nothing a good mechanic and a hammer can't fix." I hope, she added silently. And if it was beyond repair, then she would just fix the mess the way she fixed all her messes. She would pay him for it.

"What the hell did you do now?" Marcus's voice boomed into the kitchen.

Honey looked at him warily as he stormed in. "Now, see, you automatically assume this was my doing when in fact a maniac drove me off the road."

"There are no maniacs on that road!" Marcus hollered.

"I beg to differ." Honey sniffed indignantly and drew herself up to her full height, which wasn't much more than five foot three, but it would have to do.

"There's *nobody* on these roads," Gretchen fretted.

"Tell that to the scooter."

"You're coming to my wedding with a bloody face?" Marcus demanded.

Honey turned for the stairs again and looked over her shoulder at him. "Watch yourself. Don't get my dander up or I'll come to your wedding naked."

Someone hissed in a breath—maybe Gretchen, maybe Samantha. Sam was now standing in the door to the big room, propping it open with one hand, trying to figure out what was going on.

Honey dove up the stairs, desperate to get away from them all. Maybe it was as simple as the fact that twenty minutes ago she'd enjoyed the luxury of just being herself for the first time in...well, maybe in her entire life.

She reached the bell room and whipped her T-shirt over her head for the second time in the last half hour. She started to take it to the bathroom to soak the sea salt out of it but remembered that there wasn't a bathroom up here. But, she thought, neither was there a Marcus, a fussing maid or an appalled Gretchen.

She sighed and dropped the shirt on the floor. She went to one of the windows, bracing a shoulder against the frame and crossing her arms as she stared out. The *Sea Change* was still bobbing on the deep blue waters off the far south beach but she was too far away to tell if Joe had made it back on board.

"Who are you, anyway?" she wondered aloud. "What are you doing here?"

He was American, she thought. No doubt about that. And granted, she hadn't seen a great deal of the island yet, but she had the strong hunch that other than Gretchen and Kurt, Marcus and Samantha, she and Joe were the only other anglos in residence. She knew what the others were doing here. But what was Joe's story? And why had he asked her how many more people would be coming to Brunhia and how long they would stay?

Okay, Honey thought, something was wrong with this picture.

"Damn it." She dropped her arms and moved away from the window. She'd found an absolutely exquisite body attached to an intriguing man who didn't know her as Honey, didn't know her as Honor Elise, and didn't even much seem to want to come on to her...and something was definitely wrong with him.

She went to one of her suitcases for a dry top. She found

a T-shirt emblazoned with a picture of her favorite rap group, B2K. She yanked it over her head then headed back to the stairs.

She needed to speak with Kurt. He seemed honest, basic, no-nonsense. She had to find out if Joe had any connection to Marcus's wacko situation. If he did, that brought him a little too close to her world. It edged him perilously near to bam-bam-bamsville.

And if she managed to wheedle some details of Marcus's top-secret voodoo genes out of Kurt in the process, well, she thought, then that was all the better.

Honey landed in the kitchen and Rafaela looked up again and frowned. "*Senhora,* your cheek. It is still ugly."

She'd forgotten about it. "I'll clean it up in a minute. Do you know where Kurt is?"

"*Sim.* In the garage talking to my Ricardo."

Honey dodged out the back door. Just as she did, Kurt emerged from the garage. Honey jogged to catch up to him before he could get too close to the house.

"Sorry about the bike," she said a little breathlessly. She pivoted and fell into step beside him, then she put a hand on his arm to stop him.

"Don't worry about it. We keep several of them and I can't see a whole lot of our guests using them these next few days."

Honey thought of her mother on a motor scooter. "Probably not."

"Ricardo will bring it back and we'll hit the mainland for whatever parts he needs to fix it." Kurt starting walking again.

"Wait!"

He looked back at her questioningly.

"The thing is, I don't know exactly what you've been told about me, but a lunatic really did run me off the road," she blurted.

"We have a lunatic on Brunhia?"

She couldn't actually tell if he looked alarmed or disbelieving. Maybe it was a little of both. In any event, it was the opening she needed. "Marcus told me a little of what's been going on with him. The lunatic is American so I'm a little concerned that this guy might be, you know, involved somehow in the voodoo-gene thing. Marcus said a lot of people who are would be here this week."

Her blood quickened when Kurt frowned. "There's another American stalking the island? They've already nailed Zach and they almost got Gretchen so I guess they're capable of anything. Thanks. I'll look into it."

Names. Oh, yes, she was definitely getting somewhere this time. "Who's Zach?"

"I'm not supposed to tell you anything."

Honey raked her hands through her hair, then she dropped them back to her sides in frustration. "What if this guy is planning to nail *me?* He says his name is Joe and he's tucked up on that sailboat down there off the beach. And no offense but this place doesn't rank real high on the world's list of exciting vacation meccas."

Kurt's tension dissolved abruptly. To her utter disbelief, he laughed. "Joe? The guy living on the boat off the south beach? This is your lunatic?"

Honey nodded hard. Her hair danced. "That's the one."

"He's harmless."

"He's not involved in this... What did you call it again? Marcus's genetic voodoo stuff?"

His gaze leveled on hers. "Good try. I didn't call it anything."

Well, she thought, she had to admire the guy's intelligence. "Do you know Joe?"

"He's been anchored down there for a few months now."

It wasn't an answer, she thought. She tried to tell herself that Kurt had pretty much just labeled Joe as Fair Sex Game if he wasn't involved in Marcus's mess, but she was dissatisfied. "So I'm not in any danger?"

"Why would you be? The Coalition pretty much knows who they want now and it's not you."

Coalition? Honey was reasonably sure she'd never heard

the term before but it nudged something else dangling at the back of her brain.

She might work in the White House, but Honey tried very hard not to get too involved with anything political, even if she did have a poli-sci degree. Still, she occasionally picked up a newspaper and she fielded all those White House phone calls. To a large degree she knew who was calling whom and when. Sometimes she was even able to garner why.

"It's true," she said suddenly, bluntly.

"Of course it is. If I honestly believed that you were in any sort of danger, I'd tell you."

"Not that. I was talking about this whole Fight Fear campaign that President Stewart has going on. It's *true.*" Suddenly Honey had to hunt for her breath. It wanted to catch and clog. She thought about what her brother had done earlier on the roadside and the buzz of wild, panicked phone calls that had been coming into the White House these last months, and for the first time she put it together. "There *is* something to fear!"

Kurt took a wary step backward. "Got to go now."

He looked like a trapped animal, she thought. But she plunged on. "The buzz inside the White House has been that that CIA guy had some sort of nervous breakdown and he was talking nonsense."

"I have no idea what you're talking about."

"The one who went to the press blathering about designer babies, altered genes, murder, et cetera."

"Oh. That CIA guy."

"He accused the good ol' U.S. of A. of sponsoring some voodoo experiment that would create superhumans and now my own brother is running around playing superhero without a cape."

"Do you consider your brother superhuman?"

"He often thinks he is." Honey paused, remembering something else. "One of the papers said some of these experiments had actually been born."

"Was it a weekly rag with a three-headed llama on the cover?"

Honey set her jaw. "I believe it was *The Washington Post.*"

"I think the *Post* also said no one was able to find any files pertaining to such a project."

"You're lying to me. That whole project—the people who did it—they're the... What did you call it? The Coalition."

"I can state with absolute sincerity that that's not true."

Honey frowned. "Then who went after this Zach person if not the government who created the voodoo-gene babies?"

"Talk to your brother," Kurt suggested, easing away again.

Damn, Honey thought, he was good at dodging. She started to go after him, then she stalled. She was going to be here for a week. She'd get to the bottom of this sooner or later... *After* she shed her virgin status.

She followed after him back to the house. What she wouldn't give right now for her computer! She could jump online and search out all the newspaper and rag articles she'd ignored these last months and get the dirt on this situation. Why had she blown those stories off when they'd first appeared in print? Because, she thought, they hadn't been talking about Marcus then. It had all just seemed like superfluous rattle-tattle stuff, and the word winging through the Great White Hallowed Halls was that it was nonsense. She'd had a bigger stake in partying and her bam-bam-bam, rat-tat-tat problem.

Even when Marcus had sent her that letter, it *still* hadn't triggered. Because Marcus was...well, Marcus. She'd just thought he was saying that his real parents had been involved in some sort of experimental fertility project and maybe that had made him a little healthier than most. In all fairness, she thought, agitated again, that was exactly the way he'd made it sound. But since when did parents desperate to conceive a child—desperate enough to take part in an experimental study—turn around and put that kid up for adoption?

Honey shook her head dazedly. It was overwhelming.

There really were designer babies and in all likelihood her brother was one of them.

Rafaela was no longer in the kitchen when she returned there. Honey trotted up the stairs, glancing at her watch. It wasn't even two o'clock yet. That meant the day still offered plenty of beach time. She closed the bell-room door behind her and began peeling out of her clothes, putting wigged-out genetic experiments from her mind. She just hoped she wouldn't find Marcus's face in the newspaper any time soon beside a photo of Dolly the Sheep.

Half an hour after leaving Kurt, Honey stood in the barn with her beach satchel slung over her shoulder. Dressing for her next encounter with Joe-the-Inexplicable-American had proven to be just a tad tricky. True, he hadn't ignored her breasts when she'd been running around in her bra earlier. But he'd *tried* to ignore them. So she hadn't been quite sure if he would be more susceptible to her lemon-yellow thong or her teal-blue maillot suit.

In the end, she'd gone with the maillot. Just for the sheer craziness of it, and to make an impact, she'd pulled the B2K T-shirt back on again over it. She'd knotted it at her waist. Then she'd tugged on gym socks and running shoes, the better for scootering with. The whole get-up was sort of a long-distance-runner type look, although Honey never ran—purely on principle and because of the sweat quotient. But now Ricardo was balking at giving her another scooter.

"You take Cisco," he suggested, pointing at a mule.

"I ride nothing with ears longer than its tail." Honey turned away. "I'll walk, then. Tell the gang I'm sorry I'll miss dinner."

"Why you miss dinner?"

"I'll be walking that l-o-o-ng lonely road back home."

"*Senhora,* you wait."

Honey paused and grinned to herself. In the end, he gave her another scooter.

She made it all the way down to the cove without going

off the road this time. She stopped the bike behind the cabins and got off, toeing the kickstand down, going the rest of the way on foot. The beach was deserted now. There were no children frolicking and smoke was no longer belching from the little cabin's chimney. Everything seemed still and silent. Honey looked out at the *Sea Change.* There was no sign of Joe. She dropped her satchel and whipped out a beach towel, spreading it on the sand. Then she heard a shout from her right. Children were chasing several chickens around in a small pen behind one of the cabins. Without thinking, Honey stood again and went that way.

"Posso eu ajudar?" she tried in wretched Portuguese when she reached them.

The children laughed. Some apparently thought her suggestion was so hysterical, they even flopped down into the dirt.

"Guess not," Honey said.

"They think you get pretty hands dirty," said a voice from behind her.

Honey turned quickly. A young woman in a long black skirt approached. Her feet were bare and the hand she held out was rough, callused, her nails painfully short. But she was beautiful, with an ebony braid dangling down her back and soulful dark eyes.

"I am Paloma," she said as Honey took her hand. "You are from the big house, no? What you want with our chickens?"

"I have never in my life had occasion to catch one and I'm big on experiences. That's what they're doing, right? Trying to catch one?"

"*Sim.* To give back to *Senhor* Sailor."

"*Senhor—* Ah." Honey looked out at the sailboat again. She liked the tag.

An eruption of harsh Portuguese came from the nearest cabin. An older woman stomped out, waving her arms at the children. They scattered and she reached down and snagged a rooster's legs herself with a hand that moved like lightning.

"Man, you're *good,*" Honey said.

The woman studied her for a moment then nodded. *"Obrigado."*

"She say thank you," Paloma explained. "She is my mama. Her name is Lourdes. Come with me and have something cool to drink."

Honey grinned, delighted at the prospect. Then she looked back at the children.

The boys' shorts and the girls' skirts were threadbare. Their little bellies were skinny. For that matter, so were the hens who remained in the pen. Honey had the sudden, shaky certainty that she should take nothing from these people who had so very little to share. Her, a woman with a trust fund and a decent job. Then she had the unique and wonderful thought that maybe she could do something for these people later to repay this little bit of hospitality. If she put her mind to it, she could figure out a way to have a whole boatload of chickens delivered to them.

She followed Paloma into one of the little cabins. As small as the place appeared from outside, it was actually one-and-a-half stories. A loft-like space ran along just inside the ceiling. Honey saw beds stacked up there like cans of corn on a grocery-store shelf. She heard snores rumbling from that direction. Paloma put a hand to her lips to signal for quiet.

The first floor was given over to one large living area. Honey realized that she'd seen smoke earlier despite the warm day because the hearth was used for cooking. Several kettles were piled neatly beside it.

Paloma went to a crate against one wall, tucked into shadows so the sun streaming in the windows wouldn't touch it. She withdrew a jug. It dripped with melted ice. "My papa and my Adan go every morning to the mainland. They take fish to sell and the older children to school. They bring back ice and other things we must have."

"Who's Adan?" Honey asked.

"My husband."

She felt her jaw drop. "You're *married?*" Paloma looked so young.

Paloma poured from the jug into small earthen cups. "I am twenty," she said as though that explained everything.

Honey swigged from the cup without bothering to ask what was in it. Wow, she thought, it was nectar. Sweet and tart at the same time, and ice-cold. "No offense, but where I come from, twenty is just getting your feet wet."

"You have no husband?"

Something shuddered inside her as she thought of her mother's life. "No."

"Here we marry as soon as possible. For our *pais,* our parents. Getting enough fish to sell in Portimao and to feed all of us besides takes many hands. So families join by marriage and all work together." She moved for the door. "Come, we go outside. It is cooler there in the shade and quieter."

Honey followed her out of the cabin and they sat in the sand beneath one of the trees. She sipped more of the nectar. Then she saw Joe step out onto the deck of the sailboat. "Do you know what he's doing here on Brunhia?" she asked Paloma, motioning to him.

Paloma shrugged. "We are not sure, but he is a very good man."

Honey leaned closer to her. "Tell me everything."

Paloma studied her face for a moment, then gave a female grin that was the same in any culture, all the world over. "He came here one season ago. He stays out there mostly, on his boat, but sometimes he comes to village to help us. We give him chickens and fish and he always gives them back again. Sometimes not the fish," she added thoughtfully. "Sometimes he eats those."

So he had a job of sorts here, Honey thought. But chickens and fish wouldn't go far toward paying for a boat like that. She was getting a feeling for him now. He was a society dropout, content with earning a pittance for odd jobs. He didn't seem to like poultry, though.

She watched him drop over the side of the sailboat into a little skiff that was tied there. She sighed blissfully. He was coming ashore. Life was good and getting better. Honey stood. "I think I'll just wander back over to my towel and lie in the sun for a while."

Paloma gave a quick burst of laughter as she got to her feet as well. "Come back again. We talk more."

For the second time today, here was someone who hadn't a clue that she was either Honey or Honor, she realized. Here was someone who didn't know that she had once let herself get arrested for underage drinking without consuming a drop just so as not to appear sanctimonious to her pals and to get a rise out of her parents. Paloma did not know that she passed out in rose bushes when a man touched her. "I'll definitely be back," she promised.

Then she hurried for her beach towel because Joe was throwing the lines off his little boat and tugging at the ripcord of the outboard engine. Honey flopped down just as she heard the engine cough to life. She waited for the little scraping thud that told her he'd beached the craft, then she sat up to grin at him. When he noticed her, he stopped cold.

"What are you doing here?" he demanded.

All in all, Honey thought, she'd had better welcomes. She let her smile spread as her gaze coasted up and down him. "Enjoying the view."

"It's better on the other side of the island." He turned away and headed for Paloma's village.

Honey vaulted to her feet. "Hey, wait up there!"

He stopped and looked back at her. "Why?"

"Well, because..." Honey floundered. She *never* floundered. She flailed mentally for some witty response but none would come. "So we can talk," she finished lamely.

"Why do I get the feeling you'll do it whether I listen or not?"

"Ah, see, already we're getting to know each other." He started walking away again. She hurried to match stride beside him. "Why Brunhia? What brought you and your boat here of all places?"

He looked over at her with those whiskey eyes and frowned. "It's quiet here. At least, it used to be. Go away."

"I guess Lisbon could get a wee bit expensive. I imagine living is much more affordable here."

They reached the village. Paloma was no longer anywhere to be found. The children were streaming off toward the woods and more seemed to have joined them because the throng was fairly large now. Joe went that way toward a lean-to behind the cabins.

Honey ducked in after him. The side roof was low but there was enough room at the far side to stand up. His bike was there. She straddled it and pretended to rev the throttle. "No worse for the wear, I see. Mine, on the other hand, is probably still on the beach."

"Kurt will send someone after it." He went to a large metal tool chest and began taking items out.

"Yeah, Ricardo is already— What did you just say?"

"I said Kurt—" He clamped his mouth shut.

"You *do* know Kurt. All he said was that you'd been anchored down here for a while."

Damned if she didn't have a way of just sliding in on things and making him forget that he really didn't want to talk to her, Max thought. But it was gratifying to learn that Kurt had stood by him, keeping his mouth shut about his identity. He gathered up the wrenches he needed and stalked out.

"Get off my bike," he said as he passed her. "I don't trust you with it."

Honey levered her leg over again to follow him. "I'm getting better with the contraptions. I made it down here this time without mishap."

"My lucky day."

"We were talking about Kurt," she reminded him, catching up with him again.

"No, we weren't. *You* were talking about Kurt. I don't want to talk to you at all."

"Why not?"

He reached two boats that had been tugged up on shore just past the village. He kept one of the wrenches and dropped the others into the sand. Then he went to work on the outboard motor, loosening lugnuts to remove it from the stern.

He figured if he ignored her long enough, she'd eventually get pissed off and leave. He wasn't the least bit prepared for her to climb into the boat and sit on one of the bench seats facing him. She braced her elbows on her knees and her chin in her hands. Max finally stopped what he was doing to stare at her.

"They sure as hell breed them brazen on the eastern seaboard," he said finally.

She smiled. "And what eastern seaboard would that be?"

"My guess? Maryland. You're not from Virginia or any farther south, you don't have that drawl. And you're not from up north because you don't go all nasal on your vowels. So it's somewhere in the middle."

"I think those are the most words you've ever said to me all at once. I'm getting to you, aren't I?"

He laughed without knowing where it came from. "This boat belongs to a man named Lope. You didn't ask him if you could sit in it, so scoot."

"Where is he? I'd be glad to ask him."

"He's asleep. Get out of his boat," he said again.

She didn't move. "You were right, by the way. I'm from Maryland. How do you know so much about American accents?"

"I get around."

"Ah. A drifter."

Max thought about it. He hadn't drifted so much as he'd run. He reminded himself that he didn't want to discuss it with her—or anything else either, for that matter.

"So where did you begin your drift?" she asked.

He opened his mouth to tell her Paris after finding Camille in bed with that slick-tongued Francois-type character, then he choked on the words. "Remind me again how this is any of your business."

"I'm a naturally curious person."

He got the motor free and began carrying it back to his skiff. He'd work on it aboard the *Sea Change.* He'd be safe from her there. But then he found himself looking back over his shoulder at her as she clamored out of the boat. "Just for the record, you dress weird."

Honey looked down at herself. "I was making a fashion statement."

"Of what sort?"

"This is my athletic look."

He was getting it now, Max thought. Maybe he hadn't caught on before because he'd been so distracted by that yellow bra. But now he was getting it loud and clear. This was his penance, he thought, though he couldn't put his finger on what he had ever done to deserve it. He'd been scrupulously fair in all his business dealings. He'd never cheated on Camille, despite opportunity in numbers that many men would salivate over. He called his mother every Sunday night—well, he used to, before he'd dropped out—and he gave a lot of money to various charities. All the same, fate was hellbent and determined to put him at the mercy of shallow sharklike socialites who were voracious for more of what bought them the good things in life.

Max dumped the motor into his own dinghy and turned back to her. He saw it all this time. "Nothing better to do with your time than change your look, hmm?"

To his surprise, he saw her wince quickly. "It amuses me," she said.

"Living for life's amusements is important."

"I think so."

"I don't."

His voice had gone so flat suddenly, Honey thought. She was losing her stride again. Then she opened her mouth and heard some very un-Honey-like words tumble out. "Why don't you like me?"

He headed back to the spot in the sand where he had left his tools. She went after him again. "Answer me," she insisted. "Please. I really want to know."

"I'm not obligated to like you," he replied without looking at her, "no matter what life has taught you."

"What life's *taught* me?" She felt her temper tug loose. "I'll tell you what it's taught me, pal. It's taught me that it isn't the least bit difficult to push my current mood aside and be friendly to others anyway because it might just make their day if they're having a bad one, too. It's taught me that if something's wrong it doesn't matter how you go about fixing it just as long as you do, as long as you make some noise and draw everyone's attention to the problem. It's taught me that people are all pretty much the same inside—if you take the Ted Bundy-types out of it—and they hurt when they're rejected and they're touched by spontaneous kindnesses." She broke off and planted her hands on her hips. "Now look what you've done. You've made me mad."

"I made *you* mad? You're the one who was crowding me! And what the hell kind of lecture was that, anyway?"

Honey looked into his eyes. They were going very dark again. Temper, she thought. Well, at least she'd gotten a rise out of him. "My point is, there's no need to be rude to me."

"Politely telling you to go didn't work!"

"Because you didn't mean it."

"I meant it!"

"That makes no sense. I've only been friendly."

"I don't like rich girls!" he hollered.

"I'm not a girl. I'm twenty-three. I'm a woman." Then she watched him clutch his head in his hands.

"How do you wing everything around on me?" he asked disbelievingly.

"It's my gift. At least I got you to give me an answer. You don't like me because you think I'm rich." And, of course, he had so little, Honey thought. She could see where that might bother him. "How did you draw that conclusion?" Maybe she could wriggle her way out of the problem.

"You're an American lady on an obscure island who had to get to Portugal somehow and that takes money."

Honey shrugged. "You're here. Do you have money?"

"I—" He choked again.

"Although, that *is* a really nice boat." She looked thoughtfully over her shoulder at it.

"An inheritance," he said shortly. "Rich uncle."

Well, that was something, Honey thought. One more little piece of the puzzle. He'd inherited a boat, or the money to buy one, and had started drifting. And now he was doing odd jobs to get by.

Then he startled her by moving toward her suddenly and grabbing her wrist. "And *this!*" he said, shaking her arm a little.

Honey looked down at her Rolex. "Rich uncle," she said. "An inheritance." It was even true as far as it went.

He dropped her arm again to gather up his tools.

"I'm just me," Honey said, and she hated the tone of pleading in her own voice. He'd accepted her at face value earlier, the way Paloma had done. She didn't want to lose that.

Then the roar of another boat had them both looking up at the cove. Amando was back. He had four people on board this time.

Honey heard Joe swear, but when she looked around for him again, he was already at his dinghy, pushing off in a hurry.

Five

Honey forgot about Joe. She *knew* that tall and willowy brunette out there on Amando's boat. She knew the way she glanced adoringly—oh, gag me, Honey thought, grinning delightedly—at the dark-haired man standing behind her and bracing her against the jolts of the sea swells. Carey? What in the name of all the saints was Carey Benton doing on Brunhia?

Honey broke into a lope until she was standing in front of the skiff when Amando brought it in. "Hello, *bonito* missy!" he called out to her.

"Back at you!" Honey shouted. Then she stripped off her gym shoes and socks and waded out to the boat. "You're turning into a rotten influence on this woman, Tynan. She didn't say a word to me about coming here."

"Nice getup, Miss Evans," Matt Tynan replied. "Was that a fashion statement?" He gestured toward the shoes she'd left on the beach.

Honey grinned up at him. "I want to catch myself a badass body just like yours and my legs are my most alluring feature. Stop blushing, Carey." To Matt, she added, "She told me all about it. Your body, that is."

"I most certainly did not!" Carey erupted. "And why *were* you wearing gym socks and sneaks with a bathing suit?"

Honey's gaze went to Joe's dinghy, scooting neatly out to the *Sea Change* now.

Carey followed her eyes. "Who's that?" she asked.

"He's a work in progress." She looked back at them. "Just

out of curiosity, did you guys take a major wrong turn from Paris or something? What are you doing here?"

Carey's gaze slid sideways. Did she seem guilty? Honey frowned and splashed along beside the boat as Amando poled it in. Matt went off first and held up his arms to catch Carey's vault onto dry sand. She'd dig the dirt out of Carey later, she decided. Matt Tynan's arrival on Brunhia was making things more interesting. He was a White House advisor.

"So who are you?" she asked bluntly of the other couple. Ten to one, they were more government types. Was this week supposed to be an exchanging of marital vows or a Weird Genes Summit?

The man helped the woman over the bow and Tynan caught her as well. The guy seemed vaguely familiar, Honey thought, but she couldn't place him. She could know him from the Great White Hallowed Halls, or maybe he was an actor or model or some such thing. He had the looks for it in a bad-boy, biker sort of way. And...he was wearing a wedding ring.

"Oh, sorry," Carey said, jumping into introductions. "Honey, this is Ethan Williams and his wife, Kelly."

Now she knew where she recognized the guy from. "Ah, one of our Top Twenty Beltway Bachelors." He'd been featured in a magazine spread some six months ago.

"Not anymore," his wife said, grinning.

"Well, welcome to our humble corner of the world," Honey said, holding a hand out to her. Her dark ponytail was a little worse off for Amando's boat ride. "Are you all here because my brother is a genetic wonder or is this purely social?"

All four of them stared at her. Well, Honey thought, that told her something. She just wasn't sure what. Then they all began talking at once.

"Samantha and Ethan go way back," Kelly said.

"I went to high school with Samantha," Matt volunteered.

"Of course, it's social," Carey joined in. "It's a wedding."

"Well, I'll admit that Marcus's plans to hitch up are convenient.'' Honey pinned Carey with her eyes. ''And *you* haven't been able to lie worth a damn since the day I met you.''

Carey drew herself up and gave a small sniff. ''Which is why I'm not going to say anything more at all.''

''You know I'll drag it out of you, right?''

''You can certainly try. But as you've pointed out before, I don't bleat.''

Honey tucked her hand through her friend's arm and began drawing her toward the road even as Marcus appeared there with the mules and the wagon. Ethan Williams's voice shot out from behind them.

''Judas-freaking-priest! Couldn't Evans have sprung for a limo?''

Honey glanced over her shoulder at him. ''You're looking at it.'' Then she leaned close to Carey again conspiratorially. ''You can bleat to me. I'm not the press.''

''I can't bleat to anyone. I *won't* bleat.''

Marcus drew the team to a halt and jumped down onto the sand. He looked at Honey suspiciously.

''Don't worry about me,'' she told him. ''I have my own transportation.'' She let go of Carey's arm and sauntered up the road where she had left the scooter. She felt her brother staring after her.

''Ricardo wasn't supposed to give you another one of those!'' he called.

Which just went to show who was the persuasive one in this family, Honey decided.

Four more of them. Four more newcomers.

Max watched the goings-on on the beach from the door hatch that led below deck on the *Sea Change.* He tried to remember exactly what Elise had told him about what was happening at the big house this week. She'd implied that the hoopla wouldn't last forever but had she said anything about even more people arriving?

''Damn it,'' he muttered aloud. It was turning into his favorite phrase lately.

He should just pull up anchor and head into Portimao until this was over, he thought. He found himself going below for a beer instead. When he got back to the hatchway and looked out again, the newcomers were loaded into Kurt's wagon and were headed up the road. Elise was gone.

He needed to do something about her, Max thought. *Pull up anchor and head into Portimao.* Every once in a while, he liked the jolt of it, the noise and the smells and action of the mainland. He took it in small doses because Portimao was rapidly becoming one of Portugal's premier tourist spots and that was inching a little too close to civilization for his comfort. His face was known all over the world, at least without long hair and a beard.

So why hadn't she recognized him?

Maybe she had, Max thought again, going up on deck to sit in the sun now that the coast was clear. Maybe she was playing some kind of game with him. God knew that rich little socialites were aces at playing games. But he could give her the benefit of the doubt and almost convince himself that she hadn't made him because no one would expect Maxwell Strong to turn up on Brunhia.

He was dwelling on her, Max realized. Again. She confused him. He'd just pegged her for another shallow rich bitch who would only really want his money, then she'd gone off on him with all that business about smiling at strangers and making noise for good causes. He couldn't get a handle on her.

Irritated with himself, Max drained the last of his beer and went to pull up anchor.

Honey tapped her own bottle of beer against Matt Tynan's in a mini-toast.

"Truce?" he asked, widening his eyes innocently. He used charm without even thinking about it, she thought, but she couldn't dislike him for it. They'd had a falling out when he'd accused Carey of bleating some top-secret White House gobbledygook. Carey of all people, Ms. Midwest Integrity.

"Jeez, you are such a politician," she replied.

They were in the big room at the house. Ice tinkled in glasses and someone had put on a muted CD of forties classics. The chandelier was dripping golden light as, outside the windows, the day yawned from a job well done and gave up its efforts at sunshine. Delicious smells were coming from Rafaela's kitchen.

"You gave her a bum rap," Honey said, "and she's my friend."

"You collect friends like most people buy groceries, sweetheart."

Honey felt a quick, tight squeeze in the area of her heart, but he had a point. That was the rep she had created for herself. For the second time that day, she opened her mouth and something utterly un-Honey-like came spilling out. "I genuinely like Carey. She's a much better person than I am."

Tynan drank from his beer. "Now what am I supposed to say to that? If I agree, I'm putting you down. If I don't, I'm putting *her* down, which isn't happening."

"This is one of those areas where silence is the best policy," Honey advised. And then, because he seemed a little off balance, she took a shot. "So why *are* you here, Tynan? The truth this time."

"I've been friends with Sam since high school. I told you that earlier."

So much for catching him off guard, Honey thought. She rounded him for another approach. "Kurt says I'm in danger with this genetic voodoo business."

Tynan lowered his beer slowly. "Kurt said that?"

"Especially after what happened with..." What the devil had that guy's name been? "Zach," she said, remembering.

"Kurt told you about Zach?"

What was that other term Kurt had used? "He said the Coalition was capable of anything." But his eyes were doing that thing that said all his guard was going up. She'd watched him face down the press corps often enough to know the look.

"Honey, with all due respect, the word is out not to talk to you about any of this."

She frowned at him fiercely. "Now that is just ridiculous. What does everyone think I'm going to do? This is my *brother* we're talking about. I have a right to know."

"All the same, go poke at someone else. You're no match for me."

Under other circumstances, that might have made her laugh again. Honey set her jaw instead as he walked away to join Kurt and Marcus. The men were having some confab over at the bar.

"Jerk," she muttered under her breath.

"Honey, please. That whole business is water under the bridge. Don't hold it against him."

Honey turned about to find Carey. "Hey! How've you been? How's it going with the impending wedding bells and everything?" It had been a hectic few months what with Carey returning to Kansas then turning up in D.C. again—engaged, no less.

That adoring gaze of hers went to Tynan again. "I'm happy."

"I'm glad."

"I know you are." Carey looked down into her wine and sighed. Blissfully, Honey thought. "I just wish that you could feel like this. That you'd find someone."

It was an honest-to-God Kansas-Carey sentiment, and Honey loved it. "Thanks just the same."

"Honey, you can't just keep whipping through men like they were…I don't know, fast-food cheeseburgers."

"I can sure try."

"But why?"

"Ask me that in a few days after you've met the rest of my family." Then Honey heard her own voice and something like a jolt of electricity warmed every inch of skin on her body. What was happening to her today, for God's sake? Why was she saying all these out-of-character things? She never talked about her family. Maybe it was something in the Brunhia water.

"What does your family have to do with it?" Carey asked.

Honey lifted her bottle to her mouth and polished off the beer. "They want me to be my mother, and I can't be Drew or Marcus so..." She trailed off and shrugged. "I don't want to talk about me. Did I miss anything in D.C. by flying in here a little early?"

Carey scrunched up her nose. "Yesterday's tabloids from the sounds of it."

Honey perked up. "More wacko gene stuff?"

"More what?"

"You're doing it again," Honey said. "Whenever you used to pull that I-really-can't-talk-about-it routine on me, you wouldn't look at me."

"Where am I looking?" Carey's eyes came back to her.

"Three seconds ago you were finding something fascinating about the fireplace."

"It's a beautiful fireplace."

"I couldn't agree more. What was in the rags yesterday?"

Carey took a quick and basically relieved breath, which Honey didn't like the sound of. That meant whatever it had been was something she could talk about—ergo, it had nothing to do with mutant adopted babies.

"Remember that sleazy reporter who started all that mess between Matt and me?" Carey asked. "Cantrell?"

"How can I forget? But your lover boy apparently didn't take my reaction so seriously that he's stopped speaking to me. At least, he's speaking to me on subjects that suit him."

Carey sighed. "You pumped him for information, too, didn't you?"

"I tried. So what happened with the sleazebag reporter?"

"Oh! He printed that I've been seeing a sex therapist."

Honey frowned. "You? Why would he—" And then her blood established a very sudden and extreme rapport with her toes.

Carey was frowning at her. "It's not that bad, Honey. It's just more of the same gossip column stuff. This one was just so bizarre. I mean, I barely start having sex and suddenly I'm bad at it? Or Matt's supposed to be bad at it, which is even weirder what with all the testimonials to the contrary. Where do they get these things?''

From women who pass out in rose gardens, Honey thought helplessly. From women who use a friend's name to see a...well, a sex therapist. She opened her mouth and closed it again fast before the Brunhia water could do the utterly unacceptable to her again and have her blurting out the truth on this score, too.

She backed off from Carey and placed her bottle on a nearby table. ''Got to go.''

''Are you all right?'' Carey asked, concerned.

''I was out in the sun a lot today.''

''You look pale, not burned. But I meant to ask you, what did you do to your face?''

''I'm fine. It's fine.'' Honey plastered a hand to her bruised cheek and flew.

Guilt felt like a razor inside her, scraping her bones. Which was ridiculous. Given whom she was marrying, Carey was going to be written about, *had* been written about, but she sure as hell didn't need Honey's shenanigans adding to the press. Honey reached her bell room and slammed the door behind her. Then she hugged herself and wandered to the closest of the amazing, surrounding windows—her favorite, the one that faced the cove.

''What the hell is happening to me?'' she muttered aloud. In the space of a day, she'd demanded to know why a man didn't like her, as though Honey Evans would ever give a damn. She'd had some sweet, incredible drink with Paloma and had felt simply and utterly at peace for one of the few times in her life. And now she was all wacked out because she'd inadvertently hurt someone. Okay, not just someone. A friend. But still. ''No fear, no regrets,'' she whispered. It had always been her motto. She brought her hands up and framed her eyes to look out at the cove. The sky was lavender now and the view was sweetly murky. She couldn't quite see.

Then her eyes adjusted. The *Sea Change* was gone.

* * *

He'd run from her! No one ran from her. Ever. No way.

Honey stood in the kitchen the next morning and swigged coffee. Maybe she was coming down with something, she thought. Some off-the-wall Brunhia-water ailment. People who went to South America took pills first for malaria and dysentery. There was probably a pill for this place, too, and she had just missed it in her hurry to get across the Atlantic and find herself a European hottie. Something that would keep her mind sane and her life recognizable no matter how much Brunhia water she drank.

Okay, she thought. Maybe she didn't have a pill. But she did have common sense and determination by the bucket load. Maybe he'd just gone to Portimao for supplies or something. But in any event, she had a point to get across here. Said point being: Three miles of ocean is nothing, pal, because when I want something, I get it.

She'd never chased after a man in her life, she thought, slugging back more coffee and going to the urn for more. She'd always picked and chosen from those who had come after her. And then she passed out in rose gardens. But that didn't mean she couldn't change the status quo. In fact, changing the status quo was probably a very good thing. Change was what she was after, right? She'd told him her name was Elise; she was shedding her past and all those preconceived notions about her. She was going to get laid far, far removed from D.C. or Conover Pointe.

"What happened to you last night?" Marcus's voice shot at her as he came in from the dining room. "It's not like you to skip happy hour. Or dinner either for that matter."

"I was exhausted." To her great shame, she'd never made it back downstairs after discovering that Joe's boat was gone. It had depressed her. "Tell me something. If Amando brings everyone here, how do we get back to the mainland?"

"You're going home?" He looked stupefied. "What's up with you lately anyway?"

"Nothing's up with me. I just want to spend the day in Portimao."

"Why? We've got a good time going on right here."

She put her mug down on the counter. "Which I am so obviously not a part of."

"What do you mean?"

Now he was deliberately playing dense, Honey thought. She'd grown up with this guy. She knew his tricks. "Look at it this way, Marcus. If I leave for a while, all of you can whisper and commune about your nutsoid genes with utter impunity."

"Honey, you're not making any sense here. Not that you generally do." She watched him rake a hand through his hair.

Honey held her own hand up and began ticking fingers off. "We've got in residence your voodoo sister—"

"It's Gretchen's house!" His voice was rising. "She married Kurt!"

"Be that as it may. We've got her and now we've got one top-notch White House advisor holed up here, too. We've also got this Ethan Williams who—"

"Oh, come on. He's filthy rich. He just jets around. He and Sam go way back."

Honey thought about that. "Maybe he's in on this, and maybe he's not. I'll figure it out later. Right now I'm going to leave all of you to whatever it is you've told everyone not to discuss with me, and I'm going to go to the mainland and kick up my heels." She was also damned well going to find access to a computer and look up some of those old newspaper articles about designer boulder-lifting babies. Matt and Carey had probably brought a laptop with them with a wireless modem, but she wouldn't even bother to ask them if she could borrow it. She knew a brick wall when she hit one.

"How do I get in touch with Amando?" she asked again.

Marcus looked at his watch. "Go to the cove. He should be here sometime this morning. Jake and Tara flew in last night and he'll be bringing them over."

"Okay." She started to turn away, then she looked cannily over her shoulder again. "Jake who?"

"Ingram."

"Holy—" She broke off and dragged out a kitchen chair. She dropped into it hard. "And you honestly expect me to buy into this whole just-a-wedding-going-on-here-folks business?"

He stared at her unblinkingly. "Jake is a friend of—"

"Jake is a financial genius who's been hired to look into that whole World Bank Heist business!" she interrupted. And, she remembered as her heart rate escalated, he'd also called Matt Tynan once when she'd been in Tynan's office at the White House. Matt had given her some song and dance about it being a relative, not *the* Jake Ingram. She hadn't believed him, but it hadn't seemed important then.

For that matter, she'd been in his office that day in the first place to give him an envelope Carey had asked her to deliver before she'd tucked tail for Kansas. Carey had made her swear on the lives of those orphanage puppies and other assorted loved ones not to snoop and read what was inside. Honey kicked herself now for not doing it. Ten to one whatever it had been was tied to this hoopla.

So Jake Ingram was involved in this, too, and Carey and Matt were in up to their ears. Whoa, Honey thought.

"Well, he's that, too," Marcus was saying. "He's involved with the WBH investigation."

"He *heads* the investigation." Honey focused on him again. "But what does he have to do with you slinging boulders around like they were balloons?"

"Oh, for God's sake, Honey. I didn't *sling* anything and if I'd known you would react like this I wouldn't have done it in the first place."

"Too late. You did. I reacted." She tunneled her fingers into her curls and stood again. Jake Ingram. Jeez-Louise.

Marcus grabbed the full coffee carafe and began backing toward the big room again. Oh, yeah, she was definitely going to find herself a computer in Portimao, Honey decided. "I'll catch you at dinner," she said.

"What do you have up your sleeve now?" he asked warily.

"What do you have up yours?" she shot back, then she slipped through the stairs door and trotted up to the bell room.

Max was indulging himself. He rarely did, at least in this fashion, but neither did he generally come to the mainland for anything other than a specific purpose, such as supplies, or the much-dreaded bimonthly phone call to his sister in Pittsburgh. For purposes of his will—and it was a slammer—it was more or less necessary for someone in the world to know that he was actually alive. He'd chosen Elizabeth. Of all his siblings, he was closest to Liz. If she didn't hear from him every other Thursday morning by noon her time, she could sound an alarm. Other than that, she was to assume he was healthy and hale.

But this wasn't Thursday and the sailboat's larder, water and gasoline reserves were full. Max was in Portimao today for the sole purpose of escape, so he decided to have lunch at an outdoor bistro across the street from the water. Normally he soaked up a quick dose of the mainland and booked back to the island immediately. But today he had time to kill.

He was forcing himself to relax when he recognized Amando's little boat approaching the marina across the street. Elise was at the helm beside the little man. Max sat forward in his chair, bracing an elbow on the glass-topped table to stare.

"Something is wrong with your *arjamolho, senhor?*"

"Yes! No. What?" He looked up blankly at the pretty young waitress.

"Your soup."

"Fine. It's great. It's *maravilhoso.*" He jumped up and pulled euros from the pocket of his khakis. He threw the money on the table. "Got to go."

"*Senhor,* wait. Your change. You give too much."

"Keep it."

The entire process of paying his bill had taken up just as much time as Amando needed to dock the boat. When Max looked again, the man was helping Elise onto the dock.

In spite of everything he knew to be sane, Max paused then. He got frozen back in the moment when she had nearly collided with his motorbike and had gone sailing off the edge of the road. The look on her face then was the first thing he had noticed about her. Emotion so fierce and real, *he* had almost felt it. He couldn't see her face now. She was too far away. But he could have sworn the sun was brighter where she stood in a long, gauzy hot pink skirt and a very small purple tube top that didn't come close to reaching her waist. He thought her feet might be bare.

She shielded her eyes from the sun to look around. What kind of idiot would come out in the peaking heat of the day with neither a hat nor sunglasses? Max answered his own question just as he felt her spot him. Not an idiot. A woman in a hurry to track down someone she'd discovered was missing from a cove. He felt her gaze hit him like a fist.

She waved at him. Max told himself to run.

The next thing he knew she was dodging traffic, crossing the street, coming right at him. Not barefoot, no, he thought, though that would have suited her. In fact, she wore purple sandals so frail he knew they had to have cost four or five hundred bucks. When you got into the top designers, less was more. He knew. Camille had taught him so.

Too late, he started to move again. She ran to him and caught his arm, spinning him around to face her.

"Fancy meeting you here!" She grinned.

"Actually, I was trying to avoid it." What kind of woman didn't take a hint? What kind of woman actually tracked a man down? He answered himself again. A rich little bombshell who was used to getting everything she wanted. Then, for reasons that escaped him, he gave her the benefit of the doubt and asked anyway. "What are you doing on the mainland?"

"Looking for you."

Something punched him between the eyes from the inside out. "And why would you want to hunt down a man who is obviously not interested in spending time with you?"

"To convince him otherwise."

Max had no idea where the laugh came from. It erupted from belly-deep. He scrubbed his hands over his cheeks; he still hadn't shaved with this trip in mind, so the friction made his hands itch. "You're insane," he said finally.

"That's the general consensus."

She said it lightly. But her face changed, he thought, looking at her again. Max reminded himself that he didn't want to know what made her tick. Then she sat at the table he'd just vacated.

"What are you doing?" he demanded.

"You left your whole— What is that? Breakfast? Lunch?" She leaned forward from her seat to peer at his bowl.

"Lunch. People who get up before noon would know that."

"Can I have a bite?" She reached for the spoon beside his bowl.

"No!"

She looked over her shoulder at him. "Why not? You were just going to leave it from the looks of things."

He told himself he was just being obstinate when he went around to his own chair and sat again. He pulled the bowl a little closer to himself. "Mine."

She sat back in her chair with a little sigh and a satisfied smile that told Max that somehow he had played right into her hands. "Actually, I've already eaten," she said. "Twice. Rafaela is big on feeding people and Amando didn't come to the island until after noon."

Max knew who Rafaela was. Her husband, Ricardo, was somehow distantly related to Lourdes's family. Most of the villagers on Brunhia were related in some fashion, if not by blood then by marriage. He started to play dumb, just on principle, then her words finally registered. "Amando took *more* people over there?"

"Jake Ingram and one very pissed-off fiancée."

"Why was Tara pissed off?"

Honey felt her own eyes narrow. "I didn't say her name was Tara."

He took a quick scoop of food and didn't answer. "Get yourself something to eat," he suggested instead. "It's on me."

She wouldn't even contemplate it, Honey thought. She'd seen the way his boat was anchored offshore a little way, not tucked into one of the berths at the marina. He probably couldn't afford the slip fees, she realized. Neither Honey nor Honor—or the woman in between who seemed to be rearing her head repeatedly lately—could stomach letting him pick up the tab. "I'll be right back," she said.

It wasn't until she'd found a waitress and had nipped her own credit card out of her tiny purse that she realized Joe might well use her brief absence to make an abrupt departure of his own. She jerked around again to look at his table. He was still there.

Honey ordered a bottle of wine and hurried back to her chair. "I am definitely growing on you."

He lifted his gaze to hers. "What led you to that conclusion?"

"You just had ample time to run off. And you didn't."

"Maybe I'm famished."

"Then maybe you ought to stop returning those chickens to Paloma's family."

He dropped his spoon with a clatter. She'd talked to Paloma about him?

"How did you know Jake's fiancée was named Tara?" she went on.

Mind like a steel trap, Max thought, or the memory of an elephant, one or the other. "You said Ingram, right?"

He watched her mind race through her eyes. "Ah, bingo."

"The man's been on the front page of newspapers and various magazines ever since April when he was brought in to head the World Bank Heist task force."

"True."

"He's engaged to be married to Tara Linden."

"Maybe not after this little visit to Brunhia," Honey mused.

"Why not?"

"You want my guess? She's one of those silver-spoon chicks. She doesn't do sea spray unless she's standing at the rail of a yacht, and she sure as hell doesn't do mule rides."

He started to laugh again and it caught like a thorn in his throat. This woman hadn't minded the sea spray, he thought. "Do you ride mules, Elise?"

"Bite your tongue," she said. "My daddy breeds thoroughbreds."

"Why doesn't that surprise me? Who's your daddy?"

"Tom Jones," she said without missing a beat.

And in spite of himself, Max found himself laughing again, enjoying her mind.

He knows I'm playing with him, Honey thought, and grinned inside. Oh, he was a sharp one. Then the waitress brought the wine.

"What's this?" he demanded.

"It's called wine with a meal. Very commonplace where I come from. You should know that. We hail from the same place." She was going to get to the bottom of this man, Honey thought, if it killed her.

"I never said I was from the east coast," he answered.

"You knew my accent."

"I travel. Drift," he corrected himself.

"You never did tell me where you drifted from."

"And it never occurred to you that maybe there's a reason for that?"

No matter what his words said, she thought, he picked up his wineglass and drank. He wasn't going anywhere, she decided. He was relaxed. "What's the reason?"

"You're annoying."

She jolted a little, then she laughed. It felt so good to laugh like this, she thought, all the way up from her heart. "If that were true you'd have fled from this table whole minutes ago. Fifteen, at least."

Yet, here he was. He tried to find a way to answer her question without giving her the truth. "Steel-mill country," he said finally. "Trentawney High School."

"Class of?"

"Never mind."

"What did you drop out from?" she asked.

"Who said I dropped out?"

"That's what drifters do first. Before they start drifting."

His laugh touched her skin like warm sand. He didn't laugh nearly often enough, she decided.

"Okay, I dropped out," he said finally, pushing his bowl away.

It was empty now, she noticed, all but licked clean. Oh, but he had been hungry. What a shame. She needed to figure out a way to get some food to him. "You left Pittsburgh..." she prompted.

"I didn't say Pittsburgh."

"You said steel-mill country and that's the name of their football team." She watched surprise touch his eyes. Gotcha on that one, she thought. "So you left Pittsburgh where you were a..."

"Beneficiary of a rich uncle."

Her grin felt alive on her face. "Oh, yeah, I forgot that part."

"I worked in construction," he admitted. "Me and my dad."

"Sounds nice. Why would you want to bail on that?"

It was a variation of the question that had him in hiding until he could find the answer, Max realized. "I'm not sure. I'm drifting trying to figure it out."

She leaned toward him. "Isn't life funny like that? You can just be going merrily along, thinking everything is fine, then your skin starts feeling too tight for your body."

He stared at her. That was exactly how life had felt before he'd run. "Yeah." His voice was suddenly hoarse. He grabbed his wineglass again.

"Bam-bam-bam and rat-tat-tat," she said.

"Huh?"

She shrugged, looking embarrassed. "Just an east-coast expression."

"From Maryland," he clarified.

"Or thereabouts." Conover Pointe and the horses were in Maryland, but she considered herself a D.C. girl now. "What kind of construction?"

He followed her without missing a beat. "We bought old houses and renovated them, sold them again."

"There'd be a profit in that."

"There was after I got my real estate license and Dad and I could cut out the realtors."

"And you left that for your uncle's boat?"

"How many guys have a really great sailboat dropped into their laps in a lifetime?"

Well, she thought, if you were an Evans, they were a dime a dozen. "True. I guess that would change things."

But she knew that wasn't it, he thought, watching her face. Somehow, she knew. She was supposed to be a rich little princess. Why did she wear all her thoughts on her face like that?

He heard himself telling her the truth. "It got too big."

"The houses and the hammers and the nails?"

"Yeah. It started out simple. There was satisfaction with each closing, even if we only made a couple of thousand. Those houses looked a damned sight better when we were through with them than when we first bought them."

She understood, Honey thought. She understood that kind of satisfaction exactly. She'd felt it when she'd blasted that horse through the PETA protestors. She sat back and held her wineglass in both hands, staring into it. "Things should always be that basic."

"Things take on a life of their own sometimes," he said.

"Unless you fight it."

"Well, I'm fighting it."

She looked up at him again. Oh, those eyes, she thought, all whiskey brown and turbulent now. He almost looked as though he wanted her to understand. "Why do I get the idea that the houses turned into something like...I don't know, housing developments and what-not?"

"Maybe I'm as transparent as you are."

"I'm not transparent."

"Honey, you're like a pane of glass."

She almost spilled her wine. She'd been in the process of bringing her glass to her mouth when she twitched and a bit of it sloshed over the rim. Her heart rioted for a moment before she realized that he wasn't actually calling her by name. He was simply tagging her with a nickname. An endearment.

And endearments were a very, very good omen for what she had in mind with him.

Slowly, deliberately, Honey licked a drop of wine off her thumb. She saw his expression react, something flare in his eyes before they shut down, his mouth nearly kick up into a grin before he hardened it again. Sort of like when he hadn't been looking at her yellow bra, she thought.

He plowed on, giving her answers now without thinking about it because maybe he thought the answers were safer than the sight of her tongue flicking out and touching her skin. "You always start out with the idea of getting ahead. That's the goal. Make money. Succeed. Grow larger. But when it happens, all the good stuff gets left behind."

"What was the good stuff?" Honey nudged.

"The feeling of really smooth, planed wood under your palm."

"Like a woman's skin?"

"Knock it off. I'm talking here."

"And I'm interested, too. But I like making you do that thing with your eyes."

"What thing?" he asked suspiciously.

"Where you want me but lightning would strike you before you'd admit it, so you halfway look at the sky like you're waiting for it to come down."

He leaned toward her suddenly. Honey could feel the heat coming off him. Yes, he was riled.

"You know, if you were one of my sisters, my daddy would tan your hide for talking like that."

She leaned forward as well. "He'd have to catch me first." And she wondered what it would be like to have a father who tanned hides instead of looking down his nose.

"He would," Joe said. "I'd put my money on him."

"You haven't seen me run."

"Because you don't do it. You just keep encroaching. What would make you run, Elise?"

Suddenly, she was finding it hard to breathe. She took a gulp of the wine. It was really excellent wine, she thought. God bless Portugal. "Nothing."

"I don't believe that."

"I'll tell you a secret then," she whispered. "Rose gardens make me faint."

"A little prick rocks your boat?"

"One might say that."

"You're just multifaceted, aren't you?"

"You could find out." And then she heard her own words and straightened back into her chair suddenly. *What was she saying?* She wanted sex from him! Not to get to know him—other than an understanding of what he was doing here in Portugal so she knew he was safe. She definitely didn't want him to know her—not Honey who passed out at the prospect of getting laid, and not Honor who was going to be dragged to an altar like the one her mother had gotten married at unless she really kicked and screamed. This wasn't about telling him her secrets. She didn't want a friend. She wanted a one-week stand.

If Joe got too close to the heart of her, it would do the same thing to her that the townhouse had done. It would bring on the bam-bam-bam-rat-tat-tats.

Honey looked over her shoulder to buy herself time, to come up with an easy way to segue backward. But when she moved, she caught a sight at Amando's boat that froze every muscle in her body. Her father. Her mother. Drew. Boarding the skiff. Heading for Brunhia.

Honey looked back at Joe helplessly. "Sorry about this." Then she jerked to her feet and fled.

Six

A woman seated six tables down from them was wearing a wide-brimmed hat with burgundy ribbons. Honey stopped beside her, careful to keep her back to the street and the docks on the other side. "I'll give you ten bucks for that." She pointed.

"Mon chapeau?"

Honey picked up on the woman's accent. French? She was still tripping over her Portuguese.

Her father had eagle eyes. He had only to look over his shoulder to nail her, Honey thought. Best to make this quick. She didn't have time to horse around with translations. And, hey, money talked.

She dug in her purse and found a fifty. She'd never had time to convert her cash, but it would still spend. She dropped the bill on the table and plucked the hat off the woman's head. Her husband looked ready to come out of his chair and swing a fist. In for a penny, Honey thought, in for a pound. She grabbed a pair of cheap sunglasses off the table as well.

"Thanks so much!" she called back to the couple, heading up the street again.

She was shoving the glasses onto her face and piling her hair under the hat when Joe caught up with her. "Was it something I said?"

The fact that he could make her grin under this kind of duress was something she'd think about later. She peeked over her shoulder at the docks. Her family was still there.

"You're coming with me," she decided. She grabbed his arm to tow him along. When he tried to fall into step on her right, she dodged around him. "No, no, I need you to be on that side." He was big enough to shield her from view from the docks.

"It begs asking why you're acting so crazy, even for you." But he cooperated.

There was no way to tell him the truth, Honey thought. For one thing, she knew beyond a doubt that if she was going to get past the bam-bam-bam-rat-tat-tat business this time, she was going to have to do it as Elise No-Name. She couldn't have him encountering her family. Then there was the fact that the idea of squeezing back into her Honey skin felt suddenly abhorrent to her. She wasn't ready for this idyllic time to end. And she really wanted to lay her hands on a computer before this day ended. So she put a hand to the top of her head and pushed the hat down a little more firmly.

"Maybe I'm wanted in sixteen countries," she suggested.

"And maybe not."

"Maybe I decided I don't want you after all. Maybe I'm trying to scare you off."

"You already did but you won't let me go."

She smiled quickly.

"Ex-lover?" he guessed.

"Nope."

"Current lover?"

"Ha!"

He didn't understand the rough edge to that bark of laughter so he kept trying. "Seriously angry husband?" It made his stomach cramp a little. He told himself he was thinking of Camille.

Honey lifted her left hand and wiggled ring-free fingers.

"Doesn't mean a thing," he said. "My ex-wife never wore hers."

"You were married? Oh, wait, there's a cab!"

Max found himself diving into the car after her. Then his head swam all over again when she leaned forward to speak to the driver.

"Take me, *por favor,* to, uh, *uma bibloteca,*" she said.

"You want to go to a library?" Max was incredulous. "All this is about a *library?* It's a drug transaction, right? It's got to go down somewhere innocuous."

She rolled her eyes and sat back as the cab pulled into traffic again. She finally pulled off the hat and sunglasses. She breathed. Free. Still free.

Then she looked over at Joe. Funny, she thought, how the more often she looked at him, the more she liked his face—what she could see of it under all that dark beard. There was a kind of reticent character there, as though he was trying to deny what made him tick. At the moment, his whiskey eyes were challenging.

"*That* was a waste of fifty bucks," he said, pointing.

Honey looked down at the hat and sunglasses spilled in her lap. She shrugged. It was all relative.

"Ah, right," he said. "You can afford it."

"*You* decided that. I never said it was true."

"Your father—"

"Tom Jones," she clarified.

"Breeds thoroughbreds—"

"You can find the beasts in backyards all across America."

"Not the kind that would sour a woman on a good, sturdy mule."

She threw back her head and laughed. "Touché."

"And you're staying at the big house."

"What does that have to do with anything?"

"Everyone landing there this week seems to be rich and American. That makes you rich and American by implication."

"They're all politically powerful and American," Honey said, "though I'm still not sure yet where this Ethan Williams fits in. I guess most of them have some bucks, too."

"Ethan Williams? Now *there's* money." In fact, it came close to rivaling his own, Max thought. Ethan Williams was at the big house? He tried never to look squarely at Amando's human cargo when they came in because he didn't want to give anyone a dead-on glimpse of his own face. Apparently, he had missed a lot.

"What the hell is going on up there?" he asked. "Besides the taming."

"That," she said in a conspiratorial whisper, leaning closer to him, "is what we're going to a library to find out."

The car stopped in front of a large brick building that made Honey's spine tingle. She loved libraries...all that knowledge, all those words, inside one set of walls. So often they were dignified and ornate, like an old dowager inviting a young belle in for some of her wisdom. She paid the driver, opened the door and stepped out onto the street. She was so preoccupied with the building that she was halfway there before she thought to look back to make sure Joe was still with her.

He was. That could mean either that he was really curious about why she'd fled the bistro, or that he was mellowing toward her. Either way, she was pleased. She turned back to the library and pulled open the thick mahogany door.

They stepped into cool mustiness, the faint smell of thousands of old pages snuggled together. She breathed in deeply.

"What are you doing?" he asked. "Getting high on dust?"

"And you thought I was just another prima donna," she scoffed, striding forward to the information desk. "Computers?" she asked the woman there. *"Computadores?"*

"Sim, ma'am. Estąo no quarto no alto das escadas."

"Gotcha." She took off in the direction of the stairs. She'd trotted up half of them before her conscience got the better of her. She slowed down and let him catch up. She really did owe him some sort of an explanation. "There were some people back there at the marina. If they had spotted me, they would have dragged me on board with Amando and taken me back to the island. I wouldn't have gotten to come here."

"Amando's taking *more* people over?"

He seemed stuck on that, she thought. "I'm pretty sure this will be the last of them. They've run out of bedrooms."

"But they'll be gone soon? All these people?"

"Let's put it this way. We've got a White House advisor, a world-renowned financier, not to mention my fath—"

"Your what?"

Damn it, he was quick, she thought. "Not to mention Ethan Williams. *E-than.* That's what I was going to say. My point being that these sort of high-powered people generally have places to get back to in a hurry, right?"

Right, Max thought. Unless they'd dropped out the way he had. What the hell was Kurt up to? "Why would all these people not want you to come to a library?"

Honey started up the stairs again, more slowly this time, rubbing a freckle on her nose while she thought about it. "They're afraid of what I'll find out. They think I'm trouble."

He joined her in the upstairs computer room. "Ha. What a horrible misconception."

Her spine hardened to the point of pain. *Please, not from him, too.* "I don't go looking for trouble. Sometimes it just finds me."

"You damned near drove me off the road and looked ecstatic about doing it."

"I wasn't ecstatic. I was..." Honey trailed off to think about it. "Waiting to see what would happen next."

"Did broken bones enter into the picture?"

"Only briefly. Mostly I was wondering if I would need CPR and what your mouth would feel like on mine when you gave it to me."

He did it again! Oh, she loved it! His eyes got a little hotter, then they shut down. But the left corner of his mouth kept trying to tuck up. And he looked at the ceiling.

"Still waiting for lightning?" Honey asked.

"I think it's hit. I must be out of my mind."

She stepped closer to him. "Because you're still here?"

He had to turn the tables on her, Max thought. And he had to do it now. She was getting under his skin. "You'd swoon if I grabbed you and planted one on you."

She almost did. And then her heart took off at the mere

prospect. Not bam-bam-bam. Not even rat-tat-tat. It was more like it took flight. She read that as a good sign. "Dare you," she whispered.

He was staring at her mouth. And then he did it.

She hadn't really thought he would. Honey told herself that was why everything swirled inside her this time instead of outside her. He caught her elbows in his hands, and she had a second to think that they were work-roughened and that that was nice. Then he jerked her toward him, slanted his head and took her mouth with his.

She cracked one eye to be sure. The walls were where they were supposed to be. No spinning books or computers.

Then things started bubbling inside her, up from the very core of her. Like champagne, she thought, but not chilled. Tiny delicate air pockets rising and bursting as his tongue swept hers, teased a moment, then was gone. She wanted it back. She searched with her own and found his again.

And then he set her away from him.

"Never ever dare a confused man," he warned, his voice rough.

She couldn't think. She couldn't talk. She wanted to press her hand to lips that still felt on fire, but fought the urge.

"You wanted computers?" he asked, stepping away from her.

I want you. In that moment, for the first time in her life, she wanted. For herself. Not for show. Not for anything else but this thrumming blood inside her. Well, Honey thought, this certainly put a whole new slant on things. She cleared her throat carefully. "You only pushed me away first because it wasn't your idea."

His eyes heated. "I pushed you away first because we're in public."

She looked around. "Oh. Yeah. Double dare you when we're alone."

He almost made another move on her. God help him, he almost did, Max thought. How was she reaching him? She wasn't anything he wanted. And she was everything that made him feel real again.

He turned for the computers because that was safest. "What are we looking for?"

Honey couldn't remember.

She moved toward one of the desks, amazed to realize that her knees felt a little weak, as though someone had replaced the cartilage and bones there with noodles. Cooked noodles. This was a new sensation. The walls and all the books stacked upon them were still blessedly stationary, but she pulled out a chair and sat quickly anyway. She wasn't entirely sure this phenomenon wouldn't drop her, too. Why tempt fate?

She reached for the computer mouse and ran the cursor over icons until she found what she wanted. He leaned over her shoulder. He smelled like clean sea air, she thought, her mind wandering again.

"You didn't answer my question." His voice was close enough to her ear to make spiders with warm, velvety feet traipse down her spine.

This, she thought, was definitely cool. This was *not* in the same category with bam-bam-bam-rat-tat-tat. "Jake—" she began, then she choked.

"Jake as in Ingram?" he asked.

"No. Jake as in..." The only thing she could think of were the noodles in her knees. "Ziti."

"Jake Ziti?"

She had no problem with telling him the truth, but situations just like this were part of the reason everyone was closing her out, she thought. There had been occasions in her life when she had repeated things that maybe she shouldn't have. Honey took a deep, resigned breath. She had to be alone to do this, if only for her own sense of integrity. "You can go now."

"Go?"

She looked over her shoulder at him. "Yes. You know, prior to this, you struck me as a very intelligent man."

"You struck me as nuts and capricious, and you're doing a hell of a job of reinforcing that opinion."

"Thank you." Honey set her lips into a neat line.

What was her story now? Max wondered. First she'd dragged him along the street with her, and now she was trying to shake him off. Max ran his tongue over his lower lip thoughtfully and realized that he could still taste her. It made something scramble in his chest. Yeah, he should go now.

"You're planning to spend the night on the mainland?" he heard himself ask instead.

This time she turned around in her chair to look at him. "No."

"Well, Amando just left on what was probably his last trip of the day. He doesn't make the ride too close to sunset because of the shoals."

"It's only—" Her curls swirled as she looked around for a clock. "A little past four. In fact, he should even be back from dropping his last passengers by now."

"Could be. Then he'll be tucking his boat in for the night."

"You're telling me I'm stuck here?"

"Only if I leave and go back without you." He hadn't been planning on going back to the island tonight at all. Why didn't he just leave? She could afford a hotel.

She patted the chair beside her. "In that case, have a seat."

He remained standing, watching as she signed online and rooted up her own ISP.

She had a lot of e-mail waiting for her, Honey realized, but that was something she was not going to share with him—heaven only knew what she might find in there. She found her favorite search engine and tapped in Jake Ingram's name instead.

"Some Ziti."

Honey just shrugged. The screen flooded with links, most of them to newspapers and periodicals. She muttered to herself and scrolled down.

"Planning on climbing over Tara to get to him?" he asked.

Honey cast him a quick frown. "I don't even know him."

"Rich girl seeking powerful, monied husband?"

"That's precisely what I *don't* want." That would be someone her family would approve of. Honey's head filled suddenly with images of white lace and altars, baby's breath and roses, her father holding a pistol to her head, her mother delirious with happiness. Then her eyes focused hard on what she was seeing on the computer screen.

She clicked on the link. "Jeez-Louise. Zach's his *brother.*"

"Who's Zach?"

"Jake and Zach! Zach and Jake! Look!" She reared back a little to give him a clearer view of the screen, then she read aloud. "'Professor Zachary Ingram, who teaches economics at Glenlaurel University, has been reported missing. Ingram is the brother of Jake Ingram, famed economist who's been consulting with federal officials in the investigation of the World Bank Heist.'" She paused for breath. "I damned well hope he figures it out while I'm still young enough to enjoy my portfolio."

"That story is dated months ago," Joe said. "I could have told you that."

Honey glanced up at him. "Are we talking about Zach Ingram now or the fact that my stocks are currently dipping up and down like seedlings in a good wind?"

"Seedlings go back and forth in the wind, not up and down."

"Mine are going up and down."

He bit on the inside of his lip to keep from grinning again. "Ride it out. That's my best advice."

"This from a drifter whose only known possession is an inherited sailboat?"

Something happened to his face, she thought, a spasm of discomfort. What was that about? Then his voice went vague and dismissive. "Zach Ingram was in a car accident. That was the official word. He was gone for a while then he turned up at a rural Texas hospital with M. J. Dalton."

"The writer?"

"And shrink. It was all real hush-hush but no one can hide

the fact that security around Jake has jumped untold notches since then. He and his brother look a lot alike. Rumor had it that Jake was actually the target of what happened to Zach. It was in all the papers. The stories got wild for a while."

She had obviously missed those, Honey thought. "Did any of them involve a Hercules-hero type?"

"A what?"

"Guess not." She signed off the computer and surged to her feet. "I'll buy you dinner in exchange for a sail back to the island."

"I just finished lunch."

"Then you can take a doggy bag back to the boat."

He looked between her and the computer. "You broke speed records to get here and look up Zach Ingram, and now you want to go?"

Actually, she didn't really want to poke too much into the voodoo-gene babies with him watching her. It would just reinforce everyone's opinion of her. "You told me what I needed to know." Honey sailed for the stairs.

It took Max a moment to catch up with her if only because he spent a moment scratching his head. "Capricious," he said again, joining her.

"That's a pretty word," she agreed, trotting down. Her mind circled round and round what both Joe and Kurt had said as they stepped out onto the street again. Mistaken identity—the brothers looked alike. So the bad guys had grabbed the wrong man? These Coalition dudes had wanted Jake? And what did that have to do with Marcus? Was the Coalition after him and Gretchen? Kurt had said something about someone trying to grab Gretchen. Was that why everyone was nestled snug and safe on Brunhia for this wedding and what was starting suspiciously to resemble a think tank?

And now Jake Ingram was on the island. For the wedding? "My butt."

"I beg your pardon?"

She slid a smile his way. Who really cared about boulder-lifting super-babies anyway when her virginity was in such imminent promise of demise? She eased a little closer to him. ''So where are we having dinner?''

''If you're really hungry, I've got some stuff on the boat.''

''I'm really hungry.'' She ran a manicured finger down the front of his T-shirt.

He batted her hand away. ''Knock that off.''

''You say that a lot, you know,'' she murmured. ''Whenever I get too close. Or talk about sex.''

''Because most men prefer to be led on a little bit of a chase.'' They reached the street, and he started walking in the direction of the marina.

Honey hurried to catch up with him. ''Are you one of them?''

''Yes.''

''Liar. You kissed me first and I was standing right in front of you. You didn't chase at all.''

''You climbed all over me. I had no choice.''

''Ha!'' She let her head fall back and gave a hoot of laughter. The late-day sun felt delicious on her face. ''Let's buy oysters and champagne and anchor somewhere between here and Brunhia. We can kiss some more.''

''Let's not.'' But when she sneaked a peek his way, she saw the grin playing at his mouth.

They reached the piers and walked out to his dinghy. He dropped over the edge of the dock and into it and held a hand up to her. Honey smiled down at him. ''So are we going to do this your way or mine?''

''Mine. If you want a ride back to the island, get in here. No champagne.''

''You know, you're going to miss me when I'm gone.''

''How soon will that be?''

She laughed again and took his hand to get into the boat. He really did delight her with his comebacks, Honey thought.

He tugged on the ripcord and the outboard sputtered to life. Honey sat in the bow and he leaned past her to throw off the lines. His skin was tanned almost to brown. She thought of licking the sea spray off it. The thought eeled into her brain seductively, with not a bam-bam-bam or a rat-tat-tat to be found. She let out her air and breathed it in again deeply, bringing in all the smells of the water and the cafés across the street.

Then she remembered that the rest of her family was waiting for her on the island.

She pushed the thought away but it left a lingering tightness across her chest. Honey concentrated on keeping her skirt from blowing up in the backlash of air as they zoomed out toward the *Sea Change*. Then she thought, What the hell? She stood up.

What was she doing now? Max wondered. He started to shout to her over the wind, to remind her of the obvious: one good bounce of the boat on a wave and she was going overboard. Then he realized that she probably wouldn't mind.

She was like no one he had ever met before, he thought—rich or poor, pampered or straight out of the school of hard knocks, shark-grinning husband-hunter or chaste, content nun. Except no nun would stand up in a boat so the wind could beat at her skin, wearing a gauzy pink skirt that suddenly ballooned up to flash more miles of leg than any petite little hellion had a right to. Her underwear was purple this time. And he almost rammed the skiff nose-first into the transom of the *Sea Change* as he noticed.

"Get down!" he shouted, throwing the rudder to one side. The skiff veered.

She should have gone overboard. Anyone else would have. But she was like a cat on her feet, he thought, nimbly dancing a step or two to the bench seat and dropping down there. She held on to the sides of the skiff as he made a neat turn to come up on the sailboat's starboard side.

He tied up and snagged a rope ladder off the side of the *Sea Change*. "Do you have a death wish, or are you just trying to make a statement?"

The question snagged her thoughts back to Brunhia and what she would walk into when she ultimately got to the big house. Honey felt a faint bam-bam in her chest and she pressed the heel of one hand there. "Definitely the latter," she said lightly. "Are you going to help me up onto that boat?" She batted her eyes at him.

"No. I don't trust what you might do if I touch you again."

And he left her. He just...left her there, Honey thought and watched, bemused, as he went to crank up the motor on the *Sea Change.* Then it struck her that the motor wouldn't do at all for what she had in mind. She scrambled up the ladder after him.

"What's wrong with the sails?" She waved her hand at them, all neatly rolled and awaiting some other trip.

"For a three-mile scoot?"

"It could be longer." Oh, God, she thought, she didn't want to go back! She didn't want this to end yet! They were already chugging toward Brunhia.

He was watching her face. That, Honey thought, wouldn't do. She wasn't sure what he might read there right now. "What if I decided to soak up some all-over tan and got naked?"

Max kept his face expressionless, though her comment made images dance in his mind. And, he thought, a few other parts of his body stirred as well. He shifted his weight uncomfortably. "It's tough to tan by the light of the moon."

"The moon's not out yet." She could think of a few other things she'd like to do by it, though.

"The sun won't be for much longer, either."

"Maybe tomorrow." She came and sat on one of the cushions beside him. "Will you take me for another boat ride tomorrow?"

"Not on a bet." The breeze was trying to damn him, Max thought. It picked up the scent of her—the one he'd become way too familiar with when he'd bitten at her bait and had kissed her in the library—and it carried it to him, teasing him with it. It was like nothing he was familiar with, neither one of the four-hundred-bucks-for-a-teardrop's-worth fragrance that Camille had slathered on, nor any of the other top-notch scents that could cut through a man's better intentions like a razor. It was spicy and it made him think of a forest. With flowers.

Yeah, she was getting to him. And that was insanity. Because she was everything he was running from.

"It's not going to happen again," he said shortly. "I won't kiss you again."

She leaned back to rest her elbows on the teak molding. She tipped her head back and if they had still been in the dinghy, her long hair would have trailed in the water. And he knew she wouldn't have minded. "We could make a wager on that."

"I'm not a gambling man."

She straightened again. "Sure you are. You bought houses on spec to resell."

He must have been out of his mind when he'd told her that. "I wasn't gambling. I was trusting in my father's skill and my own." And it still brought pain all these months later.

"I trust in my skills," she told him.

Max really didn't want to look at her. There was something about her when she was utterly relaxed like this, the last of the sun spilling on her hair, turning strands of it to golden fire. But he found himself doing it anyway. "Which particular skill are we talking about?"

"To get what I want."

"You *are* dogged."

She laughed again, a quick peal. "If I do get you to kiss me again, you lose."

"What do I lose?"

"You have to take it further."

God help him, things weren't just stirring now. They were leaping back to life. She leaned toward him. And this time, yes, this time she smiled like a shark, like all the women he was escaping. But on her, it just looked…challenging.

"You've just pretty much insured that you won't get yourself kissed again until you leave Brunhia and find someone else to torment." His voice was going hoarse.

"Do I torment you?" she asked silkily.

"You irritate me."

"Do we have a bet?"

"No." He was out of his mind. He told himself to agree if only to end the conversation. "Sure."

They were back to Brunhia. Amen.

Max guided the *Sea Change* to his usual spot between shoals, then he went to throw the anchor over. The dinghy was still snugged against the side of the sailboat. "Let's go."

She stood and planted her hands on her hips. "You've successfully avoided having dinner with me."

This time he let himself grin fully. "I know."

He watched her gather fistfuls of her long skirt in her hands and thought about women who wore purple underwear. Then she was over the side and into the little boat.

Suddenly, there was a chugging sound overhead that made the hairs on his neck stir. *Helicopter blades.* Max looked up sharply. Paparazzi. Reporters. They'd found him. But the chopper kept going north toward the big house. This was getting out of hand, he thought. If he had a sensible brain cell going, he'd head right back to Portimao for the night.

He looked at Elise. She'd glanced at the helicopter as well. He wanted to ask her who else was scheduled to arrive at Kurt's place...and he wanted her gone before he gave in to himself and took from her everything she offered. He followed her into the dinghy, threw off the lines and headed to shore.

He expected her to linger, or try to. But she surprised him again. When they closed in on the beach, she toed off her pretty sandals and levered her legs over the side to splash into water up to her thighs, drenching her skirt. Then she waded toward the beach without a backward glance.

When she hit the sand, she tossed a single word over her shoulder. "Thanks!"

"You're welcome," Max said under his breath.

He watched those cat's feet of hers traipse across the beach, the wet skirt molding to her thighs, and he realized suddenly that the weight was gone, that heavy feeling in his chest that had made him fear that he might be having a heart attack at his father's funeral last spring. The sensation had gripped him nearly every single day since then and no doctor in any country had been able to explain it. Because there was nothing wrong with his heart, though there had been a great deal wrong with his life. The weight hadn't eased until this woman had blasted into his life, damned near ramming her motor scooter straight into his.

She'd prodded him and circled conversations around him, getting him to talk about things he'd forgotten. But she hadn't been doing all that with Maxwell Strong. She'd been doing it with Joe. And the pressure was gone. Sometime in the last two days the invisible weight on his chest had lifted.

Max knew in that moment that her yellow bra and purple panties and images of her getting naked on the bow of his boat were the least of his problems. All those things he could withstand. What was far sweeter—and far more dangerous—was the way she let him be just a guy from Pittsburgh again.

Seven

Honey puttered the scooter back toward the house at a slow crawl. She was in no hurry. The smile on her mouth felt new and incredible and she wanted to savor it. Part of it was probably the satisfaction of having outwitted Marcus and his cronies just a little. But most of it was a sense of peace that still swam in her blood, the kind of feeling that came from an afternoon gloriously spent and rife with simple pleasures.

She liked the way Joe tried not to grin at her. It tickled her. She enjoyed his dry one-line comebacks, neatly quick and clever. More than anything, she envied him, Honey realized, so deeply in her soul it was almost an ache. He could do anything he wanted to do at any given time without considering how anyone else would react.

She couldn't wait to see him again. But at the moment, duty called.

Honey was pretty sure she caught a whiff of her mother's perfume when she was still a good quarter mile from the house. She chose the front door instead of sliding in through the kitchen as had become her habit and cut a left up the long front hall. She sauntered in to the big room. Her mother had been at work. The women were all gathered around one of the cocktail tables and the men were at the bar, nicely segregated.

Honey grinned around at all of them. "Okay, I'm back. The party can begin now."

Her mother rose from the sofa in a smooth move of utter elegance and held her arms out to her. "We were just wondering what had become of you, sweetheart."

Honey went to her. Sarah Evans's hug was quick but sincere; the peck on her daughter's cheek was neat. "Missed you," Honey said, planting a sound kiss on her mother's mouth. Then she turned to the others.

Gretchen was in one of the chairs, neat and pretty in khaki slacks and a sea-green T-shirt. Samantha was perched on the arm of the sofa in a gold-and-green sundress that made Honey envy her boobs all over again. Tara Linden had been sitting closest to Honey's mother before Sarah had whooshed up to do the hug-and-kiss-daughter routine. They'd been involved in some kind of girl chat that alarmed Honey for Jake Ingram's sake.

Carey and Matt, Kelly and Ethan Williams hadn't joined everyone yet. But there was a new face standing behind the sofa. Honey pegged the woman immediately. If she wasn't a fed now, then she had at least been one at some point in time. Spend enough days in the Great White Hallowed Halls, Honey thought, and you could peg Secret Service in a heartbeat. Well, well, well, she thought.

"Hey there," Honey said, extending a hand toward the woman.

"Pleased to meet you." The agent looked at her hand briefly before she took it.

"Relax," Honey said. "It's just road dust, not any sort of chemical weapon."

"Your feet are a bit dirty as well, dear," Sarah said. "And your skirt is soaked."

"I, for one, want to hear this story," Samantha said.

Yes, Honey thought, she definitely liked her sister-in-law-to-be. "I was boating with the USDA anchored down in the cove."

"USDA?" Sarah echoed. "What in the world is that?"

Sam caught her laugh too late. A small sound escaped Gretchen as well. Honey looked at her to find that the woman had discovered something utterly fascinating about a piece of cheese she'd plucked from a tray on the coffee table.

Honey's attention went back to the woman behind the sofa. "I didn't catch your name."

"Naomi."

"Can I get you something to drink, Naomi? You're the only one without a glass."

"I don't drink."

Glory be to the flag, Honey thought. If she got any more rigid, she'd implode. "On duty or ever?"

No one answered her. Leave it alone, Honey thought. What difference did any of this make? Marcus would always be Marcus to her, even if he suddenly took it upon himself to spin around the globe with the Empire State Building on his back. She had no great interest in Gretchen's hieroglyphic talents, though she liked the woman well enough. The travails of Jake Ingram's brother had no great impact on her own life. She *should* just let all this go. And maybe she might have. Maybe. Except Marcus, as soon as he noticed her talking to Naomi, chose that moment to zoom in on her. And she caught the look Jake Ingram snapped her way as well—wary and curious.

"I want a drink," she decided, dodging past Marcus just as he got to her side. "Hi, Daddy." She leaned up to kiss her father's cheek as she reached the bar, then another big-tough-protection-type—this one a guy—came in from the kitchen with an extra tray of cheese and pepperoni and crackers.

"Honor, it's good to see you," Charles Evans said.

"Ditto. How come they have you schlepping the food?" Honey asked the new guy.

"I was going that way," the man replied.

"National crisis in the kitchen?"

"Honor, stop baiting the poor guy."

The admonition came from Drew. Honey peered around her father to grin at her oldest brother. "Hi there, Fly-boy. Missed you, too." She loved him, even if he had ruined her Girl Scout career with that damned cookie incident. He'd shown some promise toward being a normal human being once until he'd lost his best friend during a Navy Search and Rescue mission a few years ago.

She winged around to face Jake Ingram. "What's with all the armed-and-dangerous types? Are they for you?"

"I beg your pardon?" He was careful with his expressions, she thought.

"I believe Annie Oakley over there has a gun tucked into a shoulder holster under that jacket she's wearing. It's awfully warm today for a jacket, don't you think?" She reached to shake the male bodyguard's hand as well. "So what brings you to Brunhia?"

"Honey, that's enough!"

Honey sighed and turned to face Marcus. He'd stalked her back to the bar. "Are you going to send me to my room now?"

"I'd settle for you being polite and civilized."

"She's being civilized," Drew said. "I mean...comparatively. For her."

Honey graced him with one of her better grins. "Thank you."

"I swear you were born with your nose in places where it doesn't belong," Marcus said in a warning tone.

"It just strikes me that I haven't seen this much muscle in one place since the last inauguration."

"Presidential or gubernatorial?" Jake Ingram asked without missing a beat.

"The big guy. Given my family connections, state government is so...lackluster." She grinned at him. "Naomi and the pepperoni-toter weren't here when I left earlier."

Jake gave a slight frown. "Maybe a gull dropped them off."

Honey laughed. She liked him. She was too much the Evans to be intimidated by his renown and she saw right past it to a clever mental agility that reminded her of Joe. *Joe.* She wanted to be back on that boat with him, not making waves here. But since she was here, she'd splash around a bit and see what she could stir up.

"Or maybe a chopper," she suggested. "Come to think of it, I heard one when I was down on the beach. Have Naomi and Robert joined us because your family members have been inexplicably popping off recently, or is my own family involved in something I don't know about? Not counting Marcus, of course. We all agree that he's immersed in nutsoid genes right up to his ears."

"With all due respect, Ms. Evans," Jake said, "your brother feels that you're better off not being involved in this."

"That brother wholeheartedly concurs," Marcus said.

Something started pounding deep in her head. Suddenly, she'd had enough of the game. "Right." She turned away and went to the door.

"Are you leaving?" Marcus asked. "Where are you going?"

"Where I'm wanted." Though Joe didn't particularly want her either, Honey thought. But he, at least, didn't have a prayer of resisting her.

Max had had every intention of going back to Portimao until all the hullabaloo on Brunhia died down. He couldn't have said why he was still at the island when the moon rose. He sprawled in a deck chair, his feet up on the transom, nursing a beer.

Outdoor fires dotted the beaches, friendly beacons in the night. The boats had headed out again some time ago and the women were settling down for the night. As for him, he was...content, Max realized. He wasn't getting any closer to going back to his life. He was floating farther away. He was chewing on that when he picked up the indistinct and far-off mutter of a scooter engine.

His first instinct was to come out of the chair like a rocket and lunge for the anchor, fire the engine. His second was to grin. Since Elise wasn't anywhere close enough to see it, he let himself do the latter. She couldn't get out here to him anyway, he thought. Unless she swam. He realized suddenly that he wouldn't put it past her so he ended up getting to his feet after all.

He went below for two more beers and dropped over the side into the dinghy. He threw off the tether and tugged the engine into life to head for shore. When he beached the little boat, Max caught a glimpse of her in the moonlight. She'd left the scooter on the road and was walking toward Deus Fornece. Hadn't she come here looking for him? Why was she going down there? Max frowned and realized that she'd confused him yet again. Since he hadn't brought enough beer for the whole village, he called out to her to stop her.

"Take a wrong turn?"

She spun back to look for him, seeming surprised. She had to have heard the mutter of his outboard, Max thought, either that or she was really preoccupied. He wondered again if she was playing some sort of game with him. Watching her come back toward him slowly, he found that he didn't care if she was.

He waded in to the beach and joined her. The rich little lady in her mega-bucks sandals was gone now. In her place was a vision that seemed impossibly fresh and unjaded. She wore cutoffs, either white or denim that had been bleached to that point by repeated washings; he couldn't quite tell in the darkness. Her loose white T-shirt had been hacked off to stop just above her waist. She was barefoot.

Max held up the beer bottles. "Want one?"

"Did a friendly bug bite you or something?" She dropped to sit in the sand and took a beer from his hand. She twisted off the cap, letting her head fall back to drink deeply, then she tucked the cap in her pocket. "Ah. Just what the doctor ordered."

He was what the doctor had ordered, she thought. She was pretty sure he'd heard her scooter and come to shore to meet her. It was the only explanation for the two beers. She wanted to think of that as progress, but after the scene at the house things were feeling just a little bruised inside her. It was hard to get her hopes up.

"The grand soiree up at the big house tonight wasn't to your liking?" he asked.

Honey dug her heels into the sand and rested her arms on her knees. "It was less a soiree than a meeting of political minds. They'll get more accomplished with me gone."

"Political? Kurt?" He sat beside her.

She cut a look at him out of the corner of her eye. "That's the second time you've said something to indicate that you know him. Come on, cough it up. What are a few revelations among moonlight drinking partners?"

Max surprised himself with a bark of laughter. He held his bottle out to her and she clinked hers against it. "To moonlight drinking partners," he said.

"How do you know Kurt?" she asked again.

He realized that he could tell her the truth without risking his anonymity. "I met him in Cairo," he said finally. And it was true. He'd known Kurt before that, had hired him occasionally as a private investigator, but he *had* met up with the man again in a bar there. "I said I wanted to drop out and he told me about this place, said he owned it and that I wouldn't be bothered here."

"He acted like he had no idea who you were."

"That's a friend for you." Max swigged from his beer. "I told him I wanted to be left alone and he was probably making sure that that was exactly what happened."

"Hell of a loyal friendship for one meeting in a bar," she observed.

"It happens."

"Not in my experience." Something shifted inside her and it hurt a little. Carey was the best friend she'd ever allowed herself, one of the few people she'd ever dropped any of her guard with, but even Carey was excluding her from whatever was going on at the house.

"Tell me what it's like to run away," she said suddenly.

He thought about it. "It's an act of desperation," he said finally. "It has to be if you're going to leave behind everything that's familiar."

"Sometimes the familiar isn't all it's cracked up to be."

It was the second time today that she'd said something that spoke everything he felt. "I lost the best part of the familiar," he heard himself say. "I lost the one part of it that counted." She didn't ask what it had been. She didn't prod him to go on. Maybe, he thought, that was why he did. "My father died six months ago."

Honey felt her heart miss a quick beat. "Mine is often a pain in the ass, but yeah, he's one of the integral parts of who I am."

"Mine made me everything I am. But he, too, was often the source of some discomfort in my nether regions."

Honey laughed. "You do have a way with words. Forget the hammer and nails, Joe. You could have a whole new career as a speech writer." She realized that if she continued to talk she'd give away a piece of her real identity, the woman who worked at the White House. She got off that subject fast. "So your dad died and you dropped out."

"Give or take an event or two."

"I'm waiting for you to fill me in."

"Maybe I don't want to."

"And maybe you want to get it off your chest."

She saw him grin again. "Maybe *you* want me to get it off my chest." He finished his beer and nestled the bottle into the sand. "When my father died, I felt like there was no sense in building things anymore without him. I felt like a door was slamming shut on me. I stood there at his funeral and all of a sudden I knew that there was no going back."

"Going back to what?"

"I couldn't go back to refurbishing houses because I'd lost my partner."

"Couldn't you have done it alone?"

He thought about it. "It wasn't the houses. It was the feeling of loving what I was doing. I wouldn't have loved it without him."

"I never loved doing anything," she said suddenly, as though it was a revelation.

"Ever?"

"The hurdles, maybe," she said. "I did love riding steeplechase."

"On daddy's thoroughbreds," he clarified.

She flashed a grin. "I learned on his thoroughbreds then I set out to get a job riding for other farms."

"What happened?"

"I was given some of the best mounts in racing, and that was that."

"I don't get it."

"My father arranged them for me. The other jockeys—guys and women who'd worked really hard to get where they were—resented me. I didn't blame them." She paused. "I was seventeen."

"So you quit and never went back? Were you any good?"

"I never got to find out." She changed the subject back to where he knew she wanted it. "So you stopped building things and drifted off because you couldn't do it with your dad any longer."

He'd realized that the possibility of going back to Pittsburgh had been out there on the edges of his mind for a while before his father had died, tantalizing him as an escape route from an enterprise that had gotten so huge it didn't even need him anymore. "I needed to talk about it," he remembered. "My wife hadn't come to the funeral. I went to find her."

"Your *wife?*"

"Ex-wife," Max corrected himself.

"Okay. That's livable. You mentioned her before, but sort of in a past tense. I have designs on you, you know."

"Like I could have missed them."

"Tell me about your ex-wife," she pressed, unoffended.

"I caught up with her at our—" He broke off. He'd been about to say "Paris home." "At our home."

"That wasn't what you were going to say."

"Okay, I caught up with her on Mars."

"That means you're not really going to tell me where you found her."

"Nope."

"Why are you so secretive?"

"Am I?"

She laughed.

"It's part of the whole running-away thing," he admitted. And that, he thought, was absolutely true.

"We were at the part about your ex-wife," she prompted him.

"Camille."

"Pretty name. Was she beautiful?"

He looked at her. "Yes." But Camille had never talked to him like this, peppering him with questions. Camille had never cared.

"I'm guessing red hair, blue eyes, skin like ivory."

"Now how the hell could you know that?" She *did* know who he was, he thought. Or at least she knew Camille Strong.

"That's just the way her name sounds," she said.

"You're not that fanciful."

"It's fanciful to conjure an image based on a name?"

"Yes."

"Then I guess I'm fanciful."

"You're a heat-seeking missile."

Her eyes went wide as she looked at him. "Oh, I like that one."

"It wasn't quite meant to be a compliment."

"I'll take it as one anyway. So you found Camille on Mars and told her that there was no sense in building things anymore without your father?"

"Not exactly." Why the hell was he telling her this? Because, he realized, he'd told no one. Not even his attorneys. He'd held the truth over Camille's head, knowing she wouldn't want it to get out to the media in case she managed to bag another billionaire like himself. Husband Number Two might not appreciate the way she'd dealt with her first prenup agreement. In the end, Camille had walked away from his money in exchange for his silence. She'd had no choice.

If he'd talked, she wouldn't have gotten the money either. At least this left her hope on the horizon.

There had been a clause in their contract that said if they remained married for ten years she'd get a sizeable settlement in any divorce thereafter. A day less and she got nothing—unless Max called it quits first. And he could only do that in the event that she committed adultery. He'd had the foresight to walk into that Paris bedroom with a camera in his hand, if only because he'd recognized the throaty cries coming from inside.

"Deep silence," Elise observed.

"Sorry." Max shook himself out of it. "When I got home, Camille was in bed with another man."

Honey felt herself wince deep inside. "Ouch." She couldn't imagine a woman having him and wanting someone else. He was the first man who hadn't brought on the bam-bam-bam-rat-tat-tat business. And she happened to know that if he handled the rest of sex the way he did kissing, the woman couldn't have had a complaint in the world. "So *then* you dropped out and went to Cairo."

"Actually, I went to Mazatlan first." Then Greece. Then Italy.

"Convenient of your uncle to kick off when he did. Leaving you the boat and all."

"Right."

"Mazatlan must have been expensive on a carpenter's salary."

"I wasn't a carpenter. Exactly. Not at the end. The whole enterprise had sort of...expanded. And it's all in the way you travel anyway. Not that you'd understand that."

This time it hurt. Maybe it was just a lingering edginess from the scene at the house but it made something twist in her gut. "You don't know me well enough to judge me."

"Then tell me the truth. Have you ever *not* flown first class?"

"No. But that doesn't mean I wouldn't."

"There's no champagne before takeoff," he warned her.

"I prefer beer on a beach anyway."

She did, he thought. The moonlight was slanting across her face in a way that made her cheekbones seem stark and elegant, but she had shifted her weight during the course of their conversation, moving a little so that she more than halfway faced him, and she was leaning toward him urgently. Her azure eyes were clear and bright even in the murky light and that same forest-flowery scent of her was filling his head. She leaned closer still.

"What are you doing?" he demanded.

"Giving you every opportunity to kiss me again now that we've gotten all that talk out of the way."

"I already told you that's not going to happen." If he had a brain cell in his head, he thought, he'd get up from the sand right now.

"Afraid you'll lose our bet?"

"Yes."

"Tell me why you think that would be unpleasant."

"Maybe I didn't like kissing you."

"What an outrageous lie."

It was, he thought. Just looking at her mouth, he could taste her all over again. "You're one of the things I'm running from."

"The kind of woman who flies first class," she clarified.

He couldn't fall into the clutches of another Camille, he thought. He didn't have it in him to survive it twice. But he couldn't say that Camille had married him for his fortune, had played games so sterling silver in their perfection that he'd only seen the gleam. That she'd signed the pre-nup gushing that it didn't mean a thing. That she'd almost immediately begun spending most of her time in whichever of his homes he wasn't in. That she'd cooed about having his children, then had gone on the pill for those rare occasions when they had actually ended up in the same bed together. That she'd been serving a ten-year term until the pre-nup was invalidated so she could walk away with everything she'd worked for while keeping lovers in the various cities around the world.

He couldn't tell Elise any of that without having her realize that he was Maxwell Strong. And the more time he spent with her, the more he found the prospect of that appalling. He just wanted to keep on being the man he was when he was with her.

"I'm strictly adhering to women without complications at the moment," he said finally. He wondered if he was trying to convince himself. "You're the biggest basket of contradictions I ever came across."

"Yes, but in a few days I'll be gone again so what do my contradictions matter? By the way, your mouth is moving no closer to mine."

"Ah, *now* you're catching on."

He barely got the words out before she reached for the shorn-off hem of her T-shirt. Before he could blink she had it up over her head.

"What the hell are you—" He started to yell. He *meant* to yell and grab that shirt from her hand and do something with it, cover her up again somehow, anything to change the course of these events before they could turn into everything he didn't want and everything he craved. Then, defiantly, she tossed the shirt back over her head, into the sand. And there was no little yellow bra this time. There was only…her.

"I'm allowed to try to change your mind, right? That's fair play?" she asked before her hands found his shoulders and her mouth covered his.

Something was shaking inside her, Honey thought, something that knew this was outrageous, even for her. But bigger than that was the need, a clamoring urgency to escape, to run, to get lost in him. He was a place where none of the usual hurts and fears and frustrations mattered.

His mouth was hard, but only for a heartbeat. She felt his palms on her skin, a little chafing, but there was desperation there, too, as they slid up over her sides to cover her breasts possessively. *Yes, oh, yes,* was all she had time to think. And she was free of the panic. She was flying.

His mouth crushed hers and his tongue swooped. His thumb

found her nipple and circled there. An agony of delicious wanting started coiling inside her as he slanted his head for better access to her mouth. She got the idea to nip at his bottom lip with her teeth. Then he sat up hard enough and suddenly enough that he would have spilled her if he hadn't caught her.

He couldn't do this. The thought raked through Max's mind like something with claws. It wasn't because he was still afraid that she had claws of her own. He was starting to believe that she didn't.

He couldn't take her, couldn't let himself sink into her, when almost everything he'd given her of himself was a lie. Even the truths he'd told her tonight had been only half of his heart.

Maybe she didn't want more than that. But maybe he did. And he couldn't elude Max forever.

"What?" Her voice was a throaty gasp, and he heard hurt around the edges of it.

"I'm sorry." He set her away from him and stood.

Suddenly she felt nothing inside, Honey realized. Nothing at all. No shame. No desperation. Not the lancing of being rejected yet again in a single night. Nothing but stillness.

She watched him get to his feet and walk a few steps down the beach. He scooped up her T-shirt from the sand. She launched to her feet as well and went to him to grab it.

"Elise—"

"Never mind." When she *did* feel again, it was going to come crashing in on her, and she had no intention of being here on the beach with him when it happened.

"It's not you," he said. "It's me."

"I think that's on a list of clever rejection lines somewhere. You disappoint me. I thought you'd be more original." She yanked the shirt over her head again.

"I told you I was no speech writer."

"Go to hell." He'd made her feel everything—*every-*

thing—and then he'd yanked it all back from her again. "Roast there."

Then she hurried away from him because Honey Evans never cried.

Eight

She was *not* in the mood for a wedding, Honey thought early the next afternoon.

She dragged her hair out of the braid she'd just woven it into. She'd planned to thread flowers into it, but *she* wasn't the bride. And hadn't some frost-nosed etiquette expert once said something about anyone else wearing flowers to a wedding being a touch gauche?

"It was probably Mom," she muttered. "That sounds like a Mom-ism." But she slathered her hands with gel instead and mussed her curls into a riot.

As though Honey's thoughts had summoned her, Sarah Evans's voice floated through the bathroom door. "Honor, are you about ready?"

"Nobody here by that name." Then again, she really didn't know who she was these days. Honey went to the door and opened it a crack to peer out at her parents. "I need a few more minutes. Go ahead without me."

"What are you wearing?" Her mother fretted. "Not *that?*"

Honey looked down at herself. She wore a vibrant red dress with long bell sleeves and a slit up one side. It was even reasonably long, stopping just a few inches above the knee. She felt the beginnings of a headache coming on. "What's wrong with it?"

"It's rather..." Sarah trailed off. "Flamboyant," she finally decided.

"That's what I like about it." Honey stepped back and closed the door again.

She was recapping her lipstick before her conscience got

the better of her. There was nothing wrong with flamboyant, she thought, nothing at all. The dress came pretty darned close to being appropriate for the occasion. But just in case, what right did she have to screw up Samantha's wedding?

"Damn it," she said aloud. She left the bathroom and jogged back upstairs.

She dragged the dress over her head, making her curls even more wild. She stomped over to the wall where she'd hung a few hangers on pegs for lack of a closet. One by one she yanked the dresses down. No to the yellow sundress cut down to her navel, she decided. And no to the kicky green ruffled skirt that barely covered her bottom. She held up a strapless and sheer lavender sheath with a deep purple satin lining.

"What you see is what you get, folks." She snapped off her bra and slithered her way into the dress. She was halfway to the door again before she remembered to change out of her red pumps and into the Kogi sandals she'd spent the equivalent of two paychecks on.

When she reached the kitchen, she heard soft music filtering in from the big room. The wedding was starting. Suddenly her chest felt constricted. The dress was too tight. Why hadn't she ever noticed that before? She tucked into the big room just as Marcus took his place in front of the chaplain who had been boated over for the occasion.

Jimmy! She recognized the best man, Petty Officer First Class James Robinson. He was Marcus's swim buddy and best pal. When had he arrived? Probably this morning, she realized, when she had still been sleeping off the hurt of last night.

The seating was arranged on the dance floor. Honey spied an empty chair next to Carey and slid into it.

"Where were you?" Carey whispered without looking at her. She was watching the door where Samantha would be entering.

"I was trying to be appropriate."

That jerked Carey's attention back to her. "*You?* Why?"

"I had a hiccup of conscience." Honey shrugged. "It happens."

Her mother leaned forward and frowned at her from a chair on the opposite side of the floor. Ticked off because I didn't sit with her and Dad and Drew, Honey thought. Then again, Sarah would have had just as much of a cow if she'd disrupted the whole room by trying to get to the seats over there.

Her chest *really* hurt, Honey thought. She tugged at a seam under her left arm.

"Ah," Carey sighed. "She's beautiful."

Honey looked at the door. Sam had arrived and was starting up the aisle. The bride was indeed radiant. Honey caught the look the woman sent her brother. Not sappy enough to be adoring, not misty enough to be blissful. Samantha was just grinning from ear to ear.

BAM. Honey jerked in her seat at the kick of her heart. She hadn't just felt that. It made no sense. There wasn't a man within three feet of her except Matt Tynan, seated on the other side of Carey, and she sure as hell wasn't going to try to seduce him.

BAM-BAM. "No," Honey murmured aloud.

"What's wrong?" Carey whispered.

Honey shook her head. It wasn't the same thing. This wasn't a panic attack. It couldn't be. It was just the dress.

She wondered if she had ever looked at a man in quite the same way Sam was looking at Marcus now. The bride joined the men in front of the fireplace and Honey caught a glimpse of her brother's face. He was adoring and misty. "Ah, Jeez-Louise."

BAM-BAM-BAM.

Honey fixed an unblinking stare on the chaplain. He was holding candles aloft, his voice all resonating gentleness. "These two candles are symbolic of separate people in their own right. Joining the two candles into one symbolizes the strength and the unity of two joining together to become one, depicting Marcus's and Samantha's belief that together they can become greater than either could be alone. The side candles—'' he moved a bit to show them on the mantel ''—remain burning to further symbolize the continuing importance of the individual integrity within the marriage relationship.''

It was perfect, Honey thought. Way to go, Marcus. Her eyes burned a little. She used her pinky finger to wipe at one. She had to get over this crying business. Maybe that was the fault of the water, too.

BAM-BAM-BAM. Honey heard an odd noise and realized that she had groaned.

Marcus's voice was reverent. ''With this ring I thee wed. Take it and wear it as a symbol of all that we share.''

Honey felt perspiration begin to bead on her forehead. Then the bam-bam-bam went to rat-tat-tat and her lungs squeezed so hard, trying to shrink in on themselves, that dizziness swept her. She lowered her head, willing the sensations away.

I've got to breathe.

If she ripped down the zipper of her dress, her family would never forgive her. Honey got to her feet unsteadily. The room tilted slowly then righted itself. Her vision was too focused, too sharp somehow. Everything seemed etched. There was Marcus's handsome puss, scowling at her as though he was contemplating the odds of getting away with murder. Samantha was wearing a smaller frown, half of dismay, half of concern. Her father's face was reddening. Down the row of chairs, Drew's mouth was falling open. Her mother looked as if she was hyperventilating a little herself.

''I'm so sorry,'' Honey murmured aloud. Then she backed up clumsily, almost knocking her chair over. She turned and fled the room.

She reached the door before she thought she was going to and hit up against it hard. Her balance was off. The door swung wildly and she pushed through, her head pounding, a light show of white and pale-blue dots dancing around the edges of her vision. Rafaela's voice came to her from far away, a cry of concern. Honey veered for the back door.

Air. She just needed air.

Honey made it outside and ran. She figured she'd either black out at full throttle, or force her lungs into expanding again whether they liked it or not. She stumbled in her flimsy Italian sandals and paused, hopping on first one foot then the other to pull them off. She tossed them on the lawn and took off down the road.

Then she realized that in her panic, she was running straight to Joe.

She didn't want to see him. He'd rejected her last night, everything she was—really was—inside. She'd bared herself to the moon and he'd pushed her away. Not Honey. Not Honor. But Elise. And that hurt. God, it hurt. It made something small and ashamed twitch inside her and she hated it.

She damned well *did* want to see him.

She broke to a trot halfway to the beach, then she finally slowed to a more reasonable walk. Her lungs were on fire, dragging air in greedily now, sea-tangy, a little salty, sweet. Honey held a hand up. Steady as a rock, she thought, though that might change once she let her temper rip. She trudged on.

He'd pushed away a half-naked woman.

Max slammed the outboard motor back into place on the boat he was tinkering with for a man named Paco. Maybe it really was time to go back to the States, he thought—to seek psychiatric help. God knew there were those who thought he needed it after his behavior these last six months. Now he was starting to wonder if they were right.

He was also aware that the village kids were giving him a wide berth this afternoon, which said a lot about how foul his mood was. That shamed him, but not enough to snap him out of it. All the same, he forced a smile for Paloma when he saw her approaching him from across the sand. He stopped working to wait for her to reach him.

"Hello, *Senhor* Sailor."

"How are you today, *senhora?*" Something seemed different about her, he thought, though he couldn't quite put his finger on it. Her beautiful black hair streamed down her back in a ponytail as always. Her brown feet were delicate and bare, her skirt long and almost severely plain. Her face was as open and curious as ever.

"I am happy enough to touch the moon," she told him.

"Air's a little thin up there." He turned back to the boat.

"Eu implore seu pardon?"

Max paused. No, he thought, he should be begging *her* pardon. He forced himself to stop working again and face her. "Why are you so happy?" he asked politely.

She rubbed a hand in a circular motion over her tummy. Which, Max thought, could mean anything from a sexual come-on—which would be virtually unheard of here—to a sign of hunger. Or…

"Serafina tells me I have another baby," she said.

"Are you sure?" In spite of himself, Max looked around at the tiny and primitive coast. Serafina was a healer who lived down in one of the Paz cabins. He wondered about her credentials. Rumor had it that she'd never once left the island in her life and she was well into her seventies.

"Serafina is never wrong," Paloma said. "Also, I knew."

"Well, congratulations."

"Thank you. You have babies, *senhor,* back in America?"

His reaction surprised him, a heated lance through his gut as sharp and as focused as it had been when he'd counted up all his lost chances with Camille. Time wasn't healing him, he thought again.

"I guess you not need them so much where you come from," Paloma said.

"Now why the hell would you think that?" Max growled and grabbed a wrench.

"The funny *senhora* with all the yellow hair told me."

"The funny—" He broke off. Why should it surprise him that Elise wouldn't want kids any more than Camille had?

"No, maybe that was husbands she talk about." Paloma tapped her temple as though trying to remember.

Husbands, babies, what difference did it make to him? Max

thought. Her daddy bred thoroughbreds and she got whatever she wanted. Always. Except him, last night. And after that blow to her ego, he doubted if she'd be back to the beach before zooming off with Amando to the mainland and the nearest airport, whenever that would be. He was relieved, Max told himself. She'd finally leave him alone.

She didn't want a *husband* either? What did that do to his gold-digger theory? He decided Paloma's translations probably couldn't be trusted.

The threads of the screw he was working on were shot. He was going to have to abandon this quick fix for Paco until he went to Portimao and picked up new hardware, Max decided. Then Paloma spoke again.

"She is here now."

The hairs on Max's nape stirred along with a few other parts of his body. He straightened and jerked around to look in the direction of the road. Elise. And what was she wearing now? Unless her skin had turned purple overnight, the dress wasn't actually transparent. A minor technicality, he thought. It might as well have been. It stopped just above her breasts and left her shoulders bare. It also stopped a few decorous inches below parts of her he had been on the point of discovering last night. The filmy fabric didn't cling so much as it shifted with her every stride, and somehow that was even more provocative. The slight breeze molded it to her as though she had been born in it.

Paloma was gone now. Clever woman, he thought. Some things transcended language barriers—and the intent of Elise's stride was one of them.

She reached him and punched a finger into his chest. Max had seen switchblades less deadly than that fingernail. And damn it, it hurt. He rubbed his hand there.

"I was going to apologize," he said, and thought how lame it sounded as soon as the words came out of his mouth.

"Yeah, well, you've had damned near sixteen hours now to accomplish that little feat, but I didn't notice your backside at my front door this morning bearing roses."

"Brunhia is a little short on roses."

"Portimao's not."

"And precisely how does one bear roses with their backside?"

"One crawls," she snarled.

Suddenly he felt temper kick in his chest. How did he get to be the bad guy in this? "I never wanted what you were doing last night!"

"You wanted it," she grated.

"I did not."

"Listen, pal, I might be a—" Honey choked. *A virgin.* It almost slipped out of her. It had nearly slid right past her lips. What did this man do to her? How did he do it? She fell back and regrouped. "Then you'd better have a word or two with the rest of your body to make sure it's on the same page as your brain from here on in. Until then, you can just keep your hands to yourself."

"Damn it, I wasn't the one who started ripping my clothes off!"

"I ought to do it to you again right now, then just walk away and leave you feeling the way I did last night, all achy and needy!"

"You wouldn't—" He broke off when her hands began gathering fistfuls of her hem. "Of course you would." And something charged inside him at the thought of her doing it in broad daylight, at the prospect of falling into her again, into the taste of her and the heat of her.

He needed to get the hell out of here.

There was only so much he could stand, Max thought, and little lavender dresses were on the wrong side of the line. There was also something in her vivid eyes right now, something a little too stark and inching toward vulnerable, something that wanted to reach out and touch him in places he didn't want touched.

"I hurt you," he realized. Ah, God. He knew what hurt was at the hands of the opposite sex. He knew how it writhed and burned and she didn't deserve it.

"Don't flatter yourself." She turned and gave him her back. "Yeah. You did."

Max raked his fingers through his hair. "Hasn't anybody ever turned you down before?"

She almost choked. If he only knew, she thought wretchedly. "Mostly I do the turning." Voluntarily or otherwise, she thought. "My mind can be a little...selective."

"That's not necessarily a bad thing."

His voice came from closer than she expected. He'd moved, Honey realized, and now he was right behind her. She turned slowly to face him again. "We were good together. Things were happening between us these last few days." She wasn't so much the novice that she didn't know that. "It would have been so good."

"And that was precisely the problem."

He framed her face in his hands. Oh, heaven, she thought. He was going to kiss her again. She knew she ought to stop him—she had her pride, after all—but she thought, *Get out of my way, angels. I'm about to soar above you.*

But he only looked into her eyes. Something about his expression told her that he was trying to be honest.

"There are things..." He trailed off. "There are things you don't know."

She had a flash of the big room again as it had been yesterday, with everyone closing her out. "You won't get an argument from me there."

"That's why I stopped. It didn't seem fair to you."

"Fair, shmair. Okay, then, tell me what these things are."

"I don't know you well enough to trust you."

Honey wrapped her fist into his T-shirt and dragged him an inch or two closer to her. She wasn't sure what she meant to do. Punch him? Kiss him? Scream...or cry? All she knew for sure was that things were boiling inside her. They'd been boiling since she'd landed on this island. Things inside her were howling, and they gathered strength every time someone shut her out or judged her. For whole precious moments of time, she'd escaped everything here. She'd drunk nectar with

Paloma and she'd made this man laugh. She'd felt and she'd yearned and she hadn't bam-bam-bammed or rat-tat-tatted until the moment Marcus had gotten married and she'd realized that even this brother, the one she was closest to, had managed to capture something she might never find.

She was mad, Honey thought. She was furious. And not just at Joe, not just because he'd had Elise throwing herself at him and had turned away. She was jealous of Marcus and she was trapped by her parents and suddenly her Honey persona was an albatross around her neck, when just yesterday, it seemed, it had been her lifeline.

As suddenly as she had grabbed Joe's shirt in the first place, she pushed him away again. "You blew it, pal. I only beg once." She swiveled in the sand and took a step away.

Then he tackled her.

He wrapped both his arms around her waist. Their feet got tangled together. She told herself that was what happened, that he never meant to drop her in the sand the way he did. Because the alternative—a man who wanted her enough to do something so sudden and outrageous and delicious—made something go weak inside her. They stumbled together and went down, and when she twisted, he stayed on top of her. She saw his eyes.

There was a whole lot of heat there. *He wanted her.* He really did, no matter what he had done last night.

"Don't forget our wager," she whispered. "You kissed me again last night. Now you have to take it further."

"How much further?"

He was playing along. Her heart slammed, but the sensation bore no resemblance at all to the bam-bam-bam-rat-tat-tatting that had sent her rushing headlong to this beach. "All the way."

Then he was wrapped around her, on top of her, pressing her into the sand, and his mouth claimed hers fully. It was hard and urgent, something unleashed and gathering like a storm. She felt a sound vibrate in her throat, a sound of utter

THE BEST OF THE BEST™ — Here's How it Works:

Accepting your 2 free books and gift places you under no obligation to buy anything. You may keep the books and gift and return the shipping statement marked "cancel." If you do not cancel, about a month later we will send you 4 additional books and bill you just $4.74 each in the U.S., or $5.24 each in Canada, plus 25¢ shipping & handling per book and applicable taxes if any.* That's the complete price and — compared to cover prices starting from $5.99 each in the U.S. and $6.99 each in Canada — it's quite a bargain! You may cancel at any time, but if you choose to continue, every month we'll send you 4 more books, which you may either purchase at the discount price or return to us and cancel your subscription.

*Terms and prices subject to change without notice. Sales tax applicable in N.Y. Canadian residents will be charged applicable provincial taxes and GST. Credit or Debit balances in a customer's account(s) may be offset by any other outstanding balance owed by or to the customer.

If offer card is missing write to: The Best of the Best, 3010 Walden Ave., P.O. Box 1867, Buffalo, NY 14240-1867

BUSINESS REPLY MAIL

FIRST-CLASS MAIL PERMIT NO. 717-003 BUFFALO, NY

POSTAGE WILL BE PAID BY ADDRESSEE

THE BEST OF THE BEST
3010 WALDEN AVE
PO BOX 1867
BUFFALO NY 14240-9952

satisfaction. This was what she wanted, Honey thought, what she craved, and he was going to give it to her.

She managed to get her hands in his hair, all that glorious hair. She threaded her fingers through it and held his head so he couldn't release her mouth. She found his tongue with hers and played with it. His hands caught her hips and held her still when she would have writhed against him, and she could feel how much he wanted her.

"Honor!"

The voice was a mosquito, buzzing at the back of her brain.

"What the hell are you doing?"

The voice came again, static and irritating, but inside herself she answered it. I'm finding my way home to myself, she thought.

"For God's sake, is this necessary?"

Drew. Drew's voice.

"You ran out of the wedding to roll around in the sand with a stranger?"

Honey felt things go cold and brittle inside herself, like ice shattering. Joe seemed to find the intrusion a little off-putting as well. The hard proof of that moment when he had decided he really did want her was ebbing.

"I've got to go," Honey said against his mouth.

"Who the hell are you? He didn't call you Elise."

"It doesn't matter."

"You want me to trust you with my answers when you won't give any of your own?"

"I just want you to want me." She wriggled out from beneath him and got to her feet.

She was shaking again. She wasn't sure if it was rage now or desperation, or the aftershocks of needing the man who had been pressing her into the sand. All Honey knew for sure was that her eldest brother was a dead man.

When she stood and saw his face, she knew Drew was aware of that as well. He started backing off, his hands held up in surrender. "This wasn't my idea. Dad sent me."

She stalked toward him. ''You're old enough by now to make your own decisions.''

''Dad asked me to find you before you did something crazy. Again. And you did.''

She reached him and punched him as hard as she could in the gut. The air grunted out of him.

''Come on, kitten,'' he pleaded.

''Don't call me that!'' She screamed it and had no idea at all where the words came from. Somewhere deep, she thought. Somewhere visceral. *Please, please, all of you, just let me go and be myself.*

She whipped around to look at Joe again. ''We'll finish this later. You lost the bet.''

Then she left them and ran for the road to get to Drew's motor bike first. When she reached it, she scrubbed a hand hard over her eyes to clear her vision. She hiked her skirt up and swung her leg over the seat to mount the scooter. Damn it, Honey Evans *never* cried.

Max watched her go. He thought his ears might be ringing. He lifted his hands—the hands that had grabbed her—and looked at them as though they belonged to someone else. He thought he could still catch her scent on his skin. Forests and flowers and heat.

What the hell had he just done? He'd craved her, and he'd acted on it. Maybe he didn't need a shrink after all.

Then the other man cleared his throat. ''Who the hell are *you?*'' the guy demanded.

Max dropped his hands slowly. The man was itching for a fight and while a good brawl might nicely take the edge off right now, it was generally best not to wade into one when you were reeling, Max thought. ''Joe,'' he said. ''Just Joe.''

The man stared at him. Trying to place him. The pressured feeling started to come over Max's chest again for the first time in days. It had been bound to happen. All these people on Brunhia…

''Joe who?'' the guy demanded. ''What are you doing on Brunhia? You're American.''

"Last time I checked, that was something to be proud of." Max stepped around him, moving toward the shore again. *Joe who?* was a good sign. Maybe he hadn't pegged him yet. Which made it high time to get back to the *Sea Change*.

Max kept himself from jogging, but he kept his back to the guy even when he heard him call something out to him again. He shoved the little boat back into the water, jumped in and ripped at the engine cord. The motor kicked to life.

He was halfway back to the *Sea Change* before he let himself glance at the shore again. The guy was still watching him. Trying to place him, Max thought, and not quite able to do it. Because who would expect to find Max Strong on Brunhia, calling himself Joe?

The guy hadn't called her Elise, he remembered. He wanted to be pissed off by that, that she had lied to him. But the laugh that shot out of his tight throat instead was rich and deep and felt good. It was too priceless. She wasn't who she had said she was either!

He thought of going back to the beach and asking the guy about her. More than to protect his anonymity, Max didn't veer the dinghy around because maybe, just maybe, she had her reasons for going incognito, too. And maybe, he thought, they were as good and as desperate as his own.

Nine

She felt like a caldron inside, Honey thought, smoking and brimming, ready to spill over. This…this time was too much.

She zoomed the scooter straight into the garage and brought it to a stop with a squeal of tires. Why had she suddenly reached her fill of it all now? They'd always called her kitten, everyone but Marcus. The baby, the girl. It had spread so far as to include Uncle Russ's family, too. But she hadn't felt like a kitten rolling around in the sand with Joe. For the first time in her life she had craved something, had *needed* something for herself, something no one in her family could manage to arrange for her. And maybe it had been broad daylight, and maybe they *had* been right there on the beach in full view of both villages, but it had felt like what she craved, what she needed, what she had been looking for her entire life, had been right there within her grasp…until Drew had called her name.

She spied her shoes lying on the lawn. She snagged them and had her hand on the handle of the screen door to the kitchen when the scene inside made her pause. She lifted a brow, forgetting her own troubles for a moment.

Jake Ingram wasn't having such a hot day either, she realized. His fiancée faced him across the center island of the room, her palms flat on the aged brick.

"This bizarre visit to a place I've never heard of was more important than planning our own wedding?" Tara asked. Ah, my, Honey thought, a little pique there.

Jake appeared to have a strong need to crawl into one of Rafaela's cooking pots. "Marcus and I are close."

"You never even mentioned him before you dragged me on this trip!"

"I guess it was an oversight." He raked fingers through his dark hair. "You didn't have to come."

"We never see each other anymore! I *had* to come because in another week I might forget what you look like!"

"Tara, it's not that bad. And I have a lot on my plate at the moment."

"Does it involve these people?"

Honey watched Jake's eyes go slit-thin. "Which people?"

"All of them! Everyone out there! I've never even shared so much as a cocktail with any of them before and now here we are at this man's wedding!"

"There are other kinds of friends besides those you share cocktails with."

"And they include *bodyguards?*"

Honey leaned a little closer, very interested now. She was dying to hear how Jake explained Robert and Naomi.

"Whoever planned the World Bank Heist is a mastermind," he said. "Masterminds are dangerous. I'm just being cautious."

Honey sighed. The bank heist? She had been sure it had something to do with Marcus's voodoo genes.

"How are we supposed to get married, *stay* married, if we don't share each other's lives?" Tara demanded.

"We share," Jake protested.

"We share social occasions."

"Well, you like those, right?"

"Jake, you don't share anything inside you. And I'm starting to wonder if this is really such a good idea after all."

"Getting married?" he asked. The woman had to be blind as a bat, Honey thought, if she didn't see the hope that flared in his eyes for a fraction of a second there. And that, on top of everything else that had happened to her today, struck Honey as very sad.

Tara's beautifully manicured fingernails went into her

blond hair in a gesture of absolute frustration. "I need some time to think about all of this," she said finally.

"Tara, you were just complaining that I'm giving you too *much* time."

"I don't know what I want anymore."

"Then maybe we ought to just slow down a bit."

The woman looked as though he had hit her. "We were already crawling, Jake."

"I'm just saying...if you're not sure, God, what a mistake we'd be making."

"I was sure, Jake. I've always been sure. But this little trip has blown my mind. Call it a final straw. There's a whole room of people out there—" She broke off and waved a hand at the big room. "And every time I turn around, you're locked in deep conversation with one of them."

Yeah, Honey thought, and what are you all talking about anyway, Jake? Marcus's long-lost days in the old test tube?

"You won't let me in," Tara said, her voice too hushed. "I've tried to understand, but lately...I don't know what's going on with you, Jake, but it's getting worse instead of better. We're not coming together. We're growing apart."

It was a good exit line, Honey thought. She watched Tara leave through the door to the big room. Jake just stood there, looking lost. Honey swept into the kitchen.

"You've got a problem going on there, pal," she announced.

Jake seemed startled at her abrupt intrusion, then he just looked weary. "I'm not supposed to talk to you."

Something kicked in her brain, something that was ready to ignite into punishing temper all over again, but Honey crossed her arms over her chest and kept her voice level. "Do you have the energy right now for word play with me?"

"Not really."

Honey cocked her head to the side, her curls spilling that way. She studied his face. There was something almost frantic about his eyes that she recognized. She'd felt it often enough herself. "Toddies," she decided. "What you need is one of my famous hot toddies."

Jake rubbed his forehead. "I can't figure out if I'm supposed to be afraid of you or grateful."

"I'd recommend a little of both." Then she motioned at the door to the big room. "Your job is to go in there and grab me a bottle of the best whiskey you can find. I'm really not up to facing everyone at the moment." Suddenly she was bone-tired, she realized. It was a strange kind of pervasive exhaustion, as though her every cell had risen to the occasion with Joe on the beach, and when Drew had turned up, it had opened the floodgates to let everything gush out of her again.

Jake left the kitchen. She wondered if he would come back.

Just in case, she started raiding Rafaela's kitchen. She found butter in the giant, industrial-sized fridge and powdered sugar and cinnamon in the pantry. She put water on to boil. She had just pulled over a chair to root through a high cupboard for the mugs she wanted when she heard the door swish again behind her. Honey looked over her shoulder.

Jake stood there with a bottle of Bushmill's in his hand, looking as though he didn't know why he had come back.

"Oh, come on," she chided, grabbing the mugs and jumping down from the chair. "What did they tell you about me, anyway? The one about the retriever's tail?"

"I heard that one, yeah."

"What else?" She snagged the bottle from his hand and took it back to the island.

"That self-restraint isn't your forte."

"Well, that's wrong." She put the butter, sugar and cinnamon into each mug and found a spoon to mash it up. "I rarely do anything without an ulterior motive. And motives imply deliberation and thought."

She looked up in time to see one of his brows hike up. "What's your motive right now?" he asked, gesturing to what she was doing. "With all this?"

"I want to know how you and your brother fit into Marcus's Hercules act. If you could explain Matt Tynan's presence here on Brunhia as well, that would be a real bonus. In exchange, I'll make you feel better."

Something in Jake's eyes flared a little in genuine alarm.

"Not *that* way," Honey said, adding the whiskey to the mugs and topping everything off with the boiling water. She took the drinks to the table.

He followed her slowly. "Don't take it personally."

"That you don't want to jump my bones?" It should have bothered her tremendously, she thought, after Joe's rejection last night. But Joe had soundly un-rejected her this afternoon. Who knew what might have happened if Drew hadn't turned up? Then she opened her mouth and more incredible, un-Honey-like words tumbled out. "It's okay. I'm not particularly gaga for jumping yours either."

Jake laughed, a deep-throated sound that was startled around the edges, then he sat and seemed to relax. He took a mouthful of his toddy. "These are really good."

"By the end of this one, you'll be stretching your legs out in front of you and feeling every muscle in your body unclench. If we have another after this, you'll really unwind."

"Stop me before I dance on any tabletops."

"Will do."

He gave her a grin then that would have knocked her sandals right off her feet if she had still been wearing them. But her skin still tingled from Joe.

"Talk to me," she urged.

"I really can't." But he drank more whiskey. "I probably would, however, if it wouldn't mean betraying others. You've got a damned persuasive way about you."

"Either me, or it's the Bushmill's."

He laughed again. He was definitely unwinding, she thought.

She tried another approach. "How about this? Leave your brother and Tynan out of it. Just talk to me about *my* brother. You wouldn't technically be betraying anything because I have family dibs on him, right?"

"I'm not going to talk to you about Marcus," Jake said.

"He lifted a whole boulder off the side of the road the other day."

Jake stared into his toddy, then he nodded. "He could do that."

"Gretchen is part and parcel of it somehow. I know that much."

He looked up at her suddenly. "So am I."

Honey wasn't sure if she was more amazed by the revelation or by the fact that he had told her. "Whoa. *Three* of you?"

"That's the current count. Can I have another of these?" He held up his mug.

"Sure." She hopped up and went to make a fresh toddy. "So that CIA dude wasn't just howling at the moon."

"You have an interesting way with words."

"Thank you. Now give me some more of yours."

This time his laugh was more of a chuckle. "I can't, Honor. Seriously."

"Please don't call me Honor. Only three people in the world do that and I don't respond very well. Although just lately, 'kitten' seems to get even more of a rise out of me."

"I'm not sure I understand."

"You're safer that way. How did you find out?" She brought him the new drink. "I'm asking about you now," she reminded him. "You can't betray yourself. How did you find out that you're a voodoo-gene baby too?"

"We were all given a gift." Before she could open her mouth again, he held up a hand. "No. No more."

"Oh, come on. We were really communicating there for a moment."

One corner of his mouth tucked up. "I expected you to be an air-brain, not witty."

Honey leaned closer to him. "It's an act," she whispered.

"It's difficult to come off as witty when you're actually not."

She felt her mouth fall open a little. "I meant the air-brain business. You really have a one-track mind, don't you? It goes straight down the narrow and analytical road."

"It's *my* gift."

She gaped a little more, suddenly understanding. "Math. Numbers. Finances."

He smiled tiredly. That reminded her of why she'd felt he'd needed these toddies in the first place. "Tara doesn't know any of this, does she?"

He raised his mug in a toast to her. "You're intuitive, too."

"Not really. I eavesdropped on your argument for a few minutes."

He frowned. "That wasn't an argument. Tara doesn't argue."

"She's got bitching down to a fine art."

He laughed again. "God, I needed this."

"I can sympathize with her position, though. You and Gretchen and Marcus have this test-tube sorority going on—"

"We're siblings," he interrupted. "We had natural parents."

"Well, that sort of tarnishes the laboratory spin I was starting to imagine."

"Smoking beakers and whatnot? Sorry."

This time Honey laughed. "No problem. I just like a good tale now and again. How did you find out?" she asked again. He was talking, she thought, so she'd keep pushing.

"My natural mother tracked me down and told me."

"So where are Mumsy and Dad now?"

"They're both deceased."

Her heart did an odd kind of chugging kick against her chest. "Of natural causes?"

"That's doubtful." He shook his head.

"I know, I know." Honey sighed and sat back in her chair to polish off her own toddy. "You're not going to say any more." Then she grinned. "I got a lot out of you anyway. I'm taking it that not a whole lot of people know the truth about this genetics hoopla, right?"

"It's a dangerous situation. There are those who want to

gather us all up again before we can get to the bottom of it all and stop them."

"Oooh. And use you for nefarious ends?" She'd been joking, but his expression shocked her. "I just hit the nail right on the head, didn't I? It's the Coalition!"

His eyes narrowed and he straightened abruptly. "How did you find out about the Coalition?"

Honey waved a hand. "I wrangled it out of Kurt. I'm good at this, you know."

"That's an understatement."

She got up to make herself one more toddy. "This explains your problem with Tara. This is how it appears to me, as an outsider looking in. Ready? It sounded earlier as if you're heavily into pushing sweet Tara away."

"She has some unsweet moments."

"If you don't mind my saying so, those don't sound like the words of a man in love." She sipped her hot whiskey and went back to the table.

"I'm not sure what I am any longer. And I can't worry about it with all this other stuff going on."

"Could be your whole test-tube past is affecting that."

"I told you—"

"Test tube, uterus, who cares?" Honey interrupted. "The bottom line is that a whole bunch of your earlier childhood memories got somehow swiped from you, right? I can figure that out just from having grown up around Marcus."

"I'm starting to remember more."

"Well, until and unless you get it all back, maybe you're clinging to Tara for a sense of security."

"You've figured that out and you're a telephone operator?"

Honey waved a hand dismissively. "If I had said I wanted to be a shrink, my family would have set me up as Dr. Ruth by now. That's a whole different topic. I'm just saying that it only makes sense that the truth was hidden somewhere down there deep in your psyche all along. You know, here you are with your original family, and then poof! All gone. I don't know about your past, but Marcus landed with my family when he was twelve. And I'm pretty sure he had no memory of where he was before then. You can sort of feel that in another person, you know? Anyway, that's a lot of years to lose track of. And it could make you crave the stability of a relationship...say, of a steady girlfriend or a wife. Of *any* girlfriend or wife. It wouldn't matter who because you're not really going to let her in anyway."

"I might if she was as dogged as you." Jake made a sound of disbelief in his throat.

"They're good toddies, aren't they? Look at you, your legs are all stretched out."

"No tabletops, though."

"Good thing, too. You're a lot bigger than I am. I probably couldn't drag you down if I tried. And if I did, it might put us in a compromising position, in which case sweet Tara would *really* get pissed off."

He shook his head. "You're funny."

"One of *my* many gifts and I'm just your average run-of-the-mill sperm-and-egg product, too." Then she sipped her drink and got serious. "You shouldn't marry her."

He'd been staring into his mug but that made him look up at her sharply.

"I'm just saying, if you don't even feel comfortable talking to her about this Coalition and your voodoo-gene business, then you probably wouldn't make her such a hot husband."

"I can be hot."

Honey snagged his mug out of his hand. "I don't think you need any more of these."

"Tara can't handle it."

"If you're still on the subject of hot, maybe we ought to leave that on a need-to-know basis." More uncharacteristic words for Honey, she realized. Someone seriously needed to shut down this island's water supply.

"I meant I don't think she could handle the business about the Coalition," Jake said.

"Well, she's not so great with sea mist and mules, either." Honey put both their mugs into the dishwasher. "But I think she can avoid mules and mist a lot better than she'd be able to avoid what this is doing to you, so you might want to take that into consideration."

She would have said more. She *meant* to say more. She had a lot of opinions, and too few people cared about hearing them. But then the door to the big room shot open and Marcus appeared there.

"What the hell got into you today?" he demanded. "Why did you bolt out of my wedding?"

Her temper ticked again. "Did it occur to you that maybe I had a legitimate reason?"

"You don't have a legitimate bone in your body!"

"On that note, I think I'll bolt again."

Honey made a beeline for the stairs door. She was all out of fight.

Max sat on deck in his favorite chair and watched the village fishermen head out to sea as the sun went down. The women milled about the cabins after seeing them off.

Why *not* take Elise—or whoever she was—up on what she was offering? he wondered. He was looking for a way to justify taking what he wanted, he realized. What she *made* him want with her outrageous, shameless pursuit of him. In all honesty, that pursuit was flattering. He could imagine that she'd normally only have to crook one of those pretty manicured fingers of hers and men would hurl themselves into her bed. Maybe that was why she wanted him, he reflected, because he'd resisted her. If so, was there anything wrong with that?

He couldn't bear complications in his current life of stolen simplicities, but she wasn't offering any. She would be going home soon, back to the States.

She didn't seem to want more from him than sex. She couldn't want his money because he was pretty sure now that she didn't know he had it. So would it be wrong to give her what she wanted and take something for himself in the process?

He was starting to think not when she appeared on the beach. She'd changed into those cutoffs again, the white-blue ones, and this time she appeared to be wearing some sort of bathing suit top. She stopped at the water's edge, looked out at the *Sea Change* and waved to him to come to shore.

Max stood and went to the transom. He shook his head at her. He had never been a rash man. He had to consider this wager business for all pratfalls before he let himself act.

She waded into the water. She wasn't going to swim out, he thought. Yes, she was. She dove over a little wave and disappeared under the surface.

Something caught inside him, something impossibly alert and ready. His blood started heating. How many times in his life did a man stand aboard his boat and watch a mermaid swim toward him with the express purpose of seducing him?

Only a fool wouldn't help her on board, and he wasn't a fool, either. Or at least, since Camille, he liked to think he'd learned how not to be.

She broke through the water again eight or nine feet closer to his boat. Then she started angling toward him with clean strokes. Max was leaning over the transom when she reached it, looking down at her.

"You're out of your mind," he said quietly.

"The water's freezing. Help me out of here."

He didn't reach down a hand. He didn't do it because he was as glad to see her now as he had been when she'd marched up to him earlier, even knowing that there'd be hell to pay for what he'd done to her last night. Maybe he wouldn't take her up on her offer, not tonight, not yet, but there was no doubt in his mind that he was going to enjoy her visit.

"It's September," he pointed out.

"So?" She held on to the stern.

"Northern hemisphere. That's why the water's cold."

"Can I have my geography lesson somewhere warm and dry?"

Her lips were going a pale shade of blue, he realized. The

water was tepid enough at the shore line but out here the currents swept in with something more frigid. He finally put a hand down to her and hauled her up.

Honey scrambled over the transom. "Ooh, strong men give me the shivers."

"I think it's the business about September in the northern hemisphere."

"That too." Her teeth were snicking together, she realized. How very seductive. She almost rolled her eyes at herself. This was not going the way she had planned it when she'd left the house. But she rallied. "It might be best if I got out of these wet clothes."

"Nice try." He grinned. Oh, she loved his grin when he let it go all the way. "How about a shot of cognac instead?"

"You have cognac? How in the world can you afford that?" she asked, startled.

His grin faded and his face closed down again. He gave her his back and went into the galley. Honey thought about kicking herself for the question.

She was nervous, she realized. Her shivers were bone-deep and they weren't just from the cold. That was as new as the odd un-Honey-like words she kept spouting lately and the urge to cry that kept hitting her out of the blue.

He came back to her with a snifter. She took it and tossed back the shot. "I have something to say," she announced after the warmth hit her. Her shivers eased a little.

"Are you going to tell me who you really are now?"

"No."

"Why not?"

"Because I don't want to be who I am."

It hit him like a punch to the solar plexus. He might have spoken those same words himself, and none would have been truer. Max nodded.

Honey's heart swelled. He was going to let it go at that, she realized. It was a gift unlike any she'd ever been given before, and she'd spent a lifetime being given more than money had any right to buy.

She leaned to put the glass down on a coffee table. "Here's the thing. This started out being sort of a...a game." She wagged a finger between them. "Going after you. This whole sex business."

"Are you going to let me in on the rules?"

She owed him that much, she decided, and she nodded. "This had to be removed from my real life."

"Elise, I can't be a part of your real life for reasons you're not even aware of."

"What I'm trying to say is, this here, right now, isn't a part of that. I'm not here right now for the same reason I took my shirt off last night."

"You don't want sex?"

At least he looked dismayed, she thought. That was encouraging. "Of course I do. But I don't want it for the same reason I wanted it before."

"Why do you want it, then?"

Oh, God, she felt her chin tremble. "To reclaim me. To take back someone I should never have let them make me lose in the first place." She understood that now, she realized. She'd fought off her family's smothering control and expectations so hard and so well, she had even fought off herself. "Right now I want comfort and a haven, and you're it."

His face changed. There was something in his eyes that she hadn't seen before. There was empathy there and a misery of his own. Honey started shaking again. He finally put his own glass down.

"Don't you want to get out of those wet clothes?" he asked her.

The most amazing thing speared through her then. An almost debilitating flash of heat, followed by a thrumming sensation of wanting. Things tightened at the core of her. *Oh, my,* she thought, *I'm turned on.*

But then he turned away.

"Where are you going?" she demanded.

"To get you a warm blanket. Comfort and all that."

She wanted to tell him that that wasn't the comfort she'd

had in mind, but she was still too shaken by the awakening of her own body. And just because of words.

By the time he came back from the fore cabin, she'd rallied somewhat. "I just laid my soul bare, and you get me a *blanket?*"

"If your soul's getting naked, I've got a hunch that the rest of you is headed that way as well."

It happened again, she thought, but the heat was hotter and the thrumming was more intense. And things that were already tight inside her started to hurt.

He draped the blanket over her shoulders. When he was close, she angled her head up and caught his mouth with her own.

She knew immediately that he wasn't going to push her away this time. Maybe she'd convinced him not to, or maybe he had already made up his mind. But the games were over for him, too. His hands left the blanket and his fingers tunneled into her wet hair. He held her head while his mouth took over, his tongue diving in a slow dance that made her crazy. She wanted to shout with the things that were happening to her body. She wanted to grab what was within her grasp now in a heated, fierce frenzy before it could get away from her again. But he held her still for an assault of agonizing deliberation.

Just when she thought she couldn't stand it anymore, his hands moved to the straps of her swimsuit top and slid them down over her shoulders.

"You're probably still a little chilled," he said against her mouth.

"No. Yes."

He laughed, a low, throaty sound, and his fingers found the front of her top. He eased it down. The cool evening air wafting through the open cabin door tickled her skin and made her nipples pucker. She felt a shuddering deep inside herself.

"I'd ask if this is okay, but I think you've already demonstrated that it is."

"Mmm." Her voice was leaving her. Then his mouth

slicked over her neck, her throat, down lower. Honey felt her legs folding.

Not again! But she wasn't passing out. The need inside her was alive. She had no strength against it. Just when she thought she might mortify herself by going to her knees for an entirely different reason this time, his arms came around her. He picked her up and moved a few steps back to a sofa bunk, lowering her there.

"No gossamer sheets," he said as his mouth found her breast. "No elegant four-poster."

She meant to tell him that she didn't care. But her voice started escaping her in little, mewling sounds as his tongue traced her nipple, and she couldn't find words.

The tightness inside her was agony now. She wanted this to last forever, and yet she couldn't stand any more. Her hands started flying, seemingly of their own accord. Up beneath his T-shirt, over his skin, skin that still felt warm from the day's sun. Her mouth found his own throat and she tasted sea salt and man. She nipped on his earlobe and felt free, soaring, touching the sky. *Everything in my life has been leading me right to this moment.* She had the crazy thought that she'd just been in the wrong place to find it.

Her fingers found the waist of his shorts and it occurred to her that she really had no idea how to go about gracefully getting them off him. He rose off her a little and stripped them away himself.

She'd never seen a real man naked before. On film, sure. But not for real. She liked it. A lot.

A laugh bubbled up in her throat. He caught it from her mouth and swallowed it. She felt giddy, exquisitely alive. He found the zipper on her shorts and tugged it down. She wriggled to let him get them off her. Then he was pressed to her, all of him, length to length, and he kissed her hard again with a groan in his throat. And her thoughts spiraled and her mind shattered. She felt him press against her, inside…

…and pain exploded.

She'd expected it. She started to cry out anyway, caught the sound, swallowed it back. He froze.

"Don't stop," she begged.

"Elise, for God's sake—"

"No!" Maybe it was instinct. She would never know. She rocked her hips up against him until the barrier was gone and didn't matter anymore at all.

He didn't stop. She wouldn't let him. She wrapped her legs around him and her hands moved over his skin again, heated, demanding, urging him on. She caught his mouth and begged without words. And he picked up a rhythm until there were only starbursts in her head and light rained down through her body. And the tightness inside her imploded. She felt as if pieces of herself were tumbling in, crumbling into a glorious heap of embers. He groaned and tensed and his fingers spasmed in her hair.

It was a long time before he spoke. But she'd kind of expected that, too.

"You were a *virgin?*" His voice vibrated with shock, with anger.

She should have told him. She had been trying to ditch the status quo for so long, had been so busy worrying about the imminent bam-bam-bams and rat-tat-tats, it had never occurred to her to warn a man first. Maybe that had been wrong.

"Gotta go." She tried to squeeze out from beneath him, but she wasn't sure she could stand.

"The hell you are." His weight pressed her down more firmly.

She went with instinct. She had to get away. If he berated her, she wasn't sure she could bear it right now. "You don't want anyone from the house to come looking for me," she pointed out. It was a stab in the dark, but she was right on target. That possibility, for some reason, continued to quell him.

He rolled aside to let her get up. "We've got to talk about this."

"Later. After you calm down."

"I'm calm."

"You're angry."

"Damned right I'm angry! You should have told me! Who the hell *are* you?"

"Obviously not the same person who swam to your boat." She grabbed her clothing, then she went still. "Don't ruin this, Joe. I'm begging you. Please don't ruin it for me."

He didn't understand. She could see it in his eyes. But he let it go. He was a good man, she thought, inherently good. She could want him for that alone.

Honey struggled back into her clothes. She didn't want to have feelings for him. The absence of swooning and hyperventilation was precious enough. Because she wasn't in Georgetown, she told herself, hurrying out onto the deck again. That was all it was. That was why it had worked this time.

Honey looked over her shoulder. He was standing in the cabin door. She thought of saying more, changed her mind, then once again dove into the water.

Ten

The sun was high and warm when Honey woke in the morning, pouring in through the east windows of the bell room and heating her skin where it reached the cot. She rolled over onto her back and looked up at the bell.

It occurred to her to pump her hands skyward and hoot. *No longer a virgin!* But oddly, it hadn't turned out to feel like a hooting sort of occasion. For one thing, she was reasonably sure that Joe was going to have a thing or two more to say about the virginity business. That took a little of the celebratory edge off things. But she felt liquid, too, not charged, as though her whole body had gone to melted chocolate.

Then the thought that had spiraled through her mind last night came back to nip at her. *Everything in my life has been leading up to this moment.* Her stomach squeezed. But a woman could be expected to have bizarre thoughts leading up to her first orgasm, she decided, especially when it had taken her so long to grab the brass ring. There was something rather cataclysmic about the experience, after all. That was all that wayward thought meant. She'd come to Brunhia to find a lover. She hadn't come to fall in love.

She swung her legs over the side of the bed. She'd gotten away from the townhouse. That was why it had finally worked. It was just sex. How could it be anything else? She could never let him into her life. The minute he entered her *real* life and got anywhere near Georgetown, the panic attacks would come on.

She was halfway across the room to her suitcase when that thought froze her. She was going to have to spend the rest of her life flitting around the globe, she realized, just to enjoy the simple act of human copulation without coming undone.

"Honor? Are you up there?" Her father's voice shot up the stairs, jolting her with all the reasons she couldn't work up any passion in Georgetown. "I want a word with you."

Honey moved to the door and opened it. Her father stood at the bottom of the stairs, staring up. "Is there a fire?" she asked sweetly.

"Of course not."

"Then could I please brush my teeth and get dressed first?"

"Meet me in the dining room when you're ready. Rafaela will serve lunch shortly."

Lunch? Well, Honey thought, sex was obviously a real insomnia-buster. "Will do."

She closed the door again. He could be feeling cantankerous about anything, she thought, from the way she'd fled the wedding to the toddies she'd made for Jake Ingram, from the way she hadn't answered her mother's summons late last night—she couldn't bear to have Sarah ruin her mood when she'd come back to the house—to the fact that military men never slept until noon, even retired ones. She had no intention of meeting with him to find out which it was. She had two more days, she thought. Just two more precious days with Joe. Two days to explore sex and revel in it. Two days to touch and to feel, to prod him and make him laugh and to be herself. She couldn't take a penniless drifter back to Georgetown with her. Would he anchor in the Potomac while she went about her life and swam out to him nightly? Though maybe the Potomac was far enough removed from the city that it would *seem* like a different world and her psyche wouldn't avalanche on her.

In any event, she didn't intend to waste a moment of her time remaining on Brunhia. She went to the hooks on the wall and snatched her maillot off one of them, then she looked around the room for accessories. She'd been in residence just long enough that clothing was strewn all over the place. This time she decided that the long hot-pink gauze skirt would be the perfect accompaniment, that and her flat sandals, the ones in pearly pink. She felt like…

…a woman whose whole life had been leading her toward last night.

Honey growled aloud at the thought and went downstairs for a shower. The fact that she was headed right back to the beach today, even though she'd achieved her goal last night meant nothing. She just wanted to cram as much of this sex business into the next two days as she could, she told herself.

She was dressed and feeling chipper when she reached the kitchen. She was on her way to the back door and the garage when Carey came sweeping in from the big room. She was carrying the coffee carafe.

"Are you off to the beach again?" she asked when she saw Honey.

Honey grinned. "Yup."

"Your work in progress is coming along well, then?"

"Splendidly."

"Then don't let me keep you."

Honey's grin started feeling hard and stiff on her mouth. It was an odd thing for Carey to say, overly polite. "Got a burr up that cute tush of yours this morning?"

"Of course not," Carey said. Too fast, Honey thought. She watched her friend go to the urn to refill the carafe. "But why is it that the youngest woman in any crowd is always relegated to coffee duty?"

"It's a hierarchy thing designed by the male of the species."

"Well, that's just cow dung."

"Your Kansas is showing." She watched Carey hug the filled carafe to her tummy, both arms around it, and she was alarmed. "Hey, you're going to burn yourself!"

Carey realized it at the same time and put the carafe on the counter. "We haven't talked at all since Matt and I have been here," she said finally.

"You and Matt?" Honey asked innocently.

Carey sighed. "You and me."

"Well, I've been deliberately excluded from your little circle during this get-together. What else could I do but pursue sex with a hot island vagabond instead?"

Carey didn't laugh. She winced. "I'm sorry. But everyone's all here in one place for the wedding and they want to put their heads together."

"About what?"

Carey stared at her without answering. And Honey felt the hurt somewhere down deep in her gut, a twisting, cold thing. She turned away for the door.

"Honey, it was never my intention to shut you out! I'm stuck in the middle."

Honey shrugged. It didn't matter. She wouldn't let it matter. She reached for the door handle but then she paused.

Carey had said they were all in the big room talking again. About Marcus and Gretchen and Jake and the Coalition, about bad guys snapping up the wrong brother and nefarious ends? Honey still wondered how Matt and Carey fit into all that. She wondered if Kelly and Ethan Williams were in the big room, too.

She turned back into the kitchen. Carey had left. Why was she tiptoeing? The question flashed into her mind as she crossed the room again toward the door to the big room. "When a pariah," she whispered aloud, "one should always slither in."

She pressed her ear against the door. She couldn't hear a thing. Trust the marble maven to install two-inch thick wood. She leaned her weight against the door ever-so-gently and it eased open a crack. She couldn't see, but now, at least, she could hear.

"What was the message?" Jake asked.

Matt's voice answered. "'I have information you might be interested in.' Quote, unquote. Verbatim."

"All right, what's the downside of meeting with him?" Gretchen asked.

"Could be a setup," Marcus said.

"We really can't be sure which side Hatch is on." That was Samantha, Honey thought.

"I should be the one to meet with him," Marcus said.

"If Hatch isn't on the up-and-up, you could be in danger," Samantha said, quiet tension in her voice.

"That's my point. It would take three or four of them to overpower *me.*"

"It's got to be me," Matt said. "I'm the one he reached out to and we can't blow him off on the chance that he really does know something important. Lack of information is our greatest impediment."

"Violet would be invaluable right now," Gretchen said. Something in her tone, a soft and confused grief, lifted the hairs on Honey's nape. Marcus had mentioned Violet too. She obviously hadn't fared too well in all this. The short silence in the other room sounded as though people were collecting themselves so she figured Violet might be mom.

"We need to set a game plan," Jake said finally. Honey heard a bar stool move and imagined he'd gotten up to pace. "Okay, in order. I'm doing my damnedest to find Faith. We've got to alert her to the danger and bring her into the fold."

"I'm still working on decoding Henry's tapes," Gretchen said. "I'm close. If nothing else, we'll soon know exactly how they did what they did to us."

"I'm working out the best angle for a sting operation to take the Coalition down. But I need more facts to work with," Marcus said.

"Which brings us right back to Samuel Hatch again," Matt Tynan said. "The Coalition has no reason to grab me. I should be safe enough even if he is in with them."

"Except you've been asking a lot of questions about Code Proteus lately," Carey said. "They could grab you just to find out how much we've learned."

We've learned? Honey almost choked aloud. Oh, Carey, she thought, you're so deep into this and you never told me. A fresh sense of betrayal made her chest feel tight.

"*Senhora!* What are you doing there?"

Honey gave a little cry as Rafaela's voice startled her. She jerked around and forgot that the door was of the swinging variety. Her elbow hit it hard and it flared open.

The voices in the big room stopped cold.

"Me?" Honey asked. "I was...uh, going to see if anyone, uh...wanted breakfast. Lunch."

The door swung inward again so hard it slammed her in the back. She took a few startled steps forward and whipped around again. Her brother had pushed in from the big room. And Marcus was mad.

Well, so was she. "Don't say it," she hissed at him. "Don't even say it."

"What the hell were you doing? Eavesdropping?"

"She see about lunch," Rafaela said helpfully.

"Of course, I was eavesdropping!" Honey heard her own voice rise. "How else am I supposed to have any idea what's going on around here?"

"It's none of your business!" Marcus roared.

"Well, I beg to differ. They grabbed Zach instead of Jake, and apparently this Violet met an untimely end of some sort. And the last time I checked, we were related. Given what I just overheard, I actually *could* be in danger. Carey's afraid they're even going to grab Matt!"

"Honey, you've gone too far this time. You're just twisting things around as an excuse to snoop, then run around repeating everything you've heard. You have no place here!"

It felt like something with a hot, barbed tip drove deep into her chest. Honey felt her lungs trying to seize up again. First Carey, now Marcus—the two people she was closest to in the world. Both of them had had occasion to peer beneath the Honey-antics and see what dwelled inside. Apparently, neither of them had been impressed. They still wouldn't let her in.

She turned away. "Talk away to your heart's content. I won't be around to offer any input."

"Honey, for God's sake, what input could *you* possibly have anyway?"

It snapped something inside her just as she reached the back door. Honey jerked back to him. "I know Samuel Hatch."

He gaped at her. "How do you know Hatch?"

She twirled a finger at her temple. "Ex-CIA agent? A little wifty, holding on with both hands to memories of his old glory because retirement's not much to his liking? *That* Sam Hatch? A guy who would call the White House frequently just to stay in touch and who would enjoy chatting with anyone who expressed even the vaguest interest in his past?"

"What's your point?"

"Come on, big brother, we know all about your brawn but I always gave you credit for some brains, too."

She'd hurt him. Honey saw it in his eyes. That, she knew, was his Achilles heel. Sometime soon, when her temper died down, she'd be sorry. It would make her miserable. But now she had a grand exit in mind. "I'm a White House telephone operator. Duh."

She turned around again and banged out the door. She raked a hand through her hair as she strode toward the garage. It was trembling a little. She grabbed a scooter, hiked up her skirt again to mount, revved the little motor and peeled out for the beach. *Damn them, damn them, damn them!*

The women of Paz and Deus Fornece were all at the shoreline cleaning fish when she arrived. She started up the sand to find Paloma. The air was ripe with last night's catch. Honey pressed the heel of her hand to her chest. "I need to breathe," she whispered aloud.

"Talking to yourself?" came a voice from behind her.

Joe. Honey turned around. "I get the most interesting answers that way."

He didn't smile. She hadn't really expected him to. She pulled air in hard.

"You're still mad at me," she said.

"Are you crying?"

"Of course not." She scrubbed her hands over her eyes.

"You're crying. You're eyes are all shiny."

"I just had an altercation with someone I love. If you're

just going to yell at me, too, then beat it. I don't want to see you after all."

"Oh, you're going to see me. You've got some talking to do."

"I'm not up for it right now."

"It's all right for you to chase me all over Portugal, but when *I* want to talk to you, you just slam the door?"

"I did not chase you all over Portugal. It was just one small city and an island."

He closed the distance between them to stare down into her face. Honey wondered what he saw there. An air-brain? A lunatic who had swum out to his boat so she could unload her virginity on him? Or a woman who could make him smile and laugh? She waited and realized it mattered. It mattered a lot. Her eyes were burning again.

"Hey, hey," he said, then he reached with a thumb to catch a tear.

It undid her. She heard herself gulp and was mortified.

"Come on, nothing's that bad," he said quietly. "I'm not mad. I just don't get it."

"I'm not crying because of you." She sniffed. "You I can handle."

"Apparently." He took her elbow. They began walking up the sand.

Urgent thoughts spilled through her mind. "What I did to you was wrong."

"Well, you didn't exactly rope me and mount me."

"I thought of it. If you had resisted much more, I might have."

She was rewarded by a bark of laughter.

"I should have told you first," she said. "But I was... desperate."

"Desperate for sex? Honey, a woman who looks like you could grab it with a snap of her fingers."

She jolted a little again when he unwittingly used her name. That made her feel small, too, that she had lied to him about who she was. "Thank you. I think."

Suddenly she stopped and looked around. They'd passed the village and had reached the quarry. She sat down in the rocky soil and drew her knees up to her chin.

"Why were you desperate?" he asked, standing over her. "To fulfill some sort of saltwater fetish?"

A quick laugh escaped her and surprised her. A moment ago, she had thought she'd never laugh again. "It's more like a Georgetown phobia. I can blame myself for that, too. People don't have a right to whine because they've been wronged by a misconception they've created themselves."

Max felt her words like something winding through his blood, spreading light as it went. He had done that, he thought. It was exactly what he had done. Everyone had assumed he lived for the next deal, the next dollar. And when he'd tried to run from that and they'd hounded him, he'd blamed them for it.

"What?" she asked. "You look funny."

"Just thinking that you said another mouthful." He sat beside her.

"Wow, a high-water mark. Someone thinks I have insight."

"I've always thought you had insight."

Her brows climbed. "Really?"

"Why wouldn't I? You spit out things like that all the time."

She thought about it, then she picked up a stone and tossed it down the slope. It kicked up little puffs of dust as it tumbled. "I'm going to tell you a story," she decided. "About a princess."

"Would this princess's name be Elise?"

"That's one of her names, yes. Elise lived in a beautiful castle with a mom and dad who loved her very much and a nanny who thought the sun rose and set by her. Her mom and dad were always very busy so they needed someone to take care of their little girl. Her dad had to do important work and her mom had to sit just so in her ivory tower all the time.

She couldn't risk getting sticky little chocolate fingers on her pretty dresses."

"Ah. Makes sense. Ivory towers are hard to keep clean."

Honey snickered. "Yeah. Oh, and there were also two big brothers." She thought about Marcus's gift. "*Really* big, as it turned out."

"Goliaths?"

"One was. The other was just sort of...perfect."

"Did they love her very much, too?"

"Very much," Honey agreed. "The brothers and the mom and dad and the nanny never wanted anything to be hard for her. They all wanted her to be happy, so if she asked for a moonbeam, they'd lasso the whole moon. If she wanted to plant a flower, they'd rush out and make her a whole garden, so she wouldn't have to get her hands dirty, of course. And if she wanted to be a steeplechase jockey, then they made sure she had the best mounts available."

"Ah. I guess they bought up a lot of Girl Scout cookies, too."

"A lot of them," she agreed. "You have no idea how many cookies it takes to get to Disney World. Anyway, what they all really wanted was for the princess just to be still and grow up into...well, into her mom."

"With an ivory tower of her own," Joe guessed. "Nice work if you can get it."

Honey finally grinned. "The princess would have gone out of her mind."

"I know someone named Elise who would have reacted the same way. So what did the princess do about all this?"

"Princess Elise turned the castle on its ear. She sort of struck her own path doing very un-ivory tower-type things. Whenever her mom and dad tried to push her into her own tower, she kicked up her heels."

"I'll bet. How did her brothers feel about this?"

"She thought one of them understood until a little while ago." Her own smile faded. The game was over. "He's lived with my antics for so long, even he believes them now."

When Joe reached out and brushed a stray curl off her cheek, one the breeze had been teasing, her lip trembled. She pressed her cheek to his hand. He didn't pull away.

"You're right," he said, "you can't always blame the recipient of the, ah, antics."

"I know."

"People see what they expect to see."

"I know that, too." She brought her head up and looked at him suddenly. "I want to run away from it all. I don't want to be the heel-kicking princess anymore. Joe, I'm tired."

"Yeah, all those calisthenics could be wearing."

She reached up and caught his hand. "I'm serious. I want to do what you did."

He was startled. He started to tell her it wasn't that easy, but, of course, it was. If you had money. If you had enough determination. He thought she had both.

"Are you ever going back?" she asked abruptly. "Back to your real life?"

"I'm starting not to think so."

"Why?"

"Because a wise woman told me that you don't have the right to bellyache afterward if you've been wronged by a misconception you've created yourself."

Something in her eyes flared. "You can't complain, but maybe you can walk away from the misconception. That's what I want to do." Somehow their fingers had entwined. It felt good, she thought. It anchored her for one of the biggest decisions of her life. "I'm going to go somewhere where no one knows me and I'm just going to be Elise." She let her air out. She was breathing fine now.

"They'll follow you," he warned. "The mom, the dad, the brothers and the nanny."

"The nanny retired thirteen years ago."

"I speak from experience. They'll hire people to look for you. Everywhere you go, you'll have to look over your shoulder to see if they're behind you."

She frowned. "Then I'll tell them first. I'll tell them to leave me alone."

"They won't."

"Is that how it was for you?"

Max hesitated, then he nodded. She'd given him a lot of herself. He felt an overriding need to give some back. "I wasn't just a carpenter."

"I guessed that."

He nodded. "My houses really got…out of hand. But I kept working at making them bigger and better anyway so everyone just assumed I loved what I was doing. What I really wanted was to be back in Pittsburgh just wielding a hammer."

"Do you ever have trouble breathing?" she asked suddenly.

The question hit him like a punch. He didn't answer.

"You did. Do," she said, reading his face. "Like the whole world is pushing down on your chest." She came onto her knees and grabbed both his hands in hers. "Joe, let's run away together. Let's go someplace where we can both breathe."

It scared the hell out of him that he wanted to. It scared him more to find himself thinking it could work. His empire was running without him. What was another few weeks? By then someone would find them, one of them, and shatter the idyllic escape. But for a while longer he could keep being Joe and she wouldn't have to be a heel-kicking princess. They'd make love and drink up the sun, follow the dying summer as far as they could go.

It was insane. And it was perfect. As long as he was with her, he was just Joe. And Joe was a happy man.

"No questions about the past," she said urgently. "No promises for the future." Oh, she wanted this, she realized. She wanted it desperately. If they could get on the *Sea Change* and just keep sailing to the horizon, she could touch him any time she wanted to without the world spinning. She couldn't take him back to the States with her and anchor him in the Potomac. But there was no earthly reason why she couldn't drop out right along with him.

"You're out of your mind." His voice was hoarse.

He was thinking about it. "I know."

"No husband? That's not the reason you lied about your name? There won't be an armed man waiting for me at any port?"

"I'm Princess Elise."

"That guy called you something else."

"Elise is a perfectly legal alias," she assured him. "It's my middle name."

"You're actually talking me into this."

"I'm good at that."

Suddenly he tugged at her hands hard until she spilled into his lap. His skin was warm from the sun. Honey twisted around until she could loop her arms around his neck and lock her legs around his waist. She pressed herself to him to lick at his earlobe.

"How am I supposed to think when you do things like this?" he demanded.

"Maybe I don't want you to think. Maybe I want you to go with instinct."

"Dropping out works best when you've laid a solid plan ahead of time."

She reared back, grinning. "We're dropping out, then? We're really going to do it?"

"You've got to let them know that you're going. I don't want a rich thoroughbred-breeding daddy hunting me down with a shotgun either."

"He's more into Uzis." She laughed at his expression. "Just kidding."

"Tell them upfront. And you get one suitcase, rich girl. We travel light."

She frowned. "One? Oh, well. A woman does what a woman's got to do."

"And think about it. Think long and hard and be sure."

That, she thought, wouldn't be necessary, but she nodded to placate him.

"Then meet me at the beach at midnight. If you don't show

up, I'll know you changed your mind and we'll never mention this lunacy again."

"No questions, no promises, no explanations. I'll be there," she said quietly. She felt the shiver deep inside her at all the possibilities. It would be the most outrageous thing she had done yet, and it would be the first thing she'd ever really done for herself.

Then he caught the strap of her bathing suit in his teeth and need crested inside her without warning, hot and gushing.

"Am I going to get any more surprises if I peel this suit off you?" he asked.

Her voice shuddered. "Not a one."

It wasn't just anticipation building inside him now, he realized. Even as his blood rushed faster, it felt thicker. It pooled and gathered, built and demanded.

Princess stories aside, he didn't know who she was or where she had come from. He didn't know why she'd given her virginity to him. All he knew was that when she was around, he couldn't seem to think of pressures or guilt or responsibilities. When she was around, his mind had to jog to keep up, and she'd taught him how to breathe again.

He needed her, he realized. Maybe that was why he was so willing to do the incredible and sail off into the moonlight with her. Because he hadn't needed anything in a very long time.

He caught her mouth with his and fell into her again, into everything that was her. If there was a nagging uncertainty down deep at the core of him, then it left him when she threw herself into the kiss, all heat and eagerness and unabashed delight. Her hands flew over his skin, greedy. Before he could push down the straps of her suit, she was already peeling them away, clinging to him, her breasts pressed against his chest. She tore her mouth away from his and her head fell back, begging his tongue to trail over her throat.

When his mouth found her neck, she shivered again. It trembled through her, long and lingering. This was so right, she thought. Everything she had been chasing had been wrong, but this—the way he tasted and the way he touched—was perfect. *Everything in my life has been leading up to this moment.*

Honey shifted her weight and pushed up on her knees, intent upon tumbling him backward onto the ground. This time, she thought, it was her turn. Her time to do things she had only dreamed of before. She felt free, alive.

And then—no, *again*—someone called her name.

She jerked in Joe's hands as every good thing inside her fractured in disbelief. She scrambled off him and remembered to plaster the top of her bathing suit to her chest with both hands before she whipped around to look wildly in the direction of the beach. It was Marcus this time. She was still trembling as he approached, but now it was with pure fury.

His face was changing color as his gaze shifted from her to Joe then back to her again. He was pale with anger, then ruddy with embarrassment. "You're out of control," he said finally, almost wonderingly. "You've really reached the outer limits this time, Honey."

Things were pumping inside her. "Why?"

"For God's sake, I saw what you were just doing!"

She clapped a hand over her mouth exaggeratedly. "You saw?"

"It's broad frigging daylight!" he roared.

"I'm appalled. You witnessed something no other single and unattached human being has ever done in the history of the world."

Marcus's eyes narrowed. "Don't twist this."

"Is that what I'm doing?" She marched up to him and smacked her palm against his chest. "Were you a virgin before the I-do's yesterday, Marcus?"

"What the hell does that have to do with anything?"

"So we've got rules for you and a separate sheet of them for me? Why? *Why?*"

"You're a girl!"

"Well, here's a news flash, pal. I reached my majority two years ago. I own my own trust fund. And I don't need you or anyone else tailing me to hold me to lines of etiquette designed just for me!''

He opened his mouth and closed it again. ''I came looking for you to apologize.''

It almost melted her. Almost. But she knew him—and her family—too well. ''Why else?''

''Dad thought you were going to join him for lunch. You told him you would.''

''I changed my mind. Does your apology mean you're going to stop telling everyone to shut me out of whatever's going on at the house?''

''Damn it, Honey, I can't do that.''

She smiled. She felt it pull at the corners of her mouth. She didn't care anymore, she realized, because at midnight she would be on a sailboat gliding away from it all.

''I can't do this anymore,'' she said softly. And then she stepped around him and headed back for the shore.

Marcus didn't like her tone. Something in it unsettled him. Do what? Overreact and raise hairs? Kick ass in the face of Evans perfectionism? *What?*

Then he remembered the guy on the beach, mostly because the guy was trying to avoid him. Marcus felt his movement behind him. He turned to see the man stepping back toward the beach, and fresh anger scoured through him.

''She's not the way she comes off.'' He heard his own voice crack out like a bullet.

The man stopped and stared at him. ''Glad to know you've realized that.''

Marcus stared at him in disbelief. ''Me? You don't get it, do you? You're a plan for her, buddy. A means to an end. She doesn't do these things because they're what she wants. She does them because they get her what she thinks she needs.''

The guy's expression was suddenly odd, Marcus thought, but that wasn't his problem. He had to catch up with his sister. He didn't know what had gotten into her just lately, but she was starting to scare him.

He left the man and walked away.

Eleven

The closer she got to the house, the calmer Honey felt. Whatever rage she'd felt at Marcus, whatever passion she'd felt in Joe's arms, vaporized a little more with each breath she took. Both blistering emotions gave way to a steady, quiet litany in her head. *No more. No more. No more.*

She had created this mess of her life. And she could change it.

"*Senhora!* You are back!" Rafaela said when Honey stepped into the kitchen. "I fix something for you to eat. You miss breakfast, you miss lunch."

"No thanks." She cut for the bell room door just as her father came in from the big room.

"Where in tarnation have you been?" he demanded as soon as he saw her.

It was his drill sergeant's voice. Honey was reasonably sure he had never been a drill sergeant, but he could have been. She stopped and turned back slowly. "Out."

He stared at her. Her voice hadn't been flippant or impatient, she thought, just tired. And it brooked no argument. Maybe that was what quelled him. I should have thought of this recourse a long time ago, she realized, instead of killing myself with horses and PETA protestors.

Her father finally recovered. "Your mother and I think it would be best if you flew back with us in the morning," he said finally. "And if you came home to Conover Pointe for a while."

Honey frowned. What was this about? "I live at the townhouse and I have a job.'' That she wouldn't be going back to, she thought.

''I could arrange a leave of absence for you—''

''*No!* No more arranging, never again.'' From here on in she was doing things for herself and on her own terms.

His chest puffed up. ''Regardless, we're concerned about your behavior.''

''My behavior hasn't changed since I got arrested in that bar in Miami when I was seventeen.''

''That's what troubles your mother.''

Ah, Honey thought, one of *those* conversations. When he was most disturbed with her, she suddenly became her mother's daughter, as though she had landed on earth by some sort of miraculous conception. Sort of like Marcus.

Her father stole a look at Rafaela, who was pretending not to listen and struggle with their English. ''You want to talk about this elsewhere, don't you?'' Honey realized.

He let out a relieved breath. ''Yes.''

She moved for the big room. For one of the rare times since she had been on Brunhia, it was vacant. She went to the bar and stepped behind it, hunting around for the inevitable compact refrigerator. She came up with a can of orange soda.

''Want me to help you out here?'' she asked, popping the top and swigging. ''Marcus told you I was planning to take a lover on this trip, didn't he?'' She had finally figured that out. A lot of this stemmed from the bombshell she had laid on the voodoo-gene group that first day.

Her father's face went florid. ''Not in so many words but—''

''And you have therefore been running interference—or rather, enlisting my brothers to run interference—since the first moment you set foot on this island,'' Honey interrupted.

''You're my *daughter.*''

That touched her, made her feel a little soft inside. ''I shouldn't have opened my big mouth.''

''I've been telling you that for years.'' He almost smiled.

''Touché.''

"Your mother is concerned about your self-destructive behavior."

"It's not self-destructive. It's self-preservation." She stepped around the bar and kissed him on the cheek. "Relax, Daddy. I've never harmed a soul, not even myself. And I'm not ready to go home just yet." Well, she thought, that was certainly a mouthful. She left him and went back through the kitchen to the stairs.

She knew the hours until midnight would be interminable. She figured she'd put them to good use by having dinner with everyone—something she'd avoided all week. It would be a nice bon voyage, even if she was the only one who recognized it as such.

She figured she would leave her family a letter explaining what she was doing and why, and threatening dire consequences if they came looking for her. But she also wanted to write a special one to Carey. She hated to leave on the tension that had been between them this morning.

She reached the bell room and set about the chore of packing only one suitcase. She decided to divide everything she'd brought with her into halves; she was going to have to leave Marcus with one bag to deal with, and she would take the other with her. Unfortunately, the pile she wanted to take was far larger than what she wanted to leave behind.

"What's he going to do, throw me overboard if I show up with two?" No, she thought, but he'd probably throw one of her bags overboard. She found herself standing in the middle of the room grinning at that. Maybe that was why she loved him. He didn't fawn over her and he cut her no slack. He wasn't impressed with her shenanigans but neither did he seem to want a prima donna. He—

She heard her own thoughts.

"Ah, Jeez-Louise." Honey clapped her hands to her cheeks and sat down hard on the cot. "I don't love him. I *can't* love him. Sooner or later, I've got a life to get back to." Then again, did she? Suddenly she found herself wondering how long her trust fund would hold out so she didn't have to work.

"I don't love him," she whispered again. She couldn't love someone she could never take back to Washington and the world she'd created there. But she could love him forever if they just kept sailing.

"Totally unreasonable," she said aloud.

Why?

She launched herself off the bed again to tackle the contents of the suitcases. If Joe heaved one overboard, he would select it at random. Therefore, the smart thing to do was to put the almost-non-essentials into one and the I-can't-live-without-these-things into the other. If he grabbed for the latter, she'd just have to tackle him first. And it was entirely possible that he might just succumb to her persuasiveness and let her take two.

She put the Kogi sandals into the almost-non-essential bag. She just wanted them in case they made port in the Greek isles or something.

That brought her up short on the idea of money. Honey stopped in mid-motion and shoved a finger through her curls to scratch her head. He had none, and she had much. So she'd need her credit cards and her checkbook to pay off any expenses they ran up in their travels. She thought about how he had acted in Portimao about buying her lunch and stuffed her billfold and checkbook into the most-essential bag. She'd just have to be clever so he didn't realize she was paying for things until it was a fait accompli.

When she next looked around, the bell room was tidy as a pin and everything she had brought with her was stuffed into one bag or the other. She wondered if she could talk Joe into a quick romp on that sofa again before they actually set sail. She also wanted to explore the fore cabin. Then, still in her bathing suit and skirt, she headed downstairs.

Happy hour in the big room was in full swing. It took a woman a lot of time, Honey realized, to decide if the things she owned were essential or not.

There were some conspicuous absences tonight. Jake and

Tara had gone. And, not coincidentally, so had the fed types. Jimmy Robinson limped over to hug her.

"How's my favorite cause for concern?" he asked over her head during the brief moment she was in his arms.

"Still concerning." Honey grinned, then she saw Marcus over Jimmy's shoulder. He was frowning at her. Something else she had to fix, Honey thought, before she could leave in good conscience.

She disengaged herself from her brother's swim buddy and crossed to him. He looked wary. She framed his face and kissed him square on the mouth.

He jerked back, alarmed. "What was that, a kiss of death?"

"No, I'm saving that one in case you ever do such a thing again." She kept his face in her hands. "You were always the only one who didn't buy up all my Girl Scout cookies. Please don't change on me now."

"You never eavesdropped on private conversations before."

"To your knowledge," she corrected. "I caught that whole thing between you and Mary Beth Singer in your bedroom when you were seventeen."

It made him smile. "Big deal. I didn't score."

"You tried hard enough. Which just goes to prove what I said at the quarry earlier. People in glass houses—"

"Oh, shut up," he growled.

"You just hate being wrong, don't you?"

"It's my super-blood."

"Does it preclude apologizing?"

He looked miserable. "No. I'm sorry."

"Okay, then I'll give back a little as well." She leaned close to his ear. "Joe isn't just a fling."

"Joe who?"

"My drifter. He makes me happy, Marcus. He lets me be whole instead of fractured into a handful of different personalities for different people who demand different things from me."

"Whatever that means."

"Yes, I know, it's complicated. But don't worry. Please don't worry. Okay?"

"I can't give you that. I'm your big brother."

No, she thought, he wouldn't stop worrying about her. It was as much a part of his nature as slinging boulders apparently was.

People began moving toward the hall and to the dining room. Dinner was quiet, sedate. With Jimmy and her parents and Drew present, no one spoke of the Coalition. Jimmy repeated stories from his and Marcus's days with the navy SEALs. Honey felt the conversation flow around her.

She didn't join everyone back in the big room after they'd eaten. She slipped upstairs.

She spent the time until dark writing her notes and thinking of the logistics of running away. She cracked her checkbook again. It was healthy, but how long would it last supporting two people? She'd contact her accountant, she decided, at the first port they came to and have him move some of her trust fund into the account. Then she also wrote a letter of resignation to the White House and tucked that into her note for Carey, adding a P.S. that her friend please pass it on to the appropriate party.

At nine o'clock, it was full dark. Honey gathered up her two small bags and crept down the back stairs. Why wait until midnight? If she could somehow catch his attention and get him to bring the dinghy to shore, they could leave earlier. She wanted to be gone. She wanted to be free. Patience had never been her strong suit.

When she reached the kitchen door, she opened it barely a crack to peer through. Rafaela was still shoving dishes into the dishwasher. *Damn, damn, damn.* Then Ricardo stepped through the outside door and said something to her in rapid-fire Portuguese. The woman dried her hands quickly on a dish towel and scooted outside after him.

They'd need something to celebrate their escape tonight, Honey decided. She crept into the kitchen, to the fridge, and popped it open on a prayer. Bingo! Leftover wedding champagne. She snagged a bottle and tucked it under her arm, not willing to risk the time it would take to get it into one of the bags. Rafaela could come back at any moment.

She scooted up the stairs again to the second floor and went that way to the front of the house, down again to the strange, sideways hall. She couldn't take a motor bike, she thought as she stepped through the heavy double doors into the night. It would be rude since she couldn't return it this time. She'd already made Ricardo salvage one such abandoned vehicle. So she set out on foot.

Once she was clear of the house, she paused to stuff the champagne into one of her bags. Thirty-five minutes later, she reached the beach. Her arms ached a little from carrying the suitcases. She dropped both of them to the sand and took in a good, clean breath of sea air.

Free. She was free. Then she looked out at the water. The *Sea Change* was gone.

Gone? Honey frowned, cocked her head and left her bags to move closer to the shoreline. Gone, definitely gone. Then she smacked the palm of her hand to the side of her head. "Oh, damn it. You proud, stubborn ass!" He'd gone to Portimao early to stock up on supplies. He'd know that if she was with him, she'd try to pay for everything. Which she had every intention of doing. She was going to have to work harder at staying one step ahead of him with this money business, she realized. In the meantime, he'd beaten her at her own game *again.*

Grinning, she went back to her bags and dropped down to sit in the sand and wait. The villages were quiet. The men would be out fishing and the women were probably asleep. They worked so hard during the day. That hadn't escaped her. She wondered what it would be like to be so bone-tired by evening as to be grateful to slide into bed. She wondered what it felt like to know a job had been well done. Someday she would find out, she decided. After they'd sailed for a while.

She squinted out at the horizon. No sign of pilot lights yet.

She couldn't see her watch in the dark, but she figured that it was about ten o'clock. Honey sighed.

She wished Paloma were awake so she'd have someone to talk to. Then she started worrying that someone at the big house might discover her missing already. If they did, they'd come right down here looking for her again. She didn't want a confrontation. She wanted to leave everyone just as she had at dinner, with smiles on their faces.

Honey stood and gathered up her bags again, moving off for the tree line. She found a small copse with a tiny clearing inside and settled down there. If they came looking for her now, they wouldn't find her unless she sneezed or something and drew their attention.

Time crawled. Her mind wandered. She started to doze sitting up, then jerked herself awake. How long could it take to stock up on supplies in Portimao? Damn it, she needed to see her watch. Honey stripped her sandals off and left her hidey-hole to go back to the beach. There was still a fire alive on the sand in front of Deus Fornece, mostly embers by now, but still. Honey set off in that direction. When she reached the first one, she dropped to her knees and held her wrist out to the meager light.

Midnight? Honey surged to her feet again and whipped around to look out at the gulf. Joe still wasn't there.

What was going on?

Boat trouble, she thought. Maybe he'd gotten over there to the mainland and had been unable to get back. At the idea that she could be stuck here in her old life for another day or longer, her skin tightened over her muscles. She went back to her spot in the trees and sat down again to wait.

A while later she went back to the village. This time she thought to break a branch off one of the trees first. She used it to stir up the embers and focused on the time. Two o'clock.

"Boat trouble," she said again. "No one awake to fix it in Portimao in the middle of the night." Except how many times had she seen him repairing the islanders' motors? He had tools on board.

Something was wrong.

Honey moved slowly for the copse again. Suddenly she was exquisitely aware of a thousand sensations. It was as if her every nerve ending was alive and primed and anxious. She felt the cool sand squeeze up between her toes with each step. The night breeze tickled her nape where she'd tucked her hair to the side to lean over the fire. She licked her lips. They tasted salty from all the hours she had been sitting here at the beach.

Something was wrong.

She collected her bags from the copse again. When he finally arrived, she wanted to be somewhere where he could immediately see her. She was going to kick his ass. She headed for the shoreline again and sat there.

She thought about going to check the time again but she knew it was getting to the point where she wouldn't be able to get light out of those coals with an atom bomb. She dug into her bag for the champagne. Celebration. She realized that her heart was chugging slowly and thickly now. There wasn't going to be one.

Something was wrong.

She worked at the wire netting and popped the cork. When the champagne foamed up, she put the bottle to her mouth to catch it. Not quite as sweet as Paloma's nectar, but then, Paloma's nectar wouldn't pack the punch she needed right now.

He'd left without her.

Disbelief was a strange thing, she discovered, swigging from the bottle. It started out like a prickly feeling of alarm just under your skin. Then your skin went dead and numb. Like paralysis, the sensation spread. Into visceral parts, snaring, gripping in a cold fist.

Her heart was the last to go. When the spread of coldness got there, she groaned aloud. He'd left without her. He didn't want her either.

He'd been her last, best chance and Joe didn't want to let her in either.

Her eyes stung. She drank more champagne because Honey

Evans didn't cry. Why had he left without her? Honey hugged the bottle to her chest and closed her eyes. Because, she thought, wit and smiles weren't enough. They didn't count. She had them by the bushelful and people merely tolerated her. They watched over her. They arranged for her. But they never reached out to her for her grit. They reached out to the Careys of the world for that. Not to women who called themselves Honey.

She polished off the last of the champagne. She'd stood up for Carey once, against Matt, she remembered. She'd been a good friend. "I have grit," she whispered aloud. Then she lay down in the sand and dozed.

When she felt hands grip her shoulder, the sun was high and hot and searing her face. Honey's eyes flew open and she realized disgustedly that her tongue was more or less cleaved to the roof of her mouth. She was still cosseting the champagne bottle against her breasts. She forced her eyes to focus and saw Paloma leaning over her.

"*Senhora,* what is this?"

Honey sat up. She dropped the champagne bottle and dug her fingers into her hair to shake the sand out. "What time is it?"

"*Que hore e' ele?*" The woman motioned at her watch.

Yeah, stupid question, Honey thought, and glanced at it. It was nearly eleven-thirty in the morning.

She looked out to sea. Still no *Sea Change.* And no one from the big house had come looking for her, either. She let out a bark of hoarse laughter at that. "Well, I guess this tells me something."

"*No compreenda* what you say, my friend."

"It's okay. Don't worry about it." Self-pity stirred in her again, as it had last night. But this time it wasn't fueled by champagne. It started out meek and writhing, then it blasted through her. "I'll be damned. I've been dumped. By *everybody.*"

Paloma followed her gaze out to the empty cove. "*Senhor* Sailor is gone. This is why you are unhappy?"

Honey glanced over at her. ''Did you happen to notice when he left?''

''Sim, yes. Before the men go out last night.''

The fishermen always left just before dusk. He'd left that early? Honey scrolled back in her mind to yesterday afternoon...then her mind staggered. *Marcus.* What had Marcus said to Joe? Had he flung around more boulders, maybe a couple of huts and trees, warning what he would do to any man who touched his baby sister? Another laugh escaped her throat, this one thin and edging toward hysteria.

''*Senhora,* you are okay?'' Paloma asked.

''No.'' She swallowed hard on the giggle. ''No, I'm not okay at all.''

She needed to be furious at Marcus, Honey thought. If she could just find some really good blazing anger somewhere inside her, she would be okay now. But it wasn't there. Because if Joe had known her, had really known her, nothing Marcus might have said to him would have made a difference.

''I did love him,'' she said aloud. Her whole body jerked with the words, trying to avoid them, but she couldn't quite shake the truth.

''*Senhor* Sailor?'' Paloma asked. ''Yes, I saw that.''

Honey cut a look at her again out of the corner of her eye. ''You're a wise woman.''

''He love you, too.''

''Maybe not so wise after all. He dumped me.''

''We have not much to do here but work and love and read faces. I know.''

''He left without me. We were going to drop out together.''

''Drop out? This means what?''

''Trading in a less-than-satisfactory life for another.''

''It is that easy where you come from?''

''I thought it was.''

''Why you want to do that?''

This time Honey looked at her fully. ''So I could finally be worth something, even if it was just paying for his supplies.'' She stood up. ''I've got to go back to the house now.''

"What will you do? About *Senhor* Sailor?"

That stopped her just as she reached for her bags. Honey thought about it. "I don't need Joe...Joe..." She trailed off, suddenly stunned. She didn't even know his last name. How could she love someone when she didn't even know his last name?

Because he'd opened things up inside her, she thought. Because he'd let her be herself, without expecting anything back at all.

"Joe who?" Paloma asked.

"*Senhor* Sailor."

"His name is not Joe."

Honey frowned. "Of course, it is."

"His name is Max."

Max? Honey stared at the woman for a long time. Then the laughter that rocked through her this time came out strong and fierce. Oh, that was priceless. He'd even lied about who he was.

Then again, so had she. And somehow that only made the whole thing between them seem more right.

"Well, whoever the hell he is, I don't need him with me to start over." And maybe, she thought, maybe some year down the line, she would actually be able to forget about him. Honey hefted her bags again. "Thanks."

"For what?" The woman seemed startled.

"For listening to me."

She headed back to the big house.

Twelve

The first wave of the day's departures were spilling out the door—her mother, father, Drew, and Jimmy Robinson—when she approached the house. She hesitated on the road, dredging for the piss-and-vinegar that would allow her to explain why she was coming up from the beach at midday with two suitcases in tow. No witty repartee came to mind.

She felt hollowed out. She had the sense that this emptiness was merciful. She had a hunch that it was going to wear off eventually and then the aching would start. But at the moment she had a more immediate problem. Her family was loaded up in the wagon and Ricardo was snapping his reins over the team of mules to start them toward the road. Honey sighed and stepped back into the woods to hide out again.

"This is getting old," she murmured aloud.

As she waited, her mind limped back to Joe. She scrubbed her hands over her face. Why couldn't she just have gotten laid like a normal person without all this baggage?

The wagon passed by. Her mother's mouth was set into the kind of line that said there was a world of emotion swirling inside her, but she was damned if she was going to let one drop of it out, Honey thought. Her father looked a little pale. Drew was talking earnestly. His voice came to her but she couldn't make out his words over the clatter of the wagon wheels. Jimmy looked stoically straight ahead, trying politely to ignore the conversation.

They'd gotten her note, then, Honey realized. All in all, on top of everything else, it was going to be very embarrassing to turn up again when she was supposed to be on the high seas with a vagabond drifter. She wondered if there was some way she could get to Lisbon then home without having to go back into the house. Unfortunately, there was no way to tag Amando for a ride back to Portimao unless he came over here to pick up someone else. And even if she went back to the beach to hope for the best, that would involve coming face-to-face with that someone else.

Honey hefted her bags again and started on toward the house. She used the front door. Best just to get it over with, she decided. She dropped her bags in the front hall and veered left, toward the big room.

Carey, Matt and Marcus were there with Ethan and Kelly Williams. Carey cried out when she saw her and surged off the sofa to rush at her. Honey took a quick step back. "No hugging. Not a good idea right now."

Carey stopped abruptly, confused. "Why not?"

Because the slightest kindness will undo me.

"What the hell kind of flea-brained idea—" Marcus began.

Honey pivoted a little to look at him. "Stop right there." *This* she could deal with.

He scrubbed a hand over his jaw. "Damn it, how am I supposed to take all this? First I find you rolling around with some stranger in the quarry, then you're running away with him and none of us is supposed to look for you. What do you want me to do?"

"Trust me to know my own heart." He didn't seem to know how to respond to that, she realized. She looked around to include Matt and Carey. "You undervalue me. You all do. Part of that is my fault. I never tried to give you anything to respect."

"Drew's footsteps have always been hard to follow," Marcus said. His voice had changed, going more thoughtful. "Why bother?"

"Truth to tell, this genetic business of yours is going to be a little difficult to top, too."

He gave a ghost of a smile.

"So I *still* might not even try to achieve greatness. But I can tell you this. Whatever I do set about doing is going to be for my own satisfaction."

"It always is," Marcus said.

Her heart hurt. "No. It was for optimum impact, except maybe that underage drinking thing. I did that mostly out of loyalty to my friends. I didn't want them to get busted alone. I figured it would go down a lot better with the parents if we were all in it together."

He looked lost at her reasoning. Honey decided not to try to elaborate. She glanced at Carey. "When are you guys leaving?"

"Amando is coming back for us after he drops your family and Jimmy off," she said.

"I'm going with you." Her own flight out wasn't until tomorrow. She'd just hole up in Lisbon until then, Honey decided.

She turned for the door. Carey made another move toward her and Matt held out a hand to stop her. Marcus started to stay something else, then blessedly remained quiet.

Honey gathered her bags up again and went to the bell room to resort their contents. What she would need for a day in Lisbon was radically different from what she would have needed to lounge on the deck of a sailboat. Her heart rolled over. She'd kill right now for a little rat-tat-tat, Honey thought.

She was just finishing up when there was a knock on the door. Uh-oh, she thought. Someone with the temerity to come up the stairs and invade her space rather than just call up from the second floor. That would mean Carey. They grew them tough in Kansas.

She went to open it, bracing herself. Then her jaw dropped. It was Carey, all right. With Matt, Marcus, Samantha, Gretchen and Kurt. Honey stepped back from the door. "Come in, one and all. Though you'll probably find the accommodations lacking."

Marcus looked around and Honey followed his gaze. The

place was barren now that she had packed up all her personal possessions, but the view was still spectacular.

Gretchen cleared her throat and looked around herself before she finally sat on the floor. "Marcus tells us that you know Samuel Hatch," she said finally.

Honey let her brows climb. "Don't you guys have anything better to do than talk about me? It seems that with these Coalition dudes breathing down your neck, you'd have plenty to occupy your minds without worrying about my friends and acquaintances."

Marcus winced. Kurt coughed. The response was a little too forceful, Honey thought. He was disguising a laugh again. She really could have liked these people.

Marcus recovered first. "The point is, Hatch talks to you."

Honey narrowed her eyes at him. "Like clockwork. Every Tuesday and Thursday morning at about eleven for maybe six months now. He hates retirement."

"Does he know you by name?"

"He knows me as Number Twelve."

"What does that mean?" Gretchen asked.

"The White House phone staff is assigned numbers," Matt explained. "It's easier to track incoming calls that way." He looked at Honey. "So he doesn't know who you are?"

"Hard to say. He certainly has the connections to find out, but I don't think so."

"Do you take his calls at random?" Marcus asked.

"He always requests me from whoever catches him first." Something strange was happening inside her. The rhythm of her heart was changing and it was learning to ache in earnest. "What's this about?"

"Carey thinks you might be just the one to approach him," Marcus said. "And don't ask about what. You listened in on that whole conversation, so you know."

"Of course I did." Flippancy was definitely the way to go now, she thought, because she was afraid if she looked at her friend a world of gratitude would be in her eyes. No more tears, no more Brunhia water, she thought, and *definitely* no mush. In a far-flung definition, mush landed right in there with love. "You want to know what he knows about this Coalition and what he's willing to share with Matt?" she asked.

"No, you can't ask him that," Kurt said, but his tone wasn't dismissive. "He'll hold his cards close to his vest. He wants Matt."

"Then what's my mission? If I choose to accept it?"

"Feel him out, Honey," Carey said.

"*Not* with your hands," Marcus said quickly.

"Oh, cut me a break," Honey shot at him. "He's old."

"That should keep him safe enough from you," Carey said dryly. But she was smiling. "Can you do this? Try to find out if he's with the Coalition or not. Get a sense for it."

Honey made a gesture as though to dismiss the absurd. "Of course."

"I don't want to go into a meeting with him and get my head blown off or end up brainwashed," Matt said.

She remembered what Jake had said. That was all part of it—stealing years, memories, minds. "Am I supposed to just come at this out of the blue Thursday morning when he calls in? You know, like, 'Hi, Sam, by the way, got any vials of forget-everything juice stuck up your sleeve?"

Marcus made a sound in his throat. "This isn't going to work," he said.

Then Carey did something astounding. She turned around because he was standing behind her and she shoved him hard on the shoulder. Sort of like David taking on Goliath, Honey thought bemusedly. Marcus's mouth dropped. Matt made a sound in his throat that was halfway between surprise and laughter.

"Hey," Marcus said belatedly when he could close his mouth and form words again.

"Hey, yourself," Carey said. "She's your *sister.*"

"Which is why I have my doubts. I've known her longer than you have."

"You don't know her *now.*"

That plunged the room into silence. You go, girl, Honey

thought, though she really wasn't sure herself what Carey was getting at.

"She'll do what she does to you and to everyone else she doesn't want getting too close to things inside her," Carey said. "She'll talk circles around Hatch. She'll have him laughing and confused and taking two steps to every one of hers just trying to keep up with her mind. And he'll say something if she prods him right. And then we'll know if it's safe for Matt to meet with him."

Matt didn't give Marcus time to respond. "Honey, what are the odds you can get him to meet you somewhere? He won't discuss this on the phone."

She glanced his way. "Good to excellent."

"If he doesn't know who you actually are, that you're in any way involved with us, I'm thinking you'll be safe," Matt continued. "All the same, I want to arrange to have some people in place to keep an eye on things. That would be easiest at a public establishment."

Honey thought about it. "I can tell him that I recently met you." She pointed to Matt. "You're about to marry my very good friend, so I'm butting my nose in to find out if you're worthy of her. I'll say that I'm asking him because he knows everyone in Washington. That'll get him talking about you, then I can lead him to where I want him to go."

"Hatch has been chatting with her for months," Carey said emphatically. "He'd know that's precisely something that Honey would do."

"I've come up against bulldozers with less horsepower than her nose," Marcus said.

Honey batted her eyes at him. "Ah, big brother, are you making up with me?"

He chewed on his lips. "Maybe."

"Work harder at it. You still have a ways to go."

Gretchen was standing again. "Well, that's that, then."

"Honey, set up the meeting when he calls in on Thursday," Matt said, "and let us know the details so I can arrange some protection."

They began moving toward the door. "Hold it right there," Honey said suddenly, catching Carey's arm as she was about to depart as well.

Carey looked a little wary as the others headed down the stairs. "I wasn't going to ask what happened last night."

"I know you weren't. You'll just do that thing where you quietly wait for me to spill everything, knowing my tongue will eventually get the better of me." Honey found a smile. Now that everyone was gone, smiles were a little harder to come by. The ache was spreading. "Anyway, I don't want to talk about that yet. Someday maybe. Someday when it doesn't hurt as much. I owe you something."

Carey frowned. "Honey, you always owe me something. You never have cash on you and you're always borrowing five here, ten there. But your credit is really spectacular."

This wasn't going to be any easier, Honey thought, for the fact that it was the last thing Carey would expect of her. "I lied."

Carey frowned. "About what?"

"Okay, it wasn't a lie. It was kind of…of…an omission of truth."

"What are you talking about?"

Honey stepped away from her and grabbed her hair up to knot it at her nape.

"You do that when you're nervous," Carey said.

"Okay, so I'm nervous." On one hand, she really did want to ditch the un-Honey-like words and the tears and the aching and the love that this crazy Brunhia water brought on. She was starting to hurt so badly right now that every instinct in her body said to go back to familiar ground. Tweak a few nerves and pluck a few feathers. Open her mouth and let the outrageous spill out.

But she didn't have much of that in her at the moment. Her ears were still ringing from Carey's speech to Marcus, and something in the area of her heart was thrumming and picking up energy. All that energy, when it finally hit, was going to be bad. And what she'd realized on the beach still stood. With or without Joe—or Max, or whoever the hell he was—she just wanted to start over.

"I saw a sex therapist and used your name."

"I beg your pardon?"

She couldn't say it twice. "You heard me."

"Yes, but why? *You?*"

"I'd rather not go into it at the moment."

"You needed a sex therapist?"

Honey yanked her hair down from the knot again. "Oh, man..."

"That's the most ridiculous thing I ever heard," Carey said.

"Yeah, well, it gets more ridiculous when you figure the receptionist picked up on it and bleated to that reporter and next thing you know all of Washington and probably half the country thinks *you're* the one running around doing the bam-bam-bam-rat-tat-tats."

"The bam-tats *what?*"

"Can we end this conversation now?"

"I...sure."

"I just wanted to come clean. It's been bothering me."

"Apology accepted."

Honey closed her eyes briefly. If only everything were that easy. "I need to pack."

"You're already packed."

"Then you need to pack."

"Okay." Carey moved toward the door, then she paused again. "Honey, just make sure Hatch isn't a... What is that expression you always use?"

"Wack-job?"

"Right. A wack-job. Make sure before Matt meets with him. I'm putting my love in your hands."

"I'll take care of it."

Carey left and Honey moved for the cot. She sat down as her limbs folded without warning. "And thanks for the other thing, too. For telling Marcus," she said quietly when there was no one to hear.

Then it fell in on her, an avalanche of loss and change and missing something she'd only just learned how to savor. Honey flopped back on the bed, grabbed the pillow to her chest and let herself cry.

She'd almost gotten him. Almost. He'd almost believed her.

Max told himself that was why he was getting drunk. He was pissed off at himself. "Chump," he said into his whiskey. The Cretan bar was very small, utterly dark, and it smelled like cooking fat. One of the lights over the bar was on its last legs. It flickered fitfully, like a moth trying to find a place to lie down and die.

Which, Max thought, was pretty much how he felt. Like putting everything down and giving it up. He'd lost the island where he'd found peace, a woman he'd never quite been able to figure out in the first place, and the man she'd made him want to be. He'd lost any good excuse to get his hands dirty with honest work. He was a step closer to civilization, though no one would think to look for him in a dive like this on Crete. And for what? For a roll on his cabin sofa with a woman who had had a plan to use him all along.

For the thirtieth, maybe fortieth time since he'd started drinking, Max found that his mind just couldn't go there. Every time he tried to touch on the moment when she'd given herself to him—given herself for the first time—his thoughts fractured. They came back away from the memory so hard and fast, they fell apart.

"Because she never said why she did that," he muttered aloud. "Another big question mark. Surprise." She'd skirted his questions like a ballet dancer toying with her partner, a pirouette here, a leap there. She'd never actually told him anything except stories about princesses. And he'd gulped those down like nectar from the gods.

"Idiot." She'd been setting him up all along. That was why she hadn't told him why she'd decided to unload her virginity on him. What was it that guy—probably one of the brothers—had told him? *You're a plan for her, buddy.... A means to an end. She doesn't do these things because they're what she wants. She does them because they get her what she thinks she needs.*

He'd say she was another Camille, Max thought, but that would have been a disservice to her. Camille was never that good.

"Max Strong?"

The voice came from behind him and he reacted out of habit. He swiveled on the creaky bar stool. Immediately a thousand flashbulbs went off in his face, turning the dark, drab bar into the Fourth of July. "Son of a bitch!" Max grabbed for the nearest camera, almost had it, but the guy was quick. He jogged out of range. Max came off the bar stool but they were all scattering.

Too many of them to track down and pay off, Max realized. It had been a gangbang—a fast shot, in and out, taking what they wanted and gone. They'd scatter afterwards to make sure at least one of them got away with a photo.

He was going to be on the cover of the next issue of every rag in the world. Whether he was ready or not, it was time to go home.

The plane lowered itself from the sky over Dulles and met the runway with more of a thump than Honey appreciated. Maybe it was just her mood. Rough landings usually energized her.

They taxied in and rolled to a stop at the gate. She got up to gather her small bag from the overhead bin, but she'd had the window seat and the fat guy next to her and the dozing girl in the aisle seat didn't move. She was trapped. Why had she felt compelled to downgrade from first class? To prove a point to a man she'd never see again?

"Excuse me," she said succinctly. Neither passenger even looked her way.

Okay, screw this, Honey thought. She had plans to see to, a life to turn over. With or without Joe-Max-the-Rat-Bastard.

The ache was gone. It had ebbed sometime during her day

in Lisbon. Now what she felt was blazing, impotent fury—and it was looking for a way out. "Excuse me." Honey tried again.

The fat man looked up at her. "Put it back down, doll. Ain't no way to get up that aisle before most everybody's gone."

Honey lofted her brows. "You don't think so?"

"Know so. I travel a lot."

"Well, goody for you." Honey squeezed back against the window and ducked her shoulders and head until she could find room to stand up on her seat. Then she stepped over both of them using the armrests.

"Hey!" the girl yelled.

"Nice legs, at least," the fat guy said.

"Thank you so much," Honey tossed back, then she landed in the aisle.

Well, he'd had one point, she thought. The people in the aisle definitely weren't going anywhere. The guy behind her knocked her in the head when he went to the overhead bin for his carry-ons. She managed to poke someone in the ribs with her elbow when she finally got her own bag down. Then she stood in line clutching it, feeling like a refugee waiting to be marched off to camp. This was a *good* thing?

"It'll get better," she whispered aloud. "This is just practice. I'm just getting my feet wet with this changing-my-life business." She was embarking on a brand-new Honey, one who was going to get to do something important by sounding out Samuel Hatch. One who was going to ditch that silly job and do something invigorating. One who was damned well going to get laid in her own backyard if it killed her. Because she was going to move out of the townhouse, too. And she was going to make very sure that her new backyard did not include any rose gardens.

She was going to do all of that if she ever got off this plane.

The line finally started to move. She trundled off and when she got inside the terminal she breathed in the stale air there as if it was the purest mountain breeze. She collected the rest of her luggage at the baggage claim and tipped a porter generously to take it to the garage and to her car. There was only so much in her life she was willing to change and schlepping her own luggage tonight didn't fall into those parameters.

When she finally sank down behind the wheel of her Mercedes, she closed her eyes and gave a little shudder. "God, that was awful." She turned the key in the ignition, gunned the engine a little and left the garage to tear into Georgetown.

She thought about stopping by Murphy's, but maybe that guy would be there, the one she'd fainted on. Besides, she was too tired and bar-hopping a bit on the way back to the townhouse was too much like the old Honey. So she went home instead.

Naeve was gone for the night, sticking astringently to Honey's new hours, the ones she'd set before she'd jetted off to Portugal to ruin her life. "Hey, I had sex, didn't I?" It was only her own fault that she'd taken it further than that, that she'd bought into everything that jerk had pretended to be, that she'd let down her guard and had ended up getting speared right through the heart for it.

She left her bags in the foyer, too weary to carry them upstairs. Naeve would take care of them in the morning. She was on the second tread of the stairs when she stopped and looked back at them. That, she thought, was the action of a shallow, hell-bent-on-trouble rich girl. Hurting in places she hadn't known she had, Honey went back for the suitcases.

She took a long, hot shower and washed the cabin class off her skin. Then she found her favorite Elvis T-shirt, crawled into it and collapsed into bed. She hoped she didn't dream. She didn't want to dream about him. Joe or Max. Whoever he was. Bastard. She had no time for dreams. She was a jilted woman starting over.

Even with all the whiskey in him, Max wasn't able to sleep. He tossed and turned in the *Sea Change*'s V-berth for an hour before jerking suddenly to his feet. He whaled his head against the teak molding and swore, putting a hand to the spot. He expected to see blood when he brought it away. He did and that just incensed him further. So he kicked the door frame as he passed it and hurt his toe, too.

Who the hell did she think she was? Better question, he thought—who did she think *he* was? "A broke, down-on-his-luck drifter who wasn't worth anything more than to be toyed with."

But that didn't make sense. If he'd been a plan, what kind of plan would a woman like her have for a guy like he'd been pretending to be?

You *were* that man, an inner voice said to him. You wanted to be that man. She rejected *you,* the real you.

Plans only made sense if she'd known who he really was, Max decided, so she must have known all along. She'd duped him on that score, too. Now he was *really* pissed off, enough to stumble into the main cabin and rummage through everything he'd thrown on the table until he found the cell phone he'd bought yesterday in honor of his reluctant return to the world. Except how did you call a woman and give her hell when all you knew for sure was that her middle name was Elise and she lived somewhere in Washington?

"Kurt," he said aloud. "Kurt Wagner."

This necessitated a trip back down to the fore cabin to paw through a drawer under one of the bunks where he'd been shoving personal papers for the last few months. There it was. Wagner's cell number. Was she still on the island? She'd never actually said when she was going back to the States.

"She never actually *said* anything," he reminded himself.

Neither did you. The thought snaked through his head and made him drop Kurt Wagner's business card, the one he'd taken from him in Cairo. Max bent and retrieved it, then he returned to the main cabin and turned on a light. He sat on the sofa where they'd made love, then vaulted off it again when he realized what he was doing. She was making him hate his own sofa now. She should pay for that alone.

He placed the call. The line buzzed a few times and he

started trying to work out in his head what kind of time difference he was dealing with. Then he realized it didn't matter. It would still be the middle of the night on Brunhia. He probably wouldn't get an answer. Except something major was going on with Kurt and the big house lately. Maybe the guy slept with his cell nearby and on.

He did. Kurt answered, his voice sleep-rough and unhappy. "Who is this?" he demanded without a hello.

"Max Strong."

"Max..." The man needed a moment to assimilate. Then he obviously decided to be cautious, excellent P.I. that he was. "Why are you calling me in the middle of the night?"

"Sorry. I have a question about one of the people who's been at your island house."

"Where are you?"

"Crete."

"You're calling me in the middle of the night from Crete to find out about my houseguests? Ah."

"Ah? What does *ah* mean?"

"It means I make my living deducing the story behind the story. Is she a little blond hellion who can jitterbug around you with words until you realize you've told her damned near everything and she's told you nothing?"

Max almost smiled. "That's the one."

"Smart woman. Very clever."

"Who is she?"

"You don't know? You woke me up in the middle of the night because of her and you don't even know who she is?"

"She jitterbugged around me with words and I never realized until it was too late that she told me nothing."

Kurt laughed, a rich, appreciative sound. "Maybe she doesn't want you to find her."

"Oh, I'd put money on that."

"Well, you've got it to spend. So if you don't get the dirt from me, you'll probably hire guys on twelve continents until you get the answers."

He was assuaging his conscience, Max thought. He waited.

"Honey Evans," Kurt said finally. "The shipbuilding Evanses. Breeder of Just Another Heartache. You follow thoroughbred racing?"

Max almost choked. A few horses in her backyard? "Where can I find her? Is she still there on Brunhia?"

"Nope. Left two days ago. She's probably back in the States by now."

"In Washington," Max clarified. "Where in Washington?"

"I don't know. Her family's got the estate down on the eastern shore of Maryland but I'm not sure where she stays in the city. She works at the White House."

"The *what?*"

"Nothing over the top. She's with the phone staff or something. But my guess is you could probably find her there. Assuming you wanted to go back to the States."

Why would a woman like that seduce a penniless drifter? Damn it, he couldn't get a handle on this. On her. But he was going to. Oh, yeah, he was going to. He thought of those flashbulbs going off in his face and told himself his gig was up anyway. In the meantime, he wanted answers. This time she wasn't going to volley his questions around like Ping-Pong balls. This time he was going to get a word in edgewise. Then he'd be able to forget her. Max disconnected, glad to have a plan.

Honey took up her place in her own kiosk in the phone office of the Great White Hallowed Halls just before nine o'clock. She felt drugged.

This was asinine, she thought. Why had she come back to work the morning after a trans-Atlantic flight? Because the old Honey would loll in bed, she thought. And because she had to tender her resignation. And because it was Thursday. Samuel Hatch always called on Thursdays.

She settled in to work, groggy, moving by rote. Even a quick run down the hall to tag someone in the guy's gym for an important call didn't revive her. "Jet lag," she told herself, trudging back to her post. It had nothing to do with being dumped. And what if it did? she thought, sitting again and replacing her headset. What if she was just emotionally worn out? What if the Brunhia water effect had just knocked her entirely off her stride? All that blurting and loving and crying, then a night of fitful sleep and getting up at dawn to write her resignation. An incoming line rang. She snagged it and went through her welcoming routine to the White House, inspecting a chip in her fingernail as she spoke. She wondered if starting over involved giving up manicures, too.

"You abandoned me, Number Twelve. Where have you been?"

Samuel Hatch. Honey came instantly alert. And she fell right back into her game. This time it had a purpose. "Missing you, cowboy."

"You run off and get married or something?"

A shaft of something hard and hot hit her chest with enough force to take her breath. Which was purely ridiculous. She had *never* wanted to get married. She'd just wanted to escape on a sailboat. "Nope. I'm saving myself for you."

He chuckled, pleased with the response.

"Who do you want to speak to today?" she asked. "How should I direct your call?"

"Later. Talk to me first."

"Actually..." She drew it out and paused. "There's something I wanted to ask you. *Someone* I wanted to ask you about. With all your connections, you must know everyone in Washington. You must have met a million people in your line of work before you retired."

"Maybe half that. Which one do you want to know about?"

Honey sighed into the line for effect and sat back in her chair, encouraged. "I can't go into it here. Too many ears. When I tell you who it is, you'll understand."

"I'll buy you dinner, then."

"Hmm. I'd probably settle for a cocktail." This would

work easiest, she thought, if she could get him at least mildly inebriated. Did ex-CIA guys let themselves get inebriated?

"I thought you had higher standards than that." But he sounded delighted, she thought, to finally meet her.

"Not for old friends. I'll meet you for drinks. We'll talk about the weather and...this man I want to know about."

"Another man? You break my heart." He chuckled.

"It's not for me. It's for a friend."

"We'll talk. Where do you want to meet?"

She'd given this some thought. "How about the lobby bar at the Marriott Wardman Park?"

"Old man like me, I haven't had an offer like this in a long time. Tonight?"

"Tomorrow." If she knew one thing about men, it was that the longer they looked forward to something, the more agreeable they were when they finally got it. "Six o'clock. See you then. I'll be the lady in red." She was going to get some use out of the dress she'd bought for her brother's wedding if it killed her.

Honey disconnected quickly. Then she smiled slowly at the air. She'd done it. Carey had talked Marcus into trusting her, and she had done the first part of it.

Her new life was off to a rollicking start.

Thirteen

In spite of the photographers in Crete—or maybe because of them—Max kept his three-day old beard for the flight back to the States. He didn't cut his hair and he traveled coach. No one had bombarded him since the bar but it was just a matter of time now.

He knew all the signs. That photo had appeared somewhere, he thought. Now his second-in-command had called from Madrid this morning for a question he would have handled on his own a week ago. Register a cell phone anywhere in the world and sooner or later it will start to ring nonstop. As proof of that, Camille had called fifteen minutes after that to plead for a second chance.

He'd say one thing for Honey Evans. She never whined and she didn't plead. She had seduction down to a crazily defined art.

He wanted to confront her before his associates and his family, his ex-wife and the paparazzi really opened fire on him. She'd given Pittsburgh back to him with her zany wit and her utter acceptance of Joe, and then she'd yanked it all away again because she'd been just another woman with a goal line in mind after all. He had to know—*had* to know—what that had been between them back in Portugal. What game had she been playing? Had she known who he was all along and angled in for the kill by pretending otherwise? Or was she a lunatic rich girl who had just wanted a disposable boy-toy? Had she even gone to the beach that night to meet him? Or had she whispered sweet promises that she'd never meant to keep? He had to know. If she didn't know who she'd thrown away, his ego was still healthy enough to make sure she figured it out.

He told himself that the mystery of it was the only reason he couldn't get her off his mind. Then the tone of the jet's engines changed and they were coming in for landing. Amen, Max thought. After several hours over the Atlantic, his legs were cramping because they had nowhere to go. The baby in the lap of the woman next to him managed to throw up on his pants. He owned a *Lear*, for God's sake. And he was flying coach. But if he had called for his plane, it wouldn't have gotten off the runway before a crowd gathered around it.

The woman shoved the baby at him to rush off and find either a bathroom or a stewardess, something with which to clean up. Max held the little guy with two hands tucked under his armpits and held him up to eye-level. He had enough nieces and nephews to know the kid was at least nine months old because his head didn't react like a bobble-toy.

"Now that you got that up, you feel fine, don't you?" Max murmured.

The kid gurgled. And it hit Max again, the lancing bitterness of everything he had missed by picking the wrong woman. Now he had done it twice.

"I didn't *pick* Elise, damn it. She picked me."

"Are you swearing at my baby?" the mother asked sharply from the aisle.

Max cut his glance her way. "He puked on me. It's the basis of male bonding."

"He's a she. And it's just a little spit-up." The woman reached and took the baby back as if Max might be some kind of molester.

Before she could sit again and block him in, Max got up to squeeze into the aisle and go see about cleaning up. He took a step before the seatbelt light came on and a voice came over the intercom telling him to sit again. It had been that kind of several days.

* * *

At exactly 4:25, Honey plucked the headset from her ears and started winding up the cord to store it away for the night. "Hail, fellow, a job well done," she said under her breath, then she yawned.

She'd probably directed three hundred calls today. *There* was a real contribution to society. Then again, she *had* hooked up with Hatch.

A woman with long, dark hair and sloe eyes peered over the rim of her cubicle. "We're going to Nathan's for happy hour." It went without saying that Honey was invited.

"I can't go tonight. I'm beat." Honey reached for her purse.

The woman stood on tiptoe to peer over her shoulder as though expecting to see the *real* Honey Evans lurking somewhere behind this imposter. "You never get beat."

"I do when I fly in from Europe late one night and land at my desk the next morning."

The co-worker left, disgruntled, and Honey plucked a thin envelope from her purse. She took the long way to the employee parking lot, swinging by her supervisor's desk first. She slid the envelope onto the dark, rich wood.

"What's this?" the woman asked.

"My resignation. I'm burned out."

"From answering telephones?"

Honey knew Mary Cage had been at it in this same department for thirty-five years now. It would be useless to try to explain to her that her aspirations had suddenly become greater.

"There are people who would kill for your position," Mary chided.

"Not many with political science degrees, I bet." Where had that come from? She'd gotten that degree under duress from her family.

"So what, all of a sudden you're overqualified?" Mary snapped.

The conversation was draining things out of her, Honey thought, just at a point in her life when she needed to be strong. Suddenly, she felt so sad. What was it they called it in those Victorian-era movies? "Malaise," she whispered aloud.

"Come again?"

"I think I have malaise."

"Take something for it."

"I am. That's what the resignation is all about." She turned away from Mary's desk.

She left the White House and found her Mercedes in the secure lot. She chatted for a few moments with the guy at the gate then she slid behind the wheel of the car. This was the big one. This next step was huge. Her car was the image she had created for herself. Did she really want to bury Honey?

Yes, she thought, yes, she did. Even more than the car, she wanted to do what she was going to do tomorrow night with Samuel Hatch. She wanted to do what she would have done on the sailboat if that bastard Joe—Max—hadn't jilted her. She wanted to...to...*contribute.*

"All right, then," she said, and gunned the engine. She headed for the first SUV dealership she could find.

He almost missed her. If he had taken the time to rent a car at the airport, Max would have.

If he had been willing to take that final leap and surface back into his own skin, he could have called President Stewart himself to find out where the employees parked at this high-class establishment. As it was, he'd had to find a cab driver who frequented the area. He coughed up a hundred bucks of persuasion money to find out where employees generally exited from the building. From there, the parking lot was just a matter of following his nose. He had the cab drop him two blocks from the heartbeat of the nation and walked closer, following the general directions the guy had given him.

He came to a bank of shrubbery that in all likelihood concealed barbed wire. He followed it along the street to a drive cloistered by cherry trees and barred by a heavy iron gate. As a car approached, the gates gave a quick squeal, a quiet moan, then slid open relatively soundlessly. A car came through. A heavyset guy with thick glasses in a dark suit was behind the wheel. He looked like a White House employee. Max was in the right spot.

He peered through the closing gates and he saw her. She was maybe a hundred yards away, but he'd know her anywhere, and he had a moment to wonder what *that* meant. She didn't particularly dress down for her job, he thought. She wore a very short blue skirt with pale-blue poppies exploding over it. Her top was concealed by a blazer in a color that matched the flowers. She wore dagger-heeled pumps in the same tone.

He watched her go to a Mercedes SL500 convertible in the brightest red he had ever seen, and he'd seen a few. The paint job was custom. "Ha." She'd known who he was, all right. Women who had custom-painted Mercedes knew.

Which should have answered his question, should have let him finally walk away. Instead, he found himself wheeling around on the sidewalk, frantically looking for another cab so he could follow her and see what she did next. He found one just as the little red car burst through the gates and shot past him. Her gaze was grim and aimed straight ahead. She never noticed him.

"Follow her," he said to the driver, climbing into the back seat.

"Yo, mister, what are you up to?"

Max resignedly peeled another hundred from his wallet and gave it to him. The guy shot into traffic like a bullet.

She led them a merry chase. South first, then west, then south again. What the hell was she doing? She drove like a woman with a mission. Not at reckless speed, but determinedly and a notch above the speed limit. She finally tucked the Mercedes into a car dealership on the far-west side of the city.

He'd followed her for several miles. Max knew that she wasn't having car trouble and the salesmen knew it, too. They fell through the doors of the showroom when she pulled in, tumbling over one another, maybe seeing dollar signs, maybe just seeing those legs when she got out of the car. Probably a little bit of both, Max decided.

"Stop here," Max said to the cab driver.

"You getting out? That's fifteen-sixty."

"Hold on. I just want to watch this a moment. If any of them piss her off, she'll just leave again."

"Man, you *are* scaring me. I could like call one of those 800 numbers we got these days."

And he would have every right to, Max thought. He'd picked him up lurking around the White House, and now he was following an employee. This time he pulled both a hundred-dollar bill and his driver's license from his billfold. He handed both to the guy. "There's my ID. You can relax. You don't have to call anybody."

"Maxwell Strong? Hey, wasn't you on the cover of *People* once?"

And so it began again, Max thought. "Several times."

"I'm thinking about when you married that babe."

Max stared at him. "That was seven years ago. That's the picture you remember?"

"Hey, she was hot."

Not where it counted, Max thought. Although she might have been with Francois-the-Frenchman.

Honey Evans was moving again. He forgot about Camille.

She'd gone into the showroom with one of the men and now she came back out dangling a set of keys in her hand. She left the Mercedes where it sat and waited for another man to rush to do her bidding, delivering a dark-blue Jeep Grand Cherokee to a spot in front of her toes. She wiggled her fingers at them in goodbye, got behind the wheel and drove off.

She'd just bought a car. Well, a truck. No, an SUV. In fifteen minutes.

Max stared after the Jeep when it hit the road. "Go, follow her again."

"She the next Mrs. Strong?" the driver asked.

"I don't know what the hell she is," Max muttered, "but I'm damned well going to find out."

She zigzagged a trail across the city again. Once she stopped at a liquor store. Max couldn't see what she had bought, because it was in a bag. Then she was off again. East. North, to Woodley Park in the area of the zoo.

She parked curbside, got out carrying the bag and wandered into the park, eschewing the paths and the Stay Off the Grass signs. She was loaded with money, Max thought, and she felt it gave her certain rights, put her above rules made for the rest of society. Then, as he watched, she made an abrupt U-turn and went back to the Jeep.

Now what? She dug in her purse, obviously found change and shoved it into the parking meter.

Okay, so she didn't like the hassle of parking tickets, he thought. But it didn't feel right because he knew that she was a woman who wouldn't cheat the city out of a dime.

Then he figured out why she wanted to walk on the grass. She kicked off the spiked blue pumps and sat down on a bench to circumspectly peel off her stockings. She stuck the stockings in her purse. When a wino wandered by and made a move for her brown bag, she swatted at him and showed her teeth. He backed off fast. She stood again and proceeded onward, clearly digging her bare toes into the spongy lawn and grinning as she did.

She came to a tree and peeled off the blazer. It was probably worth a minimum of six hundred dollars, he thought, but she dropped it to the ground and spread it out so she could sit on it. She crossed her legs Indian-style, taking a decorous moment to tuck her skirt down between her thighs so she didn't flash the wino. Then she plucked a bottle of wine out of the bag; he couldn't see the brand but he guessed it would be good. This was followed by a corkscrew from her purse. She opened the wine, swigged from the bottle, then fell back to lie flat and stare at the sky.

That was when he finally figured out who she was.

She was everything she seemed to be. Genuine and generous, rich enough not to care, taking a potshot or two at the walls of her ivory tower. Something cramped inside him.

"I've seen enough," he told the driver. He was ready to go, to walk away now. And then the preposterous happened.

Honey was shaking inside. Jeez-Louise, she'd done it. She'd ditched the Mercedes. The monster she'd bought was definitely not a sports car, but she would get used to it. And it would serve her well. Now she could run away. Maybe not on a sailboat, maybe not to a million exotic ports. She'd never really clamored for that anyway. What she wanted—*all* she really wanted—was to be free.

She'd been to Milan and Monte Carlo and Hong Kong. But what she had a hankering for was to see Oklahoma cattle spreads. She wanted to see where the people who called the White House about land gripes actually lived. She wanted to see the Golden Gate Bridge. Mount Rushmore. Niagara Falls. She wanted to throw flowers into the Mississippi River and stroll along Rodeo Drive. Okay, she'd already done that, but this time she was going to just drop out and drive there. She was going to go on and on and on, as far as the SUV would take her. When she left notes for her family again, she was just going to say, "Please refer to the first in Brunhia. Same premise. Leave me alone."

But this time she would be doing it on her own. Nobody could let her down, and no one could steal the plans from her.

It filled her head with a giddy feeling of freedom. She felt as good as she'd felt since the first time Joe—Max—had filled her and brought her back to herself.

She laughed aloud, feeling better than she had since walking down to the beach that night to meet Joe. She sat up to drink more wine. She figured that her sex-in-Georgetown jinx would be shattered to a million pieces once she left. She'd take a lover in Miami and a new one in Baton Rouge. Maybe a farmer-type in Carey's Kansas. She would prove that it hadn't been Joe—Max—who had broken the bam-bam-bam-rat-tat-tat spell. It had been Brunhia. And she sure as hell didn't have to fly across the whole Atlantic to get away and shake the heebies of her own mind a second time.

She was drinking more wine and convincing herself of that when she saw him. Joe. Max. Whoever he was. Here. In Woodley Park, bellowing like a madman. Coming straight at her.

He'd sailed off without her half a world away. And now here he was.

Honey dropped the bottle of wine and it spilled out on the grass. She scrambled to her feet. "Before you go blasting me, *you're* the one who took a midnight powder."

But he ran right past her.

Amazed, Honey gaped after him. Then she left her blazer and her purse and the bottle of wine and she chased him.

He stopped abruptly and tackled a man. She could think of no other reasonable course of action so she jumped on his back.

"What are you doing?" she shrieked. "Are you out of your mind?"

He tried to buck her off. "Damn it, Elise! Honey! Whoever the hell you are! Stay out of this!"

"You're hurting him!" She winced when he managed to punch the poor guy in the jaw. He connected with the man's nose. Blood spurted. This was insane.

"Would you look at what you've done?" she screamed.

"I just saved your crazy ass!"

"I am *not* crazy! And you just got blood all over a really top-notch sweater—" She broke off and screamed when the stranger took the moment of Max's distraction to land a punch of his own.

They all rolled together. Honey managed to wriggle out from beneath them at the last possible moment. Panting, she came to her feet, her hands fisted at her sides. Joe was losing the fight now. Max, she thought dazedly, his name was really Max. Then the tide turned again and he had the guy by the throat and she still had no clue what was going on except that quite possibly she'd managed to fall in love with someone who'd escaped from an asylum.

Then the guy—whoever he was—got Max by the throat.

"Well, enough is enough already," she muttered. Honey jumped on *his* back.

He wasn't expecting it and he fought hard. But he couldn't shake her off without giving up on Max, and he couldn't fight Max without giving up on her. She clung to his back like a burr. She heard Max hollering. Then the stranger turned around and bashed her up against a tree.

Honey felt the air shoot out of her with the impact. It hurt. A cry of pain popped from her throat, then she was sliding off him to the grass, and he was running. She sank into a puddle at the base of the tree, breathing hard.

Max was getting to his feet to go after him. She found energy again and scrambled onto her hands and knees. Something had fallen out of the man's jacket pocket. Something silver. She crawled to it.

A gun.

"Don't touch it!" Max's voice hit the air like a thunder clap when she reached for it.

Honey looked wildly over her shoulder at him. "Is there some reason you think I should believe in your good judgment right now?"

"Think about it! He attacked you! It's evidence or something."

"*You* attacked *him!*" she shouted back. He'd come out of nowhere, she thought again, and had taken off after the guy for no plausible reason. Then again, the guy had been carrying a weapon and he hadn't been entirely kind about the way he'd removed her from his back. So maybe there had been a reason after all.

What had just happened here?

"You were oblivious to the world!" Max shouted. "He was right behind you!"

"People are allowed to walk behind other people in a park!" But this time her voice was feeble.

Then it all hit her. Max was in Washington. And a gun was three inches from her outstretched hand, a gun someone might have been intending to use on her. She thought of what everyone had been talking about in Brunhia—the Coalition and Marcus's voodoo genes—and things crashed in on her. Honey started shaking.

"Hey, hey," Max said, inching toward her.

"Stop right there." But her voice still lacked punch.

"Honey, you're losing it."

"Don't call me that. I'm not Honey anymore."

"Elise, then?" he asked placatingly.

"Kiss my ass."

"You're mad." But he stopped moving toward her.

"I'm overwhelmed." Then something inside her rallied. "And, let me tell you, that doesn't happen easily."

"I don't doubt it."

"Don't kiss up to me. I was just getting around to hating you." And God it had felt so much better than aching for him. This wasn't fair!

"Can I come a little closer and ask why that guy might have wanted to jump you?"

Honey came to her feet and began inching backward to where she had left her wine and blazer and purse. She picked up the wine bottle. "Not unless you want this cracked upside your head. What do you want from me, anyway? Why are you here?"

"I want to start over."

"Start *what* over?"

"Us."

One word, she thought helplessly. One blessed, wretched word from him. *Us.* And she came undone. She cried, and she didn't even have the Brunhia water to blame.

"What do tears mean?" he asked warily.

It meant she had to go find Matt Tynan.

She was blubbering, she was shaking, and she was staring at a gun in the grass. If she hadn't seen it fall out of that man's pocket, she would never have believed there had been any threat at all. She would have thought Max was a certifiable wack-job because he shouldn't even be here in her world. He was supposed to be on the other side of the ocean, not tackling people in a park, *her* park. But there was the business with Marcus and now a guy with a gun in his pocket had been trying to sneak up on her.

That cleared her brain a little. Some of the gray fuzziness around the edges sharpened up. Honey sniffed deeply. "What are you doing here?" she asked again.

"I just told you."

"No, you didn't. You tried to make me mushy." Which brought to mind everything he'd done to her—and the fact that he hadn't been where he was supposed to have been on one particular midnight. "You left me. You sailed off without me and left me."

He wanted to touch her, Max thought. He wanted to slide over explanations and pick up where they'd left off. He wanted it badly. But they'd left off on lies and questions and pseudonyms, and they couldn't go forward on those. He cleared his throat.

"I was in the process of hating you," he said honestly.

He expected shock, maybe fury, at least heated words in her own defense. Instead, he watched her face cave. "Marcus," she said on a ragged breath.

"The guy who chased you out of the quarry? Yeah, that's the one."

"What did he say?"

"That I was part of a plan for you."

She looked mystified. "Well, you were."

Max had expected anything but that. But she had never given him anything he expected. "And you feel no shame?"

"Why would I? I *told* you you were a plan. It shouldn't have come as any great revelation from him."

"You said you were playing a game."

"I was. Game, plan, whatever. Same thing."

His head was starting to hurt. Maybe it was from the athletics with the guy who'd been stalking her. Maybe it was from the way she was winging words around him again without saying anything. "Care to tell me what the plan was?"

Now she looked discomfited. "I'd rather not."

Max thought back to that conversation. "It had something to do with you dumping your virginity on me."

"I most certainly did *not* dump it."

"You didn't warn me."

"Of course not! What would you have done if I had?"

"Run for the hills. Except Brunhia didn't have any."

She folded her arms across her chest. "Exactly."

"Do you really want to have this conversation shouting at each other across ten feet?"

"I'm not shouting." But she took a step closer to him. She was, however, still holding the wine bottle.

"Maybe put that down?" he suggested, motioning at it.

"No. I haven't decided yet if I want to use it on you or not."

"Haven't you had enough violence for one day?"

"I'll deal with that other business later." Matt, she thought again. She was going to have to touch base with Matt and tell him about the guy with the gun. This changed things. But for the time being, she just gripped the bottle more tightly. "If I had told you I was a virgin, I'd still *be* a virgin."

"This plan—game, whatever—involved going to Brunhia to change that status quo?"

"Yes!"

"That was it? The beginning and end of your plan?"

"Of course. What did you think it was?"

There was a whole new can of worms, Max thought. He'd have to tell her—it would have to be part of the moving-forward business—but he thought he might wait awhile. At least until she put the wine bottle down. Then he thought that he should have known that if this woman had had any sort of plan, it would be something just as crazy as that.

Suddenly she frowned at him. Max took a quick step back to put space between them again, not trusting her with that bottle. "What?" he asked warily.

"How did you get here?" she asked.

"In a cab." Which, he realized, was probably still waiting for him and his fare. And the fare would be creeping upward. Ah, well, money was no object.

"Not here to the park," she said. "Here to the States."

"What difference does it make?" He wanted to move forward, he thought again, but this was more ground he'd prefer to broach when she wasn't armed.

"You couldn't have sailed across the whole Atlantic or you wouldn't be here yet," she said stubbornly. "That would take time."

"No. I mean, yeah. It does."

"So you flew. And *that* takes money."

"Not so much." The coach-class ticket had cost a hell of a lot less than fueling up his own jet.

"Where'd you get it?" she demanded.

"I have some stashed."

"All those years of hammering and sawing?"

"You could say that."

He expected her to keep pressing. Instead, she finally lowered the arm that held the bottle. She let out a long, shaky sigh and turned away from him. She went back to where she had been sitting before all this had started and she sank down on her blazer.

Max approached her cautiously. "What?"

"You spent what little money you have to fly all the way over here and find me."

Guilt churned in his stomach. "I have plenty left. It was no big deal."

She looked up at him. "Still."

"Can I sit down now?"

"After all you went through to get here, sure." When he did, she added, "This doesn't mean I'm ready to forgive you."

"I realize that." But she'd let go of the bottle, he thought. And when had it come around to *her* forgiving *him,* anyway? This had started out the other way around.

"If your boat is somewhere on the other side of the ocean, Max, then you must be planning to sleep somewhere else while you're here in Washington."

"I haven't done anything about that yet. I just got off the plane and went straight to the White House to find you."

Her eyes narrowed.

"Kurt told me you worked there."

They narrowed even more. "You've been following me since I left work?"

"More or less." But that was a lie, too. "Yes. You snooped on me, too."

"I did not. How did I do that?"

"You just called me Max." So when, he thought, had she actually discovered who he was? How long had she known? This whole reconciliation business was rife with minefields.

"Oh, that," she said. "Paloma told me."

"Paloma." She didn't know, then, because Paloma didn't know the truth. He wasn't sure if he was relieved or disappointed. Because if she didn't know, then it remained that he had to tell her.

"When she found me on the beach that morning," she continued.

"That morning?"

"I fell asleep waiting for you."

"You *waited?*"

"I got there before ten and I thought maybe you just went to Portimao early for supplies."

She'd waited all night, he thought, thinking the best of him when he'd deserved the worst. Things squirmed inside him. "So what do we do now?" he asked, half expecting that the question would bring the wine bottle back again.

She sighed. "You can stay at my place. We've got ample bedrooms."

He wasn't sure what part of that to address first—the "we" business or the implication about the bedrooms. He decided to take them in order. "You have a roommate?"

"A couple of them. But they actually live in Conover Pointe and they rarely visit."

She'd done it again. She'd just answered his question without telling him a thing. Max decided that moving forward also meant that *that* was going to have to stop if for no other reason than it made him dizzy. "But they pay rent," he persisted.

"No, the place is paid for. No mortgage."

"Do you own it?"

"They do."

This was getting him nowhere. He veered to his other question about the bedrooms. "Uh, are things curtailed between us physically? Are you making me sleep in another room?"

She sighed and it was a heartbreaking sound. "I sort of have to."

"Because of the roommates?"

"No, I told you, they're in Conover Pointe." But, Honey thought, this was Georgetown. And she knew what happened to her in Georgetown, in that townhouse.

Maybe she would decide to forgive him and take him with her when she ran away. But she knew that if she tried to make love to him here, it would be a disaster. Honey collected her purse and the wine bottle again and stood. She tugged at her blazer until he stood as well and took his weight off it. "Maybe eventually the sex thing will change," she told him. She'd probably be able to have sex and breathe at the same time on the road.

At least she was going to let him in her home, Max thought. Unfortunately, they had other problems besides their relationship, or lack of one.

The gun was still sitting in the grass. "Honey, we need to contact the authorities."

"What for? I'm over the age of consent. Though you'd never know it where my family is concerned."

That comment gave him hope. She was still thinking about sex. But Max nodded at the gun. She followed his gaze and closed her eyes briefly.

"Oh. That."

"It's a rather significant *that.*"

"You don't know the half of it."

Another comment he couldn't even begin to fathom. "We can't just leave it lying there."

"No, we can't. I know."

Honey wrapped her hand in her blazer and went back for it. Marcus and assorted others might think she was an imbecile, but she *did* watch a lot of movies. She picked up the gun without actually touching it. She inspected it for a moment, figuring there was probably a safety or some such thing involved. At least, there always was on the silver screen. She really didn't need to be shooting her own kneecap off right now. She had enough to worry about with all this life-changing business. And with Max here, and the Coalition after her.

Honey closed her eyes briefly. "I don't know that," she whispered aloud. "This could have been anything." But it wasn't, and she knew it wasn't. She'd spoken to Hatch six hours ago and now all of a sudden someone was coming after her with a gun in his pocket.

She started shaking again. She really didn't want Hatch to be a bad guy. She liked him. Maybe the Coalition just knew that she had been on Brunhia with the rest of the gene-y babies. Maybe they had decided she was somehow associated with them or with one of them. In that case, then everyone else who had been there was in danger as well, and she had a real obligation to tell them all what had happened.

But if she did that, they'd never let her meet with Hatch.

"No," she said aloud. She wasn't willing to give that up. She just wouldn't.

"You're talking to yourself again."

She jumped a little when Max came up behind her. "Do you know anything about these things?"

"A little," Max said. "Why?"

"Where's the safety?"

"Honey, what are you going to do?" he asked suspiciously.

"I'm going to wrap it up and put it in my purse. I'm going to take it home and hide it."

"Why?"

She opened her mouth and closed it again without answering. This was the other reason no one had wanted to talk to her on Brunhia—because she personally talked a lot. She wanted to tell him. She wanted to tell him the whole crazy thing. She couldn't tell Matt or Carey or any of the others what had happened today because they'd yank her back from seeing Hatch. And she couldn't confide in Max either because that was something the old Honey would have done. She would have blabbed.

She was going to start over, run away from her old life if it killed her. For the first time she realized that it was going to involve more than just ditching the Mercedes and her job. She was going to have to handle this on her own.

"Fix the safety," she said, pushing the gun at him a little. "Make sure it's on."

He watched her face and knew, for one of the few times in their acquaintance, that she was serious. Something was going on in that head of hers, but she wasn't going to tell him what it was. Max checked the safety.

She took the gun back and wrapped it snugly in her jacket, then she pushed everything down into her oversized purse. "Come on. I'll give you a ride in my brand-new Jeep. But I guess if you've been stalking me too, then you already know about that."

Before he could think of any possible answer, she set sail out of the park. Well, Max thought, when you screwed things up royally in the first place, no one gave you any guarantees that it would go easy the second time around.

He followed her.

Fourteen

"Why'd you dump the fancy car?" Max asked as they headed back to the townhouse.

That tugged a smile to her mouth. "I'm going to LaCrosse, Kansas. It's the barbed-wire capital of the world."

"No kidding." His own mouth tucked up.

She wanted to taste it again, she thought, glancing his way. She wanted it with a ferocity that surprised her. He'd dumped her, had taken a piece of her heart that she wasn't sure she'd ever get back. And still she wanted to kiss him.

"Barbed wire and a Mercedes don't seem to mix," she explained finally.

"I know a few cattle barons who might disagree with you."

That caught her. "You know cattle barons? I thought you were from Pittsburgh."

"I've traveled a lot."

Did he hesitate? Why would he?

"You were still going to run away, weren't you?" he asked. "With or without me."

"Correction. I *am* still going to run away." Honey pulled into the driveway and jumped down from the blue Jeep. She went to the door, fitted her key in the lock, then stepped inside to turn off the alarm system.

"What about the White House?"

"I quit today."

He caught her arm when she tossed her brand-new car keys on a fragile table in the foyer. "A job like that is hard to get."

"Not for me."

She looked both sad and whimsical. There were so many facets to her, he thought. Then she marched across an Aubusson rug toward the back of the house. Max followed her and found her in a small wine room off the kitchen.

"French, Italian, Portuguese or Napa?" she asked. "Hmm, Portuguese would bring back memories."

"Oh, no, you don't."

She looked at him, startled. "Don't offer you wine? I think there's beer, too."

"You spin words and you never answer my questions."

"Well, I was getting to it." She plucked a bottle of Niepoot's Redoma from the rack and squeezed past him to go back to the kitchen. "I was going to say that I don't even know why I majored in political science. I never gave it any thought whatsoever. Probably a bleed-in from everything I was trying to deny."

She found a corkscrew. He took it from her hand. "Are we back to Princess Elise?"

"Yup. But politics never interested me."

"What interests you?" He set to work on the bottle and watched her sigh and brace her elbows on a breakfast bar. Then she tucked her chin into her hands.

"Movies. People. Puzzles."

She was a puzzle, he thought. A delicious, invigorating, complicated puzzle. The more she gave him of herself, the more she was a mystery. He could live with her for forty years, Max thought, and never anticipate what she was going to say or do next.

His thoughts stalled on that. *Live* with her? How could he trust someone he couldn't figure out? Because, he thought, right off the cuff, everything she gave was genuine. A little skewed, but genuine.

"Anyway, I'm not sure it matters," she said. "Provided Jake Ingram ever gets to the bottom of the World Bank Heist, I really never have to work a day again in my life." She went to the wine room again and returned with two glasses. "So what are *you* going to do now?"

He knew then. He knew the answer as clearly as if he'd never had to drop out to find it. "I don't want to work anymore either."

She laughed, delighted. "Well, you don't, not near as I can tell. Do you think you'll get bored eventually?"

"Not as long as Kansas has barbed wire."

Her heart lurched.

Max took a mouthful of wine and put his glass down. It was time to confess. The moment felt right. She was mellow in a way she rarely was. He might be walking back to the city to find a hotel room if she blew a cork over the way he'd lied to her, but then, she apparently wasn't going to let him sleep with her tonight anyway.

And then she shattered his thoughts. She leaned close to him over the breakfast bar, stepping on one of the rungs of the stool behind her to match his height. And she touched her mouth to his. A butterfly kiss, he thought, things clenching then unclenching inside him.

"Max," she whispered, "will you still run away with me?"

Lead the way. "Did you just forgive me?"

"I'm working on it."

"Can I help things along?"

"No."

He could have sworn he saw panic cross her face. He reached for her and she backed up fast, dropping off the stool again. This time he didn't try to figure her out. His hand caught in her hair and he pulled her back toward him. Gently at first, then with more intent. Her eyes stayed on his and widened as her face came closer to his. Then she closed them and sighed.

He kissed her again, falling into her, remembering all the reasons he hadn't stopped when he'd realized she was a virgin. It was as if life vibrated through her, bubbling, waiting for something. Then she caught his wrists to stop him.

"Max, I can't do this."

"I want you."

"You don't understand. This is *Georgetown.*"

He let her go reluctantly. "To the best of my knowledge, yes."

Honey's heart was hammering. Which was worse? she thought frantically. Which was more mortifying? To simply tell him, or to swoon at his feet if she put it to the test? She gulped wine. "I don't know anything about you."

"That didn't stop us six nights ago."

"That was Brunhia."

"I'm missing the connection."

And then, although there wasn't a drop of Brunhia water anywhere to be found, the words came tumbling out of her. "I can't have sex here because I bam-bam-bam-rat-tat-tat and go down like an overripe tomato dropping off the vine!" He stared at her. Yes, Honey thought, she was mortified. "I faint."

"Sex makes you faint?"

"In rose gardens."

"We're not in a rose garden."

"I can't be anywhere *near* a rose garden! And then Marcus was getting married so I went far away, and you were there, and I was there, and wham!"

"Wham," he repeated.

"Wowza."

"It was that, too."

"You're not getting this, are you?"

"Not a bit."

Honey set her jaw. "All right, damn it. I'll *show* you."

She stepped around the bar and fisted his hair in her hands. Then she drew his mouth back to hers. He was everything she remembered once she stopped being panicked. He still tasted like sea and freedom. His tongue swept by hers and she let her fingers unclench. She slid her hands down until she gripped his biceps.

"Come on," she whispered. "Come with me."

He thought she was taking him upstairs to a bedroom. She

tugged him toward the back door instead. She did have that exhibitionist streak, he thought.

There was a rose garden six strides out the back door bordered by a sundial on one side and a quaint little potting shed on the other. She led him to it then she wrapped her arms around his neck and pressed her body to his. "I'll show you," she said again, then her lips came back to his.

And everything he thought he knew about himself started to die inside him. If Camille had kissed him like this, would he have let her roam the globe without him? If she had kissed him like this, would he ever have been able to let her go? He met Honey's tongue and she swallowed everything he used to be and wanted to forget. She took all the fear and the weariness and the pain.

She pressed her breasts to his chest and heard his breathing change. It went ragged and something inside her leaped. It made her feel light-headed...almost. She listened to the beating of her heart. It was hitting a crescendo now, but it didn't hurt.

He tugged her top from the waistband of her skirt and everything tightened inside her again. His hands slid up over her ribs and her mind shattered and she forgot to worry, forgot to think. Then he had her top over her head and his mouth fell to the swell of her breasts. Her knees wanted to give out.

Max felt her going weak in his arms. His mouth never lost touch with hers as he lowered her to the soft, mulchy ground, unzipping her skirt as they went. He flowed with her and she rolled on top of him.

They had been apart for days, she thought, and it felt like years. She needed to be with him again, skin to skin, connected. She tugged at his T-shirt, suddenly frantic. She found the fly on his jeans and tugged it down.

"This is what happens to you in rose gardens?" he asked against her mouth.

"Uh, not quite."

He caught the front of her bra in his hand until her breasts spilled from it. He unhooked it, then looped his thumb at the corner of her panties and pulled them away too. Then he left her...and everything inside her howled. No rat-tat-tat and no bam-bam-bam. Just greed and desperation, howling through her, demanding that he come back to her now. *Right now.*

He stripped out of the last of his clothes and settled his weight on top of her. Just when Honey thought the pain of wanting would kill her, he found his way inside her again, deep and strong. She wrapped herself around him and held on and rode the crest with him until things came apart inside her.

Her last thought as she went over the edge was that he'd beaten Georgetown and the de Hooch artwork. That meant Georgetown and the de Hooches had never really been the problem at all.

A strand of her hair had curled around his little finger as though to hold him. Max played with it, flat on his back in the rose garden, her warmth pressed against his side. She did have a thing for the outdoors.

His brain was still ringing. His body felt drained. And still, even still, something nagged him.

He wanted to believe that she was just what she seemed to be—quixotic and real, vibrant with touching little shadows. She was forthcoming if he pushed the right buttons. But there was still a gun in her purse and he didn't understand why.

"Why don't you want to go to the police about what happened this afternoon?" he asked again.

Honey stirred against him. *Not now,* her mind cried. *Please don't make me go there now.* For the second time in her life, she just felt...satisfied. There was nothing else she wanted to reach for beyond this garden. But he was right. There was the matter of the gun.

She sat up reluctantly and knotted her hair at her nape. "I'm not sure if I can trust the police."

"You know who that guy was?"

She shook her head fretfully. "No, I really don't."

"But you have an idea."

"I have an educated guess. There's a difference."

"And you're not going to share it with me." It hurt. That was crazy. They hadn't been together long enough for him to feel a twinge because she shut him out. Whatever it was, why she hadn't been surprised by that gun, it had all probably been going on long before he'd met her. But he lay there watching the new light of the moon spill over her skin, and he felt lost and helpless and yeah, a little bit angry. "You're in danger."

"Well, yeah. That's obvious." For the first time she considered, really considered, what condition she might be in right now if Max hadn't materialized out of thin air at that precise moment in time. Would that guy have killed her? Would she have died without ever knowing that she really had nothing against rose gardens at all, that she had only needed to escape her own chains, that she had just needed one particular man?

Honey hugged herself. "It doesn't involve me, not directly. I'm sort of attached at the fringes."

"What the hell did you get yourself tangled up with?"

"*I* didn't. But someone I love did." His eyes flared at that. "Oh, for God's sake. Not love *that* way. Love like...a brother."

"Why would anyone go after you?"

Because maybe Samuel Hatch really wasn't on the up-and-up, she thought again. Maybe he had figured out her mission. And maybe he had decided to derail her before they met. She scrubbed her hands over her cheeks. "I'm not sure."

"Can you tell this brotherly-love person what happened today?"

"No. I've decided not to. If I do, I'll lose my chance to find out what I'm really made of." She leaned forward suddenly so she was looming over him again. "Max, trust me on this. Please. I've spent my whole life denying what everyone expected from me and I was so busy doing that, I never got around to meeting myself. Now I want to see what I'm made of."

He must be as crazy as she was, Max thought, because she was making absolute sense. "What can I do?"

Her mouth trembled. "You just did it. You respected me enough to let me take care of this."

Respect had never, ever been an issue, he thought. "Lie down here with me again. It's getting cold without you."

She stood instead. "I have a better idea. Let's go to bed."

Max sat up. "Do I get to share a room with you after all or are you going to stick me in that potting shed?"

"We can share now." She finally grinned. "Georgetown is *iced.*"

She still felt replete and content when she woke in the morning. Then nerves crept in. She started rattling inside at the thought of meeting Hatch and getting a needle stuck in her that might wipe out her mind—although some would say there was very little there to wipe—and at the thought of letting Carey down. She was frightened by the possibility that maybe she wasn't made of much substance after all. She was scared because she also knew she was going to go to that meeting alone. She couldn't call Matt to arrange for the bodyguards or whatever he wanted to have in place at the bar. She was afraid that if she talked to him, she'd blurt out the whole business about the stranger in the park and the gun. And then he'd pull the plug on her whole mission.

Max rolled over to pull her close. "Come here."

Something delicious rolled through her. "I can't."

"We have to go back outside again?"

She laughed. "I need to take a shower and go to work."

"You quit."

"I gave notice. There's a difference. I'm still expected to chirp into phones today."

He groaned. "Just my luck. She's got an honorable streak, too."

Honey leaned up to look over his shoulder at the bedside clock. "Then again, I've got maybe twenty minutes to spare. Can you work fast?"

"When I have to."

As though to prove it, he rolled on top of her. He was already hard. A shiver of expectation and joy tickled through her. She wanted this. She needed this. Especially if she was going to die tonight or have her mind erased of his name.

Honey decided to go home and change after work. She hadn't wanted to wear the red dress to the White House. That was a little over-the-top, even for her.

Lines from an old Rod Stewart song rolled through her head; she loved old music the way she loved old movies, though it was a dear-kept secret from those who had orbited in her old Honey-world. *Tonight's the night.* She'd meet with Hatch and prove herself. She'd turn over whatever she learned to Marcus and Matt and the others. Then she'd hit the road in her nifty new Jeep with Max by her side.

She rolled into the townhouse driveway and jogged to the door. "Max!" She skidded to a stop in the hallway, listening for a return shout.

It came from the kitchen. Honey went that way and dumped her purse on the breakfast bar. He was sitting on one of the stools with a cell phone in front of him.

"I need a favor," she said.

"Ask. It's yours."

"I need you to come to the Marriott Wardman Park with me," she said. She'd been thinking about this all day. She didn't need Matt's protective goons if she had Max. "I have to meet someone about the gun."

He came instantly alert. "Okay."

She held up a hand. "I can't tell you. I *can't.* Not yet."

"When?"

She didn't know. Once they were on the road and out of reach? "Soon. I need to change." She turned away, then she paused and looked over her shoulder at him. "Oh, and Max. Bring the gun. Just in case."

She left him. Max watched her go, panic twitching in his gut. She thought she needed protection? He was, however, very glad that she had asked him to come along. Because if she hadn't, he probably would have followed her anyway. And yes, he would have taken the gun.

He thought back to what he had seen from the cab yesterday, that guy watching her from between two dogwood trees, watching hard enough that he'd drawn Max's own attention. The man had switched position to a bench, drawing ten feet closer to her, then moving to a patch of flowers, closer still. He had looked around for observers and had begun moving straight toward her with his hand in his pocket and his gaze unwavering on the back of her head. Max had seen the rest of it play out in his mind. He'd reach her and one arm would go around her neck. Whatever was in that pocket—at the time he'd had a certainty that it was a knife—would go to her throat. Max had figured him for taking her purse, the new Jeep keys, maybe hurting her first so she couldn't holler or raise an alarm.

He had never anticipated this. Whatever this was.

"What are you thinking about?"

Max jolted. She'd returned. And she was wearing…a flame. The dress was somewhere between orange and red, but it was less jarring than provocative, hinting of heat and something wild. It wasn't exactly short but there was a slit up one side nearly to her hip. The sleeves were long, belled. It fit like a second skin as far as her hips, then it loosened and shimmied.

"Wow," he said.

"The better to slay dragons with." Honey forced a grin to show that she wasn't nervous at all and did a little twirl to show the dress off.

"Just out of curiosity, how old is this guy you're going to meet?"

"My best guess would put him somewhere between sixty and sixty-five. Why?"

"Just wondering if he's going to have a heart attack when you walk in, or if he's going to tackle you."

She smiled, her heart feeling steadier. "Let's hope for neither."

"Okay, let's do this. Where's the gun?"

In response, she headed for the stove. "I put it somewhere no one would ever think to look." She tugged all four heating elements from the range top, then she lifted it. The gun was snugged between burners, still wrapped in her blazer.

"Good thing you canceled the maid today," Max said. "That would have been a hell of a fire show if she had tried to cook something."

"Yes, but I thought to cancel her, didn't I?" She partially unwrapped it and turned back to him to study him critically. "Where should you carry this?"

"How about the waistband of my jeans?"

"Oh, like no one would notice *that* at Wardman Park." Then she paused. "Wait, I've got an idea."

As he watched her go again, he thought how close *he* had come to firing up the stove today for the makings of a grilled cheese sandwich. He wasn't willing to call her a danger to all mankind, but she did bear watching.

She came back carrying a sports jacket and shoved it at him. "This might fit."

Max took it. "Well, since I know it doesn't belong to an ex-lover—up until Brunhia you were a little short on those—it begs asking whom this belongs to."

"One of the roommates. Try it on."

He did. It fit after a fashion, Honey thought. Not perfectly, but then the man had probably never encountered a custom-made jacket in his life so he wouldn't know the difference. It fit as well as anything could be expected to off the rack. "Good enough," she decided, then she turned for the hall. "I don't think we should arrive together."

"So you've got some preposterous alternate plan for getting me there?"

"I do, but it's not preposterous. I'm going to drop you three blocks away and you're going to walk." She glanced at him as she reset the alarm and they stepped through the front door. "I got that from a movie. Same one I got the hide-a-gun-in-the-range-top idea from. I don't remember which exactly, but I'm thinking Peter Fonda."

Honey's gut tightened as she drove. Squeezing, spasming, until she thought she might be sick. *There* would be an ignominious end to her short-lived career as a super-spy. *Hi, Hatch,* she thought, *excuse me while I vomit.* She had to get a grip.

She pulled over to the curb three blocks from the Marriott. Her heart was thrumming. "I'm scared."

"Ah, Honey, damn it." He reached for her.

She let herself lean her forehead against his shoulder for just a second. Then he spoke again, and she knew without a doubt that she really did love him.

"Go in there and kick some ass. That's what you're made of."

His words sank into her as deep as her soul. Honey straightened and drew in breath. "As you enter the lounge, the curving hem of the bar is right there by the door. Then it sweeps down the entire room. Try to get a seat as close to the door end as you can." In case they had to make a quick getaway, she thought. She wanted him covering her from there. "I'm thinking Ha—" She broke off again and restarted. "I'm thinking this guy will probably get us a table. He doesn't strike me as the sit-at-the-bar type, but I could be wrong."

Max got out of the Jeep then leaned back in through the window. "By the way, when we're done here, I'm driving home. And on all occasions thereafter."

She started to take exception to the fact that he seemed to be disparaging her driving, but she didn't have the chance. He started off down the street.

Honey looked at the dashboard clock. It was six on the dot. If she was going to be fashionably late, she had to move now.

She reached the Marriott and left the Jeep with the valet. She strolled inside to the lounge and suddenly everything within her was calm again. She thought of the man yesterday who had let a gun fall out of his pocket. She thought of poor Jake's shaky memory, which had lost whole years of his life.

Of people who would grab and hurt the wrong brother—Zach—maybe out of stupidity, maybe out of malice. She considered that they might hurt Marcus, and while she was still mildly ticked off at him, she'd die herself before she'd let that happen.

Somehow she knew Hatch the moment she stepped into the lounge. Theirs had been entirely a telephone acquaintance. She'd never crossed paths with him while he was still active because the CIA wasn't quartered in the White House. If he'd ever visited there, which he surely had done, the man would have had no call to visit the telephone operators. But she'd built up an image of him in her mind, and when he stood from a table she knew immediately that she had been right on target. He wasn't tall, but compact and solid. His hair was close-cropped and decidedly gray. No Grecian Formula for this dude, Honey thought. She wasn't quite as appreciative of his wardrobe. His khakis could have rivaled a road map of New York, and the edge of his polo shirt's collar was slightly frayed.

"Life must begin at sixty." He took her outstretched hand when she reached him.

Honey cocked her head coquettishly. "I was thinking more like twenty-three. May I?" She leaned forward quickly and brushed a kiss over his cheek. "I don't speak to many men twice a week for six months. This seems to require more than a handshake."

She expected a blush or something along those lines. But then she realized that this man wouldn't be caught off guard easily. "Ah, a heartbreaker," Hatch said equably.

Honey grinned. "If you've heard that, then I've been terribly maligned."

"Have a seat," he urged. "Please."

Honey slid onto a chair. She wondered if Max was here yet. She looked into Hatch's eyes. There was nothing doddering, senile or lonely about them. They were bottle-green and they looked as if they could cut glass. He was going to smell a lie a mile off, she realized.

A waitress came. Hatch looked at Honey questioningly, letting her order first. Old school, Honey thought. She liked that. Damn it, she didn't want to like him until she *knew*. She decided on something potent that she would sip slowly. She didn't dare order anything non-alcoholic, because Hatch would wonder why she had suggested cocktails if she didn't want a drink. By the same token, if she drank wine, she knew from past experience that she could knock back a whole glass without even thinking about it.

"Remy," she said.

"Two," Hatch agreed. "But a side of milk for me."

Then the waitress was gone and Honey felt the full focus of those green eyes. She decided to play this by what her gut was telling her. To do what she did best. She would veer off the conversation a bit then come back to it. She would make him wonder if she had any intent here at all. "Word has it that you kept a strawberry plant alive in your office against almost staggering odds. You salvaged it from your wife's garden after she died."

He looked startled, then pleased. "Did you ask about me before we arranged to meet or after, Number Twelve?"

"I didn't ask at all. Rumors follow you." The waitress brought their drinks. Honey waited until the glasses were on the table, then she leaned forward. "Want to hear what else I know about you?"

"By all means." The way he smiled told her he was enjoying himself.

"You were with the CIA, but I never heard which branch and I'm good at getting people to talk. I've also been hanging around the White House for a few years now and I know that means that whatever you did with the CIA, it was a top-secret section. Now, to my thinking, a man with *any* top-secret CIA section is going to know everything there is to possibly know about a woman he's going to meet for cocktails. Am I right or wrong?"

He lifted his drink to his mouth. Drank, put it down, lifted the milk. Drank from that as well, and put that glass down.

"Ulcers," he said to her in explanation. Then he added, "I am pleased to make your acquaintance, Honor Elise Evans."

Honey grinned. "I do so love being right."

"Then let's cut to the chase."

"You want my body?"

"I might have, thirty years ago."

"I wasn't born yet then."

"Which makes this an even more intriguing occasion."

Honey sipped the Remy. "I like a man who speaks his mind."

"And I like you, Honey."

Honey, she thought. He didn't miss a trick.

"So I'll tell you what you want to know," he said.

And that suddenly, that simply, she knew that Matt was safe meeting with this man. It was pure gut, absolute instinct. He had no memory-erasing serum stuck up his sleeve.

"You're here to give Tynan the go-ahead to talk with me. You would have been on Brunhia together last week. And now, suddenly, you want to meet me."

He'd known what she was up to all along, Honey thought. Then she met those sharp green eyes with what she hoped was a knife-edged look of her own blue ones. "I damned well want to know why I'm doing this."

"For Mr. Tynan?" Hatch asked.

"Hell, no. He already knows what's going on. For me."

Hatch laughed again. "Yes, he'd keep this close to his vest."

"That's putting it mildly."

"I'm sorry I wasn't more of a challenge for you," Hatch said.

"Not necessarily. You're not talking yet."

This laugh was deep, true. "I like you, Honor."

"Terrific. Then let's get married and run away to Lacrosse, Kansas."

"It would be my pleasure. But you've already got a man."

Honey reared back in her seat. "Damn, you're good." She

wondered for a wild moment if he knew about the rat-tat-tat-bam-bam-bam business and her rose-garden issue, too.

"And, of course, I'm going nowhere until I've ruined Willard Croft," he continued.

She tried not to react, but she knew she did. Maybe the average man wouldn't pick up on it, but this one would. "I don't know who Willard Croft is."

Hatch studied her for a moment, then he nodded. "He's behind the Coalition."

"*Them* I've heard of."

He was watching her thoughtfully. "People truly underestimate you, don't they?"

She thought again of her revelation on Brunhia, that maybe she'd brought that upon herself. "I'm going to fix that now."

He nodded. "Tell Mr. Tynan that I am merely retired after a long fight, but I am neither senile nor old."

"Well, I can vouch for that."

"Not much goes on yet that I don't know about."

"The Pres does regularly take your calls."

"It's come to my attention that Mr. Tynan has been asking many questions about Code Proteus."

Proteus. The name that had appeared in all those newspaper articles, she thought. "I'm going to take a wild leap here," she said. "I'm going to sort of think aloud."

"I'd be delighted."

She wanted to smile but she sipped her Remy instead. "The government did this to my brother. To Jake and to Gretchen and whoever Faith is, right? I heard them mention someone named Faith. The government started it by…by *creating* them."

"Yes."

"But they wouldn't do such an outrageous thing in the sixties right aboveboard where everyone could see."

"Correct."

"So Code Proteus was part of *your* deal. The CIA."

"Right and wrong."

She wanted to be angry, but all she could do was look at

him pleadingly. "Please. I just need someone to finally be honest with me here."

"They sent you in like a lamb to slaughter," Hatch mused aloud. "Didn't they?"

"No. They just underestimated both of us."

He smiled at that. "Code Proteus was never my section. But yes, they were part of the CIA. And yes, they are behind the very existence of your brother and your friends."

"What happened?"

"It fell apart largely because of the consciences of integral people. They died for it."

Her heart skipped. "Mom and Pop Test Tube?"

His mouth quirked. "Willard Croft was involved as well. When Code Proteus fell apart, I believe he continued on in a less-than-government-authorized way."

"The Coalition."

Hatch nodded. "Tell your friend Tynan that I have been watching the horizon for many years now, waiting for Croft to surface. I have been paying attention. Tell him I may have information that could prove useful to him about Croft's whereabouts."

Honey sat back. "I will."

"And alas, I think that ends our meeting. Your young man is waiting for you." He nodded at the bar.

Honey looked over her shoulder to see Max. She glanced back at Hatch. "I guess I'm pretty damned lucky you didn't turn out to be on Croft's side."

"Yes," he said. "You are."

She started to stand, then she hesitated. "I'd like to do this again sometime. For no ulterior motive whatsoever. I want to find out what happened to that strawberry plant."

"Then I'll tell you." He reached for her hand across the table. "And I will also tell you this. Regardless of the fact that my Tuesdays and Thursdays will now be bleaker, I am very glad you resigned your position. You can do more, Honey, much more than answer phones."

Her heart soared. "Thanks. I'm going to have to break some chains first, though."

He nodded. "I know."

She wondered if there was anything he *didn't* know, then she got up to go to Max.

Fifteen

Honey felt giddy with relief and happiness when she tucked her arm through Max's at the lounge door. "It went fine."

He was so incredibly glad to feel her again, to touch her again, safe and secure by his side, that he forgot all his questions except one. "I don't need to shoot anybody?"

"Not tonight." She looked up at him. "I want to go home now."

"Where are your keys?"

"You didn't mean that part about driving from now on."

"I meant it entirely."

Then again, she thought, it might be a good idea. Who knew that adrenaline and exhaustion could combine in such a numbing way? She felt suddenly shaky. She reached in her purse for the valet-parking ticket and a tip.

He was distracted enough by whatever it was that he had just witnessed that he gave the little role of ones back to her and pulled his own billfold from his pocket when the valet came back with her Jeep. Honey stared at the cash he withdrew.

"What the *hell?*" she squeaked.

Max looked down and realized what he had done. "We'll talk."

"That's a safe guess."

"Not now. At home." He didn't want her hitting him while he was driving.

"*I* have a home, pal. Last I heard, you were a vagabond."

"And I intend to continue to be one for some time to come." He peeled off several ones. He was normally more generous but discretion seemed the better part of valor at the moment. "Hungry?" he asked.

"Damned right I am. For answers." Suddenly her heart was thudding sickly.

"We can share some over dinner." *Share,* he thought, being the operative word.

"I'll cook." She grabbed the passenger-door handle and yanked it open before the valet could do it for her.

"You can't cook."

"The hell I can't."

"Name one thing." He went around to the driver's side, glad for the reprieve.

"Fondue."

He got behind the wheel and looked at her. Her arms were crossed over her chest. "Wow. You can melt cheese?"

"Sure. Throw in some beer, some spices, and you're good to go." She sniffed. "It helps if you have one of those electric pots that melts everything for you."

"Do you have one?" He drove back onto the street.

"Of course, I have one. The maid has nights off and it's the only thing I know how to make."

Max laughed. God, he loved her.

That staggered him and filled him with something bright and white and overwhelming. He was going to tell her the truth about himself. And then he was going to marry her. The man from Pittsburgh was going to take a wife.

"You're taking me home," she said when she realized where he was driving. "I thought I just successfully convinced you to take me to a restaurant."

"I had this image of you melting cheese naked."

"That could be arranged."

"Why didn't I doubt it? You've gotten naked on a beach—"

"Half-naked," she corrected.

"You stripped down to your bra the first time I met you—"

"You were bleeding. You needed a tourniquet."

"It wasn't a tourniquet. And we made love last night in a rose garden."

"I had a very big point to make with that."

"I guess you made it."

She grinned at him, the wad of his money forgotten. "So you want me to take my clothes off to make the fondue?"

"I wouldn't mind."

Life, she thought, was good. Then they turned onto her street and she saw a sight that drove every sweet, satisfied cell right out of her blood. Her father's Rolls. Honey made a gargling sound.

Max looked at her. "What's wrong?"

"Roommates are back," she said shortly.

He saw the Rolls Royce too. "You travel in high places."

"You knew that. Keep driving," she decided.

"No, I want to meet them."

"No, you really don't." She twisted in her seat to look at him. "Want to do something really outrageous?"

"Define outrageous."

"Keep driving. We've got the Jeep, I've got my credit cards, you've got that bulging roll of cash, so let's just run. Now. Right now."

"You want to run without clean underwear?"

"I can afford to buy more. And so, from the looks of things, can you."

"That might be the last cash I have to my name."

"Doesn't matter. I've got my American Express."

He pulled into the driveway anyway. Honey slid down into her seat and covered her face in her hands. Then she thought of what she had said to Hatch. *Break the chains.*

She opened the Jeep door. "Brace yourself, pal. This is going to get ugly."

She left him and strode to the door. Halfway there, she realized she was furious. Yes, she'd made her own bed with her family, and she'd lain in it, too. She'd determined what everyone thought of her by her own behavior. But she'd done it to fight back. Against them. Against this. She wondered if

Drew was here, too. Marcus? Had they all ganged up on her? Were they here to drag her off to Conover Pointe and keep her under lock and key so she couldn't get away?

She slammed through the front door and felt Max come in behind her. He mother's voice came from the living room. Honey veered that way and was immediately besieged by hugs and kisses. They loved her, she thought. They just didn't love her enough to let go.

"This is a surprise, Mom. Hi, Daddy." She smacked her lips against their cheeks.

"You're here. You're in Georgetown," her mother said, relief palpable in her voice.

"Well, where did you think—" Then she remembered the runaway note she had left them in Brunhia. "I'm still going to run away. I just stopped at home to tidy things up first." She turned back to Max. "This is who I'm running away with."

Stony silence fell over the room. Honey watched everyone looking at each other.

"I know you," her father said.

"Of course you know me—" Honey broke off. He wasn't looking at her. He was looking at Max. She pivoted on her heel to glance at Max as well. "You know each other?"

Her father came forward fast and urgently, his hand held out to Max. "Pleased to make your acquaintance." He pumped Max's hand hard.

Somehow this felt...bad, Honey thought. She looked at her mother. For one of the few times in her life, Sarah Evans seemed poleaxed.

"Honey, you didn't tell us," she said.

"Tell you *what?*"

"I was going to tell you last night," Max said to her.

"You know," she said huffily, "we've got a lot of people here telling things to each other, or not telling them, and just for the record, I'm lost."

Her father looked at her. "You've been seeing Maxwell Strong?"

"Maxwell what?"

It came to her slowly. They were all staring at her. And the name meant something to her. Of course, it did. But she had to reach for it. She liked movies more than reading. She hadn't even known Zach Ingram had been abducted until she'd gone to that library.

Maxwell Strong.

Billionaire Maxwell Strong.

Multi-billionaire Maxwell Strong.

Real estate developer. Things inside her exploded.

She veered back to him. *"Hammers and nails?"*

"Lord, Honor, your voice," her mother chastised.

Honey whirled to her. "Stay out of this. You just stay out of this."

"Honey, for God's sake," Max said. "I just needed some time."

She went at him, her claws bared. Her father caught her from behind.

"We need to speak quietly and concisely here," Charles Evans said.

"Screw concise," Honey hissed.

"Please, let's just sit down," her mother fretted. "We need to make sense of this."

"I already have." Honey jerked away from her father. She had so much to say. So much to say to all of them. It was pounding inside her. She wanted to scream, yell, be all the things her mother hated. But there was enough Evans in her that she took a deep breath instead. "I'm leaving now. But don't any of you—" She broke off and spun to Max. "Don't *any* of you dare to follow me."

"Honor," her father began.

"I haven't been Honor since I was thirteen!" Her voice was rising again, she thought. "And damn it, I'm not Honey either."

"Darling, you're making no sense," her mother said. "We came here to find you, to learn what's troubled you so that you'd want to run away."

"Then I'll tell you." She chugged in more air. "I'm not you. I'm not Drew and I'm not Marcus. Perfection leaves me cold. I hate politics and I…and I…" She trailed off, feeling helpless. How to say it? "I was miserable. I was bam-bamming and rat-tatting, and I was heading down, and it wasn't about sex at all. It was *me!*"

"Honor, please speak English," her father said.

Honey gripped her head in her hands. "I don't want to have to fight back anymore. I just want to be left alone to do what I do best. And I didn't even know what that might be until tonight." Maybe she *wasn't* making sense, she realized. They were all looking at her, stupefied. She glanced over her shoulder at Max again. "You promised me a new start but you lied. You lied about who you are and what you had to offer me. I thought you had *nothing* to offer me but yourself and that was exactly what I needed." She jerked around fully and headed for the door.

With nothing. No clean underwear. Just the keys she snatched out of Max's hand as she passed him, and the credit cards in the purse she still clutched in her hand. Honey fled.

It took Max a long time to recover after she bolted out the door. He didn't know what to say first. Then words came to him. "I love her."

Charles Evans remained stone-faced. Sarah Evans began fanning herself before she sank down onto the sofa. "This is an utter scene."

Max was gathering himself. "Maybe I can explain."

"Would you like a drink?" Charles asked.

He almost laughed. Upper-crust and polite to the end. Sometime, someday again, he'd appreciate that. "I'd love one."

Charles poured. Whiskey for himself and Max, a sherry for his wife. Somehow, Max thought, they ended up seated across from each other in the living room as though a mini-tornado had not just whipped in and out.

"I love her," he said again. Now, Max thought, now was the time to come up with his official press release for his retirement. This could be a dry run. "I've had an excellent go at things."

Sarah nodded. "One might say so," Charles agreed.

"Then my dad died."

Sarah began looking around for something with which to dab her eyes. "I'm sorry. This is all so shocking."

Max knocked back the shot of whiskey in one gulp and it spread through him, warm. "They haven't really found me yet—the press, my associates. But they're getting closer. And I'm ready. I've been ready since my father died. I just didn't know it. I needed your daughter to show me. I thought I was courageous slinking off in the night. She showed me the way in the light of day."

Charles nodded. Sarah looked teary-eyed again.

"She's sharp as a tack," Max said. "She's clever and she's wily, and she's as bright as the sun and as dark as a new moon, and no one knows that. No one knows it because you keep pushing her into…into…an ivory tower. And she keeps clamoring to get out and no one ever hears her over her shouting. She's not like any of us. She has to go her own way."

"Are you going to marry her?" Sarah asked hopefully.

And Max understood, in that moment, some of Honey's frustration. "I'm going to find her," he said quietly, standing again and putting his glass down on the nearest table. "Which may be a little like traveling after a whirling dervish."

"She'll go home now," Charles said.

Max looked at him, wondering if the man had suddenly gone insightful or if he had lost his mind. "She just blasted out of home," he reminded him.

"No. *Home.* She loves the horses. And we're here and she doesn't want to see us. So she'll go home."

Sarah stood, suddenly assertive. "Conover Pointe. It's on the eastern shore. She likes you. You can talk sense into her."

More than likely, Max thought, he'd just aid and abet her—assuming she ever spoke to him again. He started for the door, then he paused. He struggled with himself. At first it was a battle, viciously waged. More betrayal on one side, honesty on the other. But he couldn't lose her. "Do either of you happen to know why someone would be stalking her with a gun and why she would meet with a man at the Marriott about it?" he asked.

They looked dumbfounded, he thought. So much for enlightenment.

"Never mind," he said, and headed out the door.

No wheels, he thought, no boat. He turned about again and went inside. "On second thought," he said to Charles and Sarah Evans, "I need directions and I need a car."

She had no idea where she was going, Honey thought, and she didn't care. *If he had to be a lie, why did he have to come back and find her again?*

She'd been all right when she left Brunhia. Not good, not by a long shot, but all right. Then he'd come blasting out of nowhere to tackle that guy in the park. Why had he followed her home if it had all been lies?

The sensible thing to do now would be to find a map and head straight for Lacrosse, Kansas. But God, she was so bone-tired.

Her parents were in Georgetown. Conover Pointe would be safe at least until tomorrow. They could return at any time, but at least she had tonight. Maybe that was all she needed.

She was bleeding inside. Love sucked. Especially when you loved a liar.

Charles looked at Sarah again when they were alone. She sat neatly on the sofa, hands tucked in her lap. She'd reclaimed some of her serenity. That serenity had not filtered down to their only daughter.

"Maxwell Strong?" She breathed it, still amazed.

"Honor has always gone for the outer limits."

"Yes."

"I think he'll find her."

"If she *isn't* at home, he certainly has the financial wherewithal to track her down."

It was everything they'd ever wanted for her, Charles thought. A good marriage to a man who could provide for her. But yet, thinking that, he felt as though he was cheating her somehow. "Are we absolutely certain we got the right baby out of the nursery?" he asked.

She cracked a smile. "I have never been sure of that."

"She's the brightest star."

"Of all our children? Yes, she is."

"Sarah, I'm very concerned about Maxwell's comment regarding guns and stalkers and meeting men in hotel bars."

"Do you think it has something to do with Marcus's bizarre difficulties?"

"I do." He went to the phone to call his youngest son. He should be back in the States by now. There was more going on there than what that young man was telling them.

Honey smelled the horses when she was halfway down the long drive to the coast. It was one of those unique smells that could either turn a person totally off or bring them peace. It had always brought her peace.

She'd grown up here. In the mornings, after the maid had made bacon or ham and eggs, some atrociously cholesterol-laden breakfast, Honey had always snagged carrots from the fridge and gone out to the barn. Before school, before anything, because of the smell. The hay had almost a sweet edge. The wood shavings that they bedded the stalls with had the ripe cut of cedar. Bins of sweet feed for the lactating mares and the breeding stallions carried the aroma of molasses. And sure, that thing underneath, the touch of manure, but all of it came together in an overriding aroma that meant peace to her.

She didn't even go to the house when she made it home. She stopped the Jeep in front of the first barn. And when she strode in, it came to her. Here was the only place in twenty-three years—before Max and Brunhia—that she'd ever been real.

That made her want to cry. So she did, but she made it into a stall first. She didn't know the mare inside. One of the new ones, she thought. Her father was always buying and selling them. This was a chestnut with a golden mane and tail who paused only a second in munching at her feed trough to observe Honey's intrusion.

"Just going to sit a minute," Honey told her, "if that's okay with you."

She could have sworn the mare nodded.

Honey sat down against the stall wall. She drew her knees up. "He lied to me. That's the biggest thing. He lied to me. I feel like such an idiot! Do you know how much I worried about him not having any money? He probably thought I was stupid enough to buy the charade and I *was*."

The mare looked at her, chewing oats, as though to say: *Get real. If you had wanted to see the truth, you would have seen it. All the signs were there. You didn't want him to be Maxwell Strong because then he'd be the kind of man your family wants for you.*

"Yeah, yeah, I know in the beginning I said I was Elise and he said he was Joe. That doesn't bother me. We were just…you know, flirting then. But when you follow someone back to the States, that sort of takes it a notch or two above flirting."

It takes it a notch or two above just running away, too, said the mare. Then she gave a friendly whinny to a stallion a couple of stalls down.

"Oh, please," Honey responded. "It was more than sex. He believed in what I gave him and I just gave him myself."

Did you? the mare asked. *Then how come you didn't tell him who that sports jacket belonged to tonight? How come you didn't say, "This is my dad's"? How come you didn't let him get that close to Honor Elise?*

She was starting to hate this horse, Honey thought. "There were things I couldn't confide in him. I couldn't tell him the Marcus thing. That wasn't mine to tell."

The mare stopped eating and folded her front legs to lay down with a big huff.

"Ah, I'm boring you."

The mare closed her eyes.

"Good point. It's late. I'm tired. I'll sort this out tomorrow." She reached outside the stall for a horse blanket, then she lay down in the wood shavings with the mare. She'd deal with it all tomorrow, after her parents came home. Then she'd have to run again. But for now she was where she had always needed to be.

Honey woke in the morning to shouting. The mare was agitated enough that she almost stepped on her. Honey scrambled out from beneath the horse blanket and laid a hand on her long, glorious neck. "Easy, babe, easy."

When the horse was calm, Honey poked her nose out of the stall. And saw Max at the mouth of the barn. "This is not a safe place for you to be right now!"

"You're a reasonable woman. Let me explain."

"You must be thinking of another lover you lied to. I am *never* reasonable. Ask anyone in my family."

"You need to listen to me, Honey."

"Give me one compelling reason." At least she'd had the foresight to hole up somewhere with weapons. She let herself out of the stall and went to the feed room where she found a pitchfork. "I'm armed! Say whatever you have to say, then retreat before someone gets hurt!"

"I love you!" came Max's voice.

Her legs buckled. That was certainly compelling. "Liar!"

"I couldn't tell you who I was at first because I didn't want to be him anymore!"

Oh, God, she thought, oh, God. Did he have to say something she understood so well? "You are not reaching me at all!"

"Liar!"

How could she laugh with so much emotion inside? That ticked her off enough that she let the pitchfork fly. She was gratified by another shout. Finally, she went to the barn door. "Speak."

"You caught me when I was undercover. And by the time I wanted to tell you the truth, I was someone else. I wasn't Max anymore. You gave me myself back again. I didn't want to lose that."

Damn it, she was *not* going to cry. She'd been away from that Brunhia water for a week now. "That works."

"I'm not going back to that, Honey. I'm retiring. I don't want you to marry me. I want you to marry Joe."

She understood. God help her, she understood. "You're paying for the gas."

"I can do that."

She sighed and sat down suddenly in the barn alley. "I need to stay mad at you. But the mare was right."

He wasn't even going to touch that one, Max thought.

"You played me for an idiot, but I kept things from you as well."

"Maybe we both just needed to be somebody else for a while before we definitely decided to change our skins." And, he thought, their someone-elses matched perfectly. But there was still a big question mark. "Honey, I really need to know about the guy at the Marriott and the gun. I asked you once, back on Brunhia, if firearms were going to enter into this running-away business, and you said no."

Honey let her air out. Suddenly she was exhausted. But she found the energy to tell him. She *was* going to marry him, after all.

She told him what Marcus's letter had said and the cracks that Hatch had filled in. She told him why she'd gone to the Marriott. "Hatch is as clean as they come. I think he wants Willard Croft as much as the gene-y babies do. He's been keeping an eye out for the man for years and he knows something about him that he's willing to share. I've got to tell Matt Tynan to meet with him. Except…"

Max's expression turned wary. "Except? What did you do now?"

"They're all going to be pissed off at me for going into that meeting alone. None of them will ever understand why I had to do it."

He finally hunkered down next to her. "You didn't go in alone. You had me."

A smile tickled her mouth, then it faded. "If Hatch wasn't in on what happened at the park, then that means the Coalition is coming after me now, too." Maybe to grab her, she thought, and coerce Marcus into those nefarious deeds to save her.

Max's expression turned tormented. She put a hand to his cheek and said, "They're going to have to find me first, though, remember? I'm leaving. *We're* leaving."

"Can I take that as agreement that you'll marry Joe?"

"You might want to rethink that offer. You have no idea what kind of family you'd be marrying into."

"I proposed to Elise, not Honor."

Suddenly she felt sad. "We can't escape our real lives forever."

Max stood, caught her hand and tugged her to her feet again. "Why not?"

She stared at him. Why not indeed? Then she laughed. She laughed long and hard and fully. "Right. I'll race you back to the Jeep. I can call Marcus from the road."

And he did it, she thought, he really did it. He took off jogging so that she had to fly to catch up. When she reached him, she caught her arms around his neck from behind and they tumbled into the dirt.

When he trapped her against the ground and pinned her with a kiss, she was finally free.

* * * * *

There are more secrets to reveal—
don't miss out!
Coming in January 2004 to
Silhouette Books

Dr. Faith Martin arrived in Montana to help find a cure for a deadly epidemic, but found much more when she started to remember her mysterious past and the one man who could heal her aching heart…

FEVER
By
Linda Winstead Jones

FAMILY SECRETS: *Five extraordinary siblings. One dangerous past. Unlimited potential.*

And now, for a sneak peek,
just turn the page…

One

Faith was scared. So scared. Her heart was beating a hundred and twenty beats per minute, she had begun to sweat and she couldn't breathe deeply. No matter how she tried, she could not take a deep breath.

She was frightened and confused and running for her life, and she was ten years old again.

There were five of them…and then there were four. Where was Gideon? Faith's heart began to pound. She was lost in darkness, but at least she wasn't alone. Run. Hide. Stick together, now and forever. She couldn't see, but she could hear the frantic footsteps of her siblings. She could not see their faces, she did not know their names, but she knew they were a part of her. They were family.

A loud noise, a flash of light, flames, and suddenly Faith was no longer running; she was drowning. Water filled her lungs, a strong current dragged her down, and there was a bone-chilling darkness. *I'm going to die.*

Just when she thought there was no hope, strong arms captured her, steadied her and pulled her to the surface. She knew, with a surge of hope, who had saved her in her darkest moment. It was Mark who had dragged her from the depths of the ocean and into the light. Mark. Her brother.

"Faith!" Mark cried. She almost saw his face, through her tears and the salt water in her eyes, but he remained an elusive figure. "Breathe. Please breathe."

She blinked, and his face became more defined…but his features were not crisp enough to suit her. They faded and blurred in the most frustrating way. She wanted to see Mark so badly. More than that, she *needed* to see his face. He had the brightest smile....

"Dammit, Faith!"

The sharp words dragged her clumsily and quickly into the world of the waking. The dream was gone in an instant, and as soon as her eyes were open, she began to forget. For a moment she tried to hang on to that feeling of belonging that had cut through the fear, but it all faded, as she looked up and directly into Luke's worried face.

He sat on the side of her bed, one hand still gripping her arm too tightly.

"What are you doing here?" she asked, shaking off what remained of the dream.

"I came by to pick you up," he explained, "as planned." A muscle in Luke's jaw twitched; his neck corded with tension. He abruptly released her arm. "I pounded on the door for several minutes, but you didn't answer. I got worried so I called your room on my cell phone. When you didn't pick up, I phoned the clinic to see if you were there. When Dr. Helm said he hadn't seen you since you left last night, I panicked."

Faith glanced at the bedside table. Not only had her internal alarm clock failed her, but she'd slept deeply while the phone not two feet from her head rang. "How did you get into my room?"

"I woke up Eugene, the motel manager," Luke explained. "He's the one who let me in." Suddenly the man hovering above her looked less anxious and more than a little sheepish. "It was either that or break down the door."

"I can't believe I was sleeping so deeply," Faith said. She realized that her gown was twisted—and too thin to wear in mixed company—so she pulled the bedcover to her chest.

Faith had never had a man sit on the edge of her bed as she came awake. And this wasn't just any man, it was *Luke.* He was a vision any woman might like to wake up to, very masculine, enticing even to a woman who was *never* enticed. Dressed in flannel and denim and a heavy coat, his hair slightly mussed as if he'd run his fingers through it several times this morning, his shoulders broad and his legs long, he was unexpectedly tempting. Even in her waking moments, Faith Martin never gave in to temptation!

Luke's weight made the mattress dip, and it was an effort for Faith to keep herself from gently sliding into him. She still remembered last night's kiss. How could she not? The position she found herself in this morning was very intimate, intriguing. Something deep inside her wanted to let loose and drift into and against the man on her bed. Faith pointedly ignored that temptation, as she ignored all others.

Luke reached out and touched her face, very gently. Faith reacted, tensing momentarily then relaxing and allowing herself to enjoy the caress.

"A deep sleeper," he said. "I'm glad that's all it was. I feel like an idiot for overreacting, but..."

"But what?"

"I thought you were sick," he said gently. "You've been handling the virus more than anyone. I know you've been careful. I know you claim you never get sick. Still..." He shrugged his shoulders and glanced away. "Let's just say I was worried and leave it at that."

Faith nodded. What had she been dreaming about that made her tremble still? It was more than Luke's presence here that made her quiver. Something of a dream clung to her, made her blood rush cold through her veins. She could not remember the nightmare, and in truth she didn't want to. This moment was much nicer than any dream, good or bad.

"The rescue was unnecessary, but I do thank you," she said. "It was very nice of you to be worried."

When Luke did not respond, she glanced up to see that he had his eyes locked on her in an intense and not entirely casual way. She shivered, but hid the response by shifting the covers and pulling them closer.

"Who's Mark?" he asked in a lowered voice.

Wide-eyed and confused, Faith answered. "I have no idea."

"You called out his name in your sleep."

"I don't know anyone named Mark." She believed that statement for a moment, and then a few of Jake Ingram's words penetrated the fog. *Don't you remember Mark? The two of you were so close.* "No," she said more forcefully. "I don't know anyone by that name."

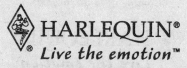

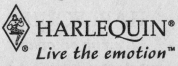